TEAM PLAYER

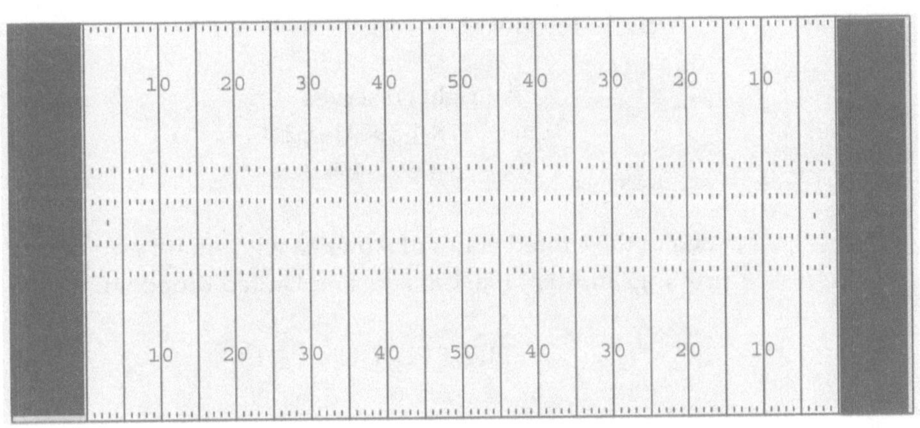

Jack Travers

TotalRecall Publications, Inc.

TotalRecall Publications, Inc.
1103 Middlecreek
Friendswood, Texas 77546
281-992-3131   281-482-5390 Fax
www.totalrecallpress.com

Copyright © 2013 by: Jack Travers

All rights reserved
ISBN: 978-1-59095-052-4
UPC: 6-43977-40526-5

Printed in the United States of America with simultaneous printings in Australia, Canada, and United Kingdom.

FIRST EDITION
1   2   3   4   5   6   7   8   9   10

To my wife and best friend, Janice

Author

Jack Travers, a social studies teacher and longtime football coach at Boston College High School, lives in Lynn, Massachusetts along with his wife Janice and their two children, Gina and Joseph. Jack holds a Bachelor of Arts and Master in Arts and Teaching from Boston College and a J.D. from the New England School of Law. As a native of Greater Boston and a twenty eight veteran of the classroom, Jack is thoroughly familiar with the themes that permeate his young adult novel, Team Player.

Introduction

Kyle Donovan, a seventeen year old star running back from the privileged suburb of Fairview, Massachusetts, is devastated when his seemingly idyllic world falls apart. The collapse of his father's computer company and the divorce of his parents force Kyle to live with his blue collar curmudgeon of a grandfather in the gritty and ethnically diverse Boston suburb of Crandall. Can his love for football, the loyalty of a new group of multicultural friends, and most importantly, the special bond between grandfather and grandson, help Kyle rise above his circumstances and understand that the ultimate value of a person is not measured by wealth and social status?

CHAPTER ONE

I glanced up from the huddle and took a good look at the scoreboard:

Fairview   28

Crandall   24

My left shoulder ached. I tried to flex my fingers and bend my wrist but the pain darted directly to my shoulder. I winced as I adjusted my shoulder pads. Twenty seven rushes into the Fairfield defensive line had done some damage. On both sides. They had scouted us well...our best passing play all year was a flea flicker thrown by the fullback, but today it fooled absolutely no one. We had to grind it out.

The crowd noise was deafening. I had been playing football since I was nine years old, but I had never before played before twenty thousand screaming maniacs. And these fans weren't sitting on their hands. After all, this was for the State Championship with several college scouts watching intently. To say nothing of the bitter feelings between the two teams.

I looked around the huddle, at these ten other guys...some were black, some were white and some were brown. I realized that I could call every one of them a friend. I couldn't say that in August but it was November now and things had changed.

And now there were eight seconds left for the Crandall

Hawks to accomplish something that at one time seemed unthinkable: beating the mighty Fairview Eagles.

Conversation was sparse during this timeout, the final timeout of the season and the prelude to the last eight seconds of ever playing organized football for many in the huddle. I quickly scanned the bleachers for a familiar face but the pain and the drizzle had transformed the crowd into a blur of colors and patterns and shapes that were unrecognizable.

I could hear the Fairview students huddled on the track just south of the goalpost. I heard them scream my name.

"Donovan, you're awful!"

"How are things in the slums, Donovan?"

"No way, Donovan! You're going home in an ambulance!"

I smiled at the taunts. Somewhere deep inside of me I knew that it was my destiny; it was Crandall's destiny to be in this situation on this day, at this time.

I snapped back to reality as our quarterback, Sal LoGrasso, returned to the huddle. We all clasped hands and Sal called our last play, "Four yards, boys. Going to the bread and butter. This is it...Tight I, toss right on one, on one, ready BREAK!"

As the linemen jogged to the line of scrimmage, I patted the right tackle, Eduardo Loureiro and said, "Nos necessitamo-lo, Eduardo." He turned and smiled.

I lined up directly behind the fullback and squeezed my hands...I would not allow myself to fumble. I closed my eyes for a split second, took a deep breath. Here we go, who would have thought three months ago that life would lead me to this moment. No time for thinking anymore...

I looked around my room...at the Class B Pop Warner championship photo on the wall above the television. Signed by Steve Grogan at our banquet. The trophies on top of the bureau, a Christmas card I made for Mom and Dad in the fourth grade...I guess I can take all this stuff with me when I move.

I repeated those words to myself: 'when I move.' Until fifteen minutes ago, who thought about moving? It was August and I'm two weeks away from my junior year at Fairview Prep. Football double sessions begin in a week with me, Kyle Donovan, the starting tailback, the featured star in Coach Pearson's wishbone offense. Heck, I was elected captain by my teammates, only the third junior captain in Fairview history. And now here I am, lying in my bed, staring at old Pop Warner photos and thinking about moving.

After I left the kitchen, I ran to my room and cried for about ten minutes. I'm usually not a big crier, but I couldn't help myself. So I buried my head in my pillow and the tears just flowed. Made me feel a little better but it didn't change anything. In three days, I'd be unloading furniture. Sixteen years in this house, my whole life...until now. Life sure stinks sometimes.

There was a gentle knock on the door and I heard my mom say, "Kyle...can we come in?" I just cleared my throat because I didn't want my voice to crack. I guess they heard my grunt because the door slowly opened and my parents walked into my room. I wanted to avoid eye contact but with my parents I never could.

My mother sat on the end of my bed and Dad stood just

inside the doorway. Mom put her hand on my arm and said, "We didn't get a chance to tell you everything, honey." She glanced back at Dad who looked really tired...more tired than I've ever seen him. Mom sighed and said, "You'll be moving in with Grandpa Butch, Kyle."

I pushed my mother's arm away and sat up. "Grandpa Butch!" I said. "He hates me...and he drinks, right Dad? You told me that yourself. Remember? You said Grandpa Butch has a drinking problem. We can't go live with Grandpa Butch. Plus, he lives in...Crandall! How can we go live in a place like that?" I plopped back on my back and tried to fight the tears.

My father rolled an office chair towards the bed. "There's more, Kyle." He closed his eyes and breathed deeply through his nose. "You'll be moving in with Grandpa Butch. Mom and I won't be going with you." I stared at a spider on the ceiling. This was just a bad dream...I'd just ride it out and then I'd wake up and my life would be back to normal. But then Dad started talking again and it didn't seem like a dream.

"Mom and I are separating...just for a while, we hope." I saw Mom turn away...I knew she was crying. Now I felt like crying again. "It's been tough, Kyle. I'm sure you've noticed things haven't been great around here lately." Yeah, but I figured everyone's parents fought about money and stuff like that. You just don't split up because you don't have enough money. Didn't the priest say "till death do us part? They must have forgotten that part of the wedding.

"You're not saying anything, Kyle," Dad said.

"Got nothing to say."

"Mom's going to get away for a while. She's going to stay with Aunt Janice and Uncle Ray in Vermont." Mom ran from the room. Dad looked back but didn't follow her...in fact, it almost seemed like he didn't really care. "I need to look for a job, Kyle. There's a couple of opportunities in New York, some connections I've built up through the years. So we're both going to be gone for a while." Dad looked away and I noticed his eyes were moist. He took a handkerchief from his pocket and wiped his eyes. He was only forty three and I used to think he looked young. But now he looked pretty old...in fact, he looked a lot like Grandpa Butch.

I sat up and Dad hugged me. I was pissed at him and pissed at Mom and pissed at the banker who was going to sell our house and pissed at all the businesses that wouldn't buy Dad's software anymore but I hugged him anyway. We held each other tight and Dad seemed to collapse right there in my arms. My hands were on his back and I felt his body shake. It was weird but I didn't feel like crying anymore as I held my father. I patted his back, looked at the empty doorway and wondered where Mom went.

Dad left and I tried to make some sense out of everything. Of course, that was useless so I grabbed my cell phone and called Paul Elliott, my best friend.

"Speak," Paul said. As usual, he was chewing on food probably of the fast food variety.

"Hey, I gotta talk to you."

"Like I said, speak."

"No, really, I have to see you."

There was a silence for a moment and then Paul said, "I'll be there in ten minutes."

Paul had turned seventeen in June and he had gotten his license before any of his friends. His father was a medical malpractice lawyer in Boston and his mother was also a lawyer. She worked for one of those big defense firms in town. His parents divorced four years ago and they basically hated each other. Paul would stay with his Dad in the Back Bay for a month or two in the summer and live with his mom here in Fairview the rest of the year. Paul said the only benefit to having divorced parents was that they both tried to out-do each other with presents. When Paul got his license, his dad bought him a new BMW. To compensate, his mom threw him the biggest birthday party in Fairview history when he turned seventeen. Mrs. Elliott actually hired a band and made sure there was a minimum of adult supervision. I'm surprised that Snoop Dogg and Lebron James didn't show up. My parents' divorce held no such promise...everyone was broke.

I heard the Beamer's horn and I rushed down the stairs. Dad sat in the kitchen, poring over some documents that must have something to do with our world falling apart.

"I'm going out, Dad," I shouted as I opened the front door. Dad said something in return but I honestly didn't really care what he had to say.

Paul had Kanye West blaring through those impressive German speakers. He'd been listening to Kanye 24-7 for around three months straight. It was beginning to get on my nerves.

"What's going on?" Paul asked. He had grown his sandy hair down to his shoulders and sported a couple of day's growth of beard. Paul had started shaving really early in life, probably in sixth grade. That made him a hero in junior high school especially for me. I still only had to shave every third day. Unlike Paul, I kept my blonde hair cut very short year round. Paul would have to get his hair chopped off in a couple weeks anyway when football started. Coach Pearson wouldn't allow any hippies on his team.

"How you doing?" I said.

"Where we going?" Paul asked as he sped away from my house on Lambert Way. As we drove past the rest of the recently built colonials in the neighborhood, it struck me that this would no longer be home in a couple of days. I felt like crying again but that could never happen in front of Paul despite the fact that he was my best friend.

We drove to Fairview Center which was actually a collection of stylish boutiques, antique stores and a couple of very expensive restaurants. There was a Whole Foods that took quite a while to construct so the builders could ensure that the storefront matched the 'character of the neighborhood.' Did I mention that Fairview was probably the wealthiest community in the Commonwealth of Massachusetts?

Fortunately, there was one small breakfast/coffee shop in the Center. It was owned by Andy Bronson who had lived in town forever.

Paul parked the BMW in the small parking lot and we entered Andy's. We had driven in silence the entire trip, which wasn't really that unusual.

After we sat down, Paul picked up a menu which was completely unnecessary since we had it totally committed to memory. "Alright, so what's going on? Is this a date or something?" he asked.

I chuckled and responded "Well, I got some news, buddy." I looked out the window and tapped the table. "I'm moving, probably in the next couple of days. I won't be going to the Prep anymore."

Paul dropped the menu to the table. "Come on, don't screw around. What's really going on?"

I shook my head. "That's it, I'm telling the truth. You're not gonna believe where I'm moving."

"Wait a minute. You're serious? What the hell happened?"

I sighed. "Long story."

"Do I look like I have anything to do?" Paul asked.

"My parents lost our house. The business just fell apart I guess...I'm not really sure, to tell the truth. I knew something was messed up but I didn't know it was that bad. So the bank's coming to take the house and...my parents are getting divorced."

Paul slumped back in the booth and looked at the table. "Divorce? Definitely?" I nodded. "That sucks."

We were quiet for a minute and than Paul said, "Hey maybe you can come live with me? Come on, we have like seven bedrooms and it's just me and my mom. My sister's at college and she never comes home anyway. Then you can still go to Prep."

"Thanks a lot, man, but we can't afford the Prep now. I think we barely afforded it last year. I know we got a lot of letters from the treasurer's office." I braced myself for my next sentence. "So I'm going to live in Crandall with my grandfather. My dad's looking for a job in New York and my mom just has to get away for a while I guess."

Paul's eyes opened wide in surprise. "Crandall? You gotta be kidding me. That place is a hole."

It was kind of weird but I already felt a little defensive about living in Crandall. "Come on, it's not that bad. My grandpa lives in a nice neighborhood."

"Hey, I'm sorry. I'm just pissed off at everything. This mean you're going to Crandall High?"

I nodded slowly.

Paul put his hands on his face. "You gonna play football?"

I nodded again. Nothing more had to be said. Crandall High School had played Fairview Prep in the state Super Bowl three years earlier. There were still a lot of bad feelings left over. I remember Paul, me and some other kids watching the game from the sidelines as eighth graders. I also recall being scared out of my mind by the Crandall fans. But really, what choice did I have? Football was sometimes the only thing that made sense to me when things were going good. There was no way I could survive all this crap without playing...even if it was for Crandall High School.

All the Prep kids thought the Crandall kids were punks. I suppose the Crandall kids thought the Fairview kids were rich snobs. The truth was probably somewhere in the middle.

"You talk to Ashley yet?" Paul asked.

I probably should have told Ashley right away but for some reason, I just couldn't.

"You better call her, pal."

I sighed and nodded. I picked at the scrambled eggs on my plate and thought about Ashley Novack. I'm not sure that I loved her but it had to be something close. She was just so different from the other girls at the Prep. First of all, she was better looking than ninety percent of them with her long blonde hair and green eyes. She dressed preppy like everyone else at the school but she never dressed to impress...she just dressed the way she was raised to dress, I guess.

Her father was a cardiologist in Boston who became famous for developing some sort of piece that attached to the arteries leading to the heart. Ashley tried to explain it to me a few times but I just pretended to understand. Actually, I had no idea what she was talking about.

So Ashley was rich, which didn't make her different than anyone else in Fairview. Yet she and her family seemed different. On many weekends, the whole Novack family went into Dorchester to work at a food bank. I went with them a couple of times and was surprised that Dr. Novack knew some of the people that came to get food. Ashley said that her father was born in Dorchester and volunteered at the health clinic there every month.

I made fun of Ashley because it seemed that she always wanted to save something or help someone...the poor people of Boston, the kid with MS in our class who traveled in a wheel chair, the skinny dog she found in the woods behind the golf course. I wonder how she'll feel about a boyfriend who was about to drop about seventeen rungs on the socio-economic scale. I'd find out soon enough.

"You gonna say anything at all?"

I looked up and saw Paul staring at me. "What?" I asked.

"I've been talking to you for five minutes now and all you're doing is turning over those eggs. Either eat them or let's get out of here."

I rose from the booth and said, "Yeah, let's get out of here."

Paul dropped me off at St. Monica's Church, the only Catholic parish in Fairview. I had made my First Communion, labored through CCD classes, and was eventually confirmed in the church. I had strayed away from the faith during the past couple of years...I wasn't really sure why. My parents were never regular Mass goers and, after I entered high school, didn't push me to go.

I'm not sure why I wanted to visit St. Monica's...I just knew that I had to find some answers. No one around me had any so maybe God knew something.

St. Monica's was built in the 70's, one of those churches constructed when folk music and priests with sideburns seemed like the future. It didn't have the feel of my grandfather's church in Crandall. No statutes and very limited stained glass.

I blessed myself with holy water, genuflected, and knelt in the back pew.

I didn't pray much, so I said an Our Father, Hail Mary, and Act of Contrition. Seemed like a good way to start...and I remembered all the words.

The church was empty and almost eerily quiet. I sat back, closed my eyes, and began to think about what had happened. I knew it wasn't a dream, but I asked God anyway. Was it possible to make sense of any of this?

Some kids at school wore those WWJD wristbands. I thought of that and asked myself: what would Jesus do if he were me? I'm pretty sure he wouldn't feel sorry for himself. I had read enough of the Gospels to know that. He wouldn't get mad...he couldn't, with all that talk about turning the other cheek. I chuckled to myself. Turn the other cheek. Did he really mean that?

I blessed myself and left the church. I had to make one more stop...and it wouldn't be easy.

Chapter Two

I rang the doorbell at the Novack residence and I felt that same sense of apprehension that I experienced on our first date. I wasn't intimidated by the size of the house...I was pretty used to mansions. I just hoped that Dr. Novack wasn't home. I know that he was supposed to be a great guy and he did all sorts of great things but to be truthful, the guy scared the wits out of me. He was a doctor but his hands were immense and looked like my Grandpa Butch's hands--in other words, hands that could do some serious damage. But my grandfather had been a carpenter for fifty years and Dr. Novack was a...doctor.

So I waited at the front door and prayed that Dr. Novack wasn't home. He never said much to me, just kind of stared. And the guy was huge and had this big mane of grey hair and bushy black eyebrows. I was in great shape, worked out all the time but I never had any doubt that Dr. Novack could kick my butt at any moment.

Thankfully, Mrs. Novack answered the door. They say that opposites attract and it was definitely true in this case. Ashley's mother was small, blonde (I think it was her real hair color), and sincerely kind and polite.

"Kyle, what a pleasant surprise...come on in," Mrs. Novack said.

Mrs. Novack didn't work and I think that she spent most of

each day doing social and charitable work. I walked into the immaculate living room and waited for Ashley to come down from her room.

Ashley's mother offered me some coffee cake but I had no appetite which was very unusual for me.

I was sitting on the couch when Ashley came down the stairs, looking good even though she was wearing sweats with her hair pulled back and no makeup.

We hugged and walked out the back door. There was a slate patio and small sitting area facing the pond that Dr. Novack had installed a couple of years ago. We sat on the stone wall surrounding the patio and just looked out on the pond for a minute or two.

Ashley held my hand and said, "Well, are we speaking today?"

I shrugged and realized that the tears were sneaking back into my eyes. What was happening to me?

Ashley must have sensed something was wrong...she always seemed to have a sixth sense regarding other people's emotions. "Is everything alright?"

I looked away and noticed a rabbit bounding across the lawn. "You get coyotes back here don't you?" I asked. Probably the most ridiculous question I ever asked but I tend to do that when I don't know what to say.

Ashley laughed softly. "Oh, I'm sure they're around but I've never actually seen one. You want to talk more about coyotes now? They actually resemble large dogs, be sure not to feed them because they're still wild animals, don't leave garbage outside, and be sure to..."

"Okay, okay, I didn't come over to talk about coyotes. I got something to tell you." I stopped speaking and felt myself choking up again.

I looked at Ashley and saw her eyes well up. "You want to break up?" she asked.

"No, no, no...nothing like that," I said. I breathed. "I'm moving, Ash...moving to Crandall, probably this week. My parents are splitting up, we're losing the house, and things are pretty bad." I took another deep breath. I had just spit out my life story in about four seconds.

She put her arm around me and said, "Oh my God, I'm so sorry Kyle." We sat in silence for a moment. "Crandall?" Ashley asked, with just a hint of condescension.

For some strange reason, I wanted to leave. I wanted to move out of Fairview today. My whole life had been spent in this town and now I wanted out immediately.

How could my father be such a moron? His business gone? Why couldn't he see it coming? Who loses an entire business? The marriage all done? My mother seemed like a zombie this morning. And the house? The bank was going to auction off the house? Didn't he have any self-respect at all? Was he that much of a pathetic loser?

I stood up quickly and avoided eye contact with Ashley. "I gotta go, Ash."

I ran from Ashley's house and sprinted down her street and into the woods bordering the road. I stopped and bent over, trying to catch my breath. I screamed at the top of my lungs, grabbed a broken branch and banged it against huge oak tree. I tossed the branch and sat on the dirt. I screamed again but with a little less volume. I put my face in my hands and cried again. This time the tears flowed like a broken water spout and my tee shirt was soon soaked.

I stood up and tried to pull myself together. I wiped my eyes with my shirt and shook my head violently, trying to get all this crap out of my mind. I couldn't change what happened and I tried to convince myself that none of it was my fault. But maybe I could have worked more during the summer, made some more money. That might have helped. Maybe I should have seen what was happening with my parents. I knew they were arguing a lot...I'm not a complete idiot...there was something wrong. Basically, I didn't care...my little world wasn't being disrupted. What a self-centered jerk.

I had to take some blame. Maybe I could help fix some of it...probably not. Anyway, I had to pull myself together; acting like this wasn't helping anyone. There was a shortcut through the woods to Lambert Street. I started walking and tried to convince myself that things would get better.

No one in our little family could bear to hang around while the bank auctioned our house away. Two days before the auction, people started coming around the house, peeking through the window and trying to open the garage door. I was out back just standing around when some couple sauntered right into the yard. I know they saw me but that didn't make a difference. So they took out a tape measure and began measuring the yard with me standing right there. It was as if I didn't even exist. At that moment, I knew that it was really time to leave.

A moving truck came and put the furniture in storage. Dad rented a small U-Haul van and he, Paul and I loaded up all of my belongings which didn't take very long.

When we finished packing, I thanked Paul and saw that despite a Herculean effort he looked like his dog had just died. "I think we're all ready for Dr. Phil now," I said. We both maintained that we would get together and chill every weekend, but I think that both of us realized that this was really goodbye. Let's face it: kids from Crandall and kids from Fairview don't make it a habit to hang out together. I don't think that's unique to Crandall and Fairview...it's just a fact of life.

Mom had taken off for Vermont in the morning with Uncle Ray and Aunt Janice. It was so strange to see her leave and have no idea when I'd see her again. She had seemed kind of in a fog for the past week and I noticed that Uncle Ray was extremely careful as he helped her into his old Taurus station wagon. Mom pressed her hand against the rear window as the wagon departed and I almost ran down the street chasing the car. I honestly feel like I'm living through some Lifetime channel movie.

Dad put his arm around me but I shrugged him off, not in an overtly disrespectful manner but in a way that he'd know I wasn't ready for any father-son bonding.

We both stood in front of the white colonial with the black shutters and brick side porch. I closed my eyes and tried to remember the smell of the place...I knew that I'd never forget how it looked. As I closed my eyes, the memories came rushing back: broken windows caused by wild pitches, the annual summer block party, the ping pong table in the basement, my mother planting flowers along the front walk...mostly, I thought of my father and mother and me laughing and joking. Just the three of us. It was a great place to grow up. Now I guess it was time to grow up for real.

I felt my father's hand on my shoulder. "Let's go son," he said.

It was only eleven miles from Fairview to Crandall but the two communities might as well exist in different time zones. We drove north to Route 128 and then caught Route 93 South. I noticed the "Hubbard Square" exit and knew that this was where Grandpa Butch lived. My cell phone rang and I saw Ashley's number appear. She had called a few times and we spoke briefly yesterday but I just couldn't bring myself to see her. So I let the phone ring until it finally stopped.

"Who's that?" Dad asked.

I shrugged and looked out the passenger window and knew that we had entered Crandall. We drove through Hubbard Square which sure didn't resemble Fairview Center. I counted three liquor stores, four bars, a check cashing center and a new CVS Pharmacy. There was a Dunkin Donuts at the edge of the square and I recalled that Grandpa Butch had once said that Crandall was home to twenty three Dunkin Donuts establishments. I also remembered that he had announced this fact with some serious pride. When I told him that Fairview had no Dunkin Donuts at all, it was as if he found out there was no Santa Claus.

Main Street ran through Hubbard Square and I noticed that many of the old shops along the street now sported signs in Portuguese. We left the commercial section of Main Street and here the road was dominated by two and three family houses of varying condition. There seemed to be a lot of brick and wrought iron and I counted seven statutes of the Virgin Mary on one stretch of the street.

About a half mile out of Hubbard Square, Dad turned right onto Lodge Avenue which I recognized as Grandpa Butch's street. "We're almost there," Dad said. "It never looks that much different."

Dad pulled the van in front of Grandpa Butch's house, a tan, vinyl sided two family with dark brown shutters, a paved over front yard with a few flower pots lining the front of the house and a narrow driveway. In the driveway, Grandpa Butch's five year old navy blue Buick Regal still appeared brand new.

Grandpa Butch came out on the porch dressed in a white undershirt, jeans and work boots. Except for my cousin's wedding, I'm not sure I'd ever seen him dress any differently. I just hoped he owned more than one undershirt. He waved to us and descended the stairs slowly.

"How you doing, Dad?" my father said as he shook my grandfather's hand.

"Okay for an old man," Grandpa Butch responded. He looked at me standing in front of the van. "All your stuff in the van, Kyle?" he asked.

I nodded. I had always been a little scared of Grandpa Butch. His crew cut was snow white and his skin was brown and leathery. Two tattoos marked his body, a shamrock on his right forearm and the Marine Corps symbol on his right bicep. When he shook your hand, it felt like a vise. Grandpa Butch's sky blue eyes could laser right through you and he constantly smoked those old Camels. Second hand smoke was something else I'd have to get used to.

I opened the rear door of the van and began unloading my various belongings. Grandpa Butch was soon beside me trying to squeeze my mattress out of the van. "I got it, Grandpa," I said.

Grandpa Butch snickered and lit one of those unfiltered cigarettes. I coughed as the smoke invaded my face. "Okinawa and fifty years of banging nails and lifting plywood. I can handle it, son."

Okay, I said to myself. Let the old man have a heart attack. Maybe then I wouldn't have to move to this hole.

I stood back and watched Grandpa Butch angle the mattress out of the van. He hoisted it on his shoulder and said, "Excuse me, Kyle."

I tried not to act too impressed and said, "Can I help you now, Grandpa?"

I saw his mouth turn into a smile ever so briefly. "Yeah, I guess you can help now."

Three generations of Donovan men finished the unloading pretty quickly. The contrast between Dad and Grandpa Butch was striking. Even when doing manual labor, Dad was all Fairview. He wore a green Polo shirt, khakis and boat shoes. His hands were soft and nails expertly manicured. It was hard to imagine Dad living here in Crandall and playing football and baseball at Crandall High. But he had the yearbook to prove it, although Dad never really seemed that proud of his Crandall background.

We sat in Grandpa Butch's living room which also served as the TV room...not quite the Great Room like we had at Lambert Lane. There were many family pictures on the walls, including photos of me in various football uniforms. My eyes caught the picture of Dad and Mom cutting the wedding cake. I didn't linger too long on that particular image.

I walked through the dining room into the kitchen to grab another diet coke. I opened a cabinet to find a glass and noticed the heaviness of the door. Inside the door I saw the initials "FXD" and "TWD." I'm no aficionado of the Home and Garden Channel but even I could see that these cabinets were incredibly well made. All the hardwood floors in the house were shiny and clean. In fact, the house was just as clean as our home on Lambert Lane. I was a little surprised.

When I returned to the living room (although Grandpa Butch and Dad both called it the 'parlor'), Dad and Grandpa were making small talk. There wasn't much closeness between the two and Dad appeared particularly uncomfortable.

"Hey Grandpa, what's the initials inside the cabinets mean?" I asked.

Grandpa Butch shot a glance at Dad who looked away. "Those are my initials, Francis Xavier Donovan. Don't you know my real name?"

"I thought Butch was your real name." Grandpa Butch laughed but Dad continued staring out the front bow window. "How about the other initials?"

Grandpa Frank again looked at Dad. He sighed and said, "Timothy William Donovan, your father. We built those cabinets twenty five years ago when your Dad was a senior in high school."

"Oh yeah, Timothy William Donovan." Made sense now.

Dad stood up and said, "Okay, Kyle, I gotta go. I have a

flight to New York at seven tonight." He glanced at his watch. "It's already three and I have to return the van."

Grandpa Butch stood and the two stiffly shook hands. "Thanks for doing this, Dad. I owe you one."

Grandpa waved his right hand and said, "This is what family's for, Timmy."

Dad raised his eyebrows and motioned for me to walk out the house with him. We strolled to the van and Dad stopped and put both his hands on my shoulders. "Okay, Kyle...I don't know what to say." He looked down at his feet. "This is only temporary, I promise. I'm gonna get this straightened out." He looked up at Grandpa Butch standing on the porch in front of the storm door. "Be patient with your grandfather. He's...you know...he can be kind of difficult but he means well most of the time. Been so much better since he quit drinking." Dad cleared his throat. "Anyway, I'll call you tomorrow. Remember, this is only temporary until I get on my feet again."

"What about Mom?" I asked.

Dad closed his eyes and shook his head. "I don't know, Kyle. Things are very...well, they're so screwed up right now. Maybe time will help. I don't really know."

I felt some serious pity for my dad at that moment. The anger subsided and I returned his hug.

I watched the van pull away and turned to walk up the brick and limestone front steps. Grandpa Butch snuffed out his cigarette in the ashtray and said, "You hungry?"

I nodded and we entered the house.

Chapter 3

I sat at the butcher block kitchen table while Grandpa Butch rummaged through the freezer looking for supper. "Eureka...fish sticks...and fries. What do you think?" he asked. Before I could offer an answer, Grandpa was sticking a plateful of fish sticks and fries into the microwave.

He sat at the table across from me and rubbed both eyes with the palms of both hands. He reached into the pocket of his tee shirt, pulled out a business card and silently handed it to me.

> **Anthony Bonfiglio**
> **Athletic Director/Football Coach**
> **Crandall High School**

There was a note on the back of the card that read:
"Hi Kyle,
Double Sessions start in a week. Hope you're interested. Stop by for Equipment when you register for school."

I placed the card in my pocket, looked up and noticed Grandpa Butch staring at me.

"I guess you gotta register for school tomorrow," he said.

I nodded. "Yeah." School. Crandall High School to be exact. I was still waiting for all this to sink in.

"You know Coach Bonfiglio?" Grandpa Butch asked.

I again nodded. "Yeah, we scrimmaged their freshmen when I was a freshman. He reffed the game. Seemed like a decent guy."

"A good guy. Former Marine...got shot up pretty good in Vietnam. He was real interested when I talked to him about you playing football for Crandall."

To be honest, I wasn't even sure that Grandpa Butch knew I played football. I only saw him a couple of times a year...Christmas and usually once or twice during the year. When I was little and my grandmother was alive, we'd visit a lot more. Once Grandma died, any visit to Grandpa Butch's house seemed almost forced, like something my parents were obliged to do. I remember Mom in the kitchen on her cell phone while Dad and I sat watching television with Grandpa in the living room. I know that Dad planned the visits when there was a Red Sox game on TV. If there were no game, he and Grandpa would actually have to talk. I don't know what happened between the two of them but it sure made for many uncomfortable moments.

"So you gonna play?" Grandpa asked as he stood to remove our supper from the microwave.

"I have to play. It's the only thing that makes sense right now. Moving, parents divorcing...but it's still four downs and ten yards for a first down, you know what I mean?"

Grandpa Butch turned and smiled. I hadn't seen him smile much but I could tell this was a genuine smile. His blue eyes crinkled up and his eyebrows rose. "It does make sense, doesn't it kid? It always made sense for your father when his old man acted like a jackass."

I never really thought of Dad actually playing football. I

know that he played...Grandpa Butch had the pictures to prove it. But I just had trouble imagining Dad making a tackle or blocking a linebacker. In fact, I had difficulty thinking of Dad living in this house or growing up in Crandall. He just seemed like he lived in Fairview his whole life.

"You want ketchup?" Grandpa Butch asked.

We sat and ate fish sticks, fries and onion rings.

"I guess you're not on the Atkins Diet, Grandpa," I said between bites.

Grandpa Butch burst out laughing. If his smile was surprising, imagine how shocked I was by actual laughter. But the way he laughed seemed like he really laughed all the time.

After we both finished our third glass of root beer, Grandpa said, "Life dealt you a pretty crappy hand here, Kyle. It all happened at once, didn't it? I wish I knew what was going on with your parents. I wish...I..." His voice trailed off and he gathered up the plates and brought them to the sink.

"I don't know, Grandpa. It was just a big shock. I lived in the house and never saw anything coming. What kind of son does that make me?"

Grandpa Butch turned and said, "This has nothing to do with you, Kyle. Remember that. Sometimes, things get messed up. There was nothing you could do about it. Remember that, okay?"

I grabbed a sponge and wiped down the kitchen table. I checked the clock on the microwave and thought that it had to be much later than 8:15. I yawned loudly.

"Hey, before you fall asleep and I have to carry you up to your room, go unpack and get to bed. We have to go down to the school tomorrow."

"Okay, Grandpa. Thanks for supper."

Grandpa waved his right arm as he continued to wash the dishes.

I made my way to the staircase and heard his voice.

"The 214 yards against Davis Prep, Kyle. That was your best game."

I was going to respond but I was too tired and confused. The anger was gone for the most part but the fatigue and guilt were still going strong. It was time for bed.

So this was Dad's old room. All the times I'd visited Grandpa Butch, I never entered this room. The door was always closed. I avoided the upstairs anyway unless I had to go to the bathroom. It just seemed kind of dark and creepy up there. I always got the scent of mothballs too.

The room was immaculate. Clean sheets, perfectly made bed, a small closet, some more pictures of Dad: the whole room seemed frozen in time. I still caught a slight whiff of mothballs but it didn't bother me that much anymore for some reason.

I was very impressed with the cleanliness of the room and Grandpa Butch's entire house. I pulled down the spread, took off my sneakers and lay down to rest for a couple of minutes. God, I was tired. I closed my eyes and tried to process the events of the day. I was usually pretty good at processing but fatigue got the best of me. I drifted off to sleep with Grandpa Butch's comment about my 214 yards against Davis Prep the last thing I remembered.

"Rise and shine, sonny boy."

I rolled over and hoped this was a nightmare. But the sight of a freshly shaven Grandpa Butch in a crisp white tee shirt was as real as it gets. He sounded like an elderly drill instructor or what I imagined an elderly drill instructor sounded like.

"Come on, Kyle, feet on the deck," Grandpa Butch said as he pulled down the spread.

"Okay, okay, I'm getting up." I slowly pulled my legs over the side of the bed and my feet hit the floor. I rubbed the night out of my eyes and looked up at Grandpa Butch standing over me, hands on hips. "What time is it?" I asked.

Grandpa Butch looked at his watch. "Seven thirty, sweet pea. Supposed to be at the school at eight thirty."

The smell of bacon wafted through the air. "You make breakfast, Grandpa?"

He nodded. "Yeah. Bacon, eggs, and pancakes."

I couldn't remember the last time Mom or Dad actually made breakfast. Everyone was always rushing out of the house to go to school or work. I'd grab a pop tart or a breakfast bar. That was breakfast at the Donovan house and that was probably breakfast at most people's houses, I guess.

"You slept in your clothes?" Grandpa asked.

I nodded. "Yeah, once I lay down, I just went out like a light."

"Well, hurry up and shower."

After I showered and changed, I devoured two plates of bacon, eggs and pancakes. Grandpa Butch used the Mrs. Butterworth syrup, not the low fat stuff that tasted like polyurethane.

After I finished eating, I was ready for a nap but Grandpa had other plans. We climbed into his Buick Regal and headed for Crandall High.

"Smells like smoke in here, Grandpa," I said while opening the window. "You smoke in the car, you never get rid of the odor, you know what I mean?"

I'm almost positive my words of wisdom had no effect on Grandpa Butch who was busy turning up the volume on the all sports station.

We rode in silence and Grandpa pulled the Regal into the parking lot of the high school. The school was located on Main Street and it looked kind of out of place next to the row of sub shops and hair salons on either side. I couldn't find a blade of grass in the whole complex. Even a tree grew in Brooklyn...but not in Crandall, I guess.

Grandpa Butch and I entered the principal's office which wasn't hard to find. There was a pretty casual atmosphere in the office, it being August and all. A middle aged secretary named Carol looked up and said, "Can I help you?"

Grandpa pulled a sheet of paper from his back pocket and handed it to Carol. "I think everything's filled out correctly," he said. Unfortunately, the paper definitely smelled like cigarette smoke.

I stood there with my hands in my pocket and began to wonder what I was doing at Crandall High School in the middle of August. I should be in the Fairview weight room, pumping iron, messing around with my friends. I thought of Ashley and knew that I should have spoken to her but I just couldn't...I just couldn't.

Carol studied the paper like it was an IRS tax form. Finally, she stood and said, "I think Mr. Amaral would like to see you. Hold on for a minute, please."

I glanced at Grandpa Butch who just shrugged. About thirty seconds later, a dark skinned, powerfully built gentleman emerged from the back office. He was about 5"9 and must have weighed around two hundred pounds. Mr. Amaral smiled at us and silently offered his hand to me. I shook and immediately attempted to tighten my grip since his handshake was like a vise. He then shook hands with Grandpa Butch and said, "Please, come into my office."

We followed Mr. Amaral into his cramped office and took seats.

Mr. Amaral leaned back in his office chair and said, "Kyle Donovan. We're very happy to have you here at Crandall. I checked your transcripts and you were quite a student at Fairview Prep. Well, we offer plenty of advanced placement courses so I'm sure you'll find what you'll need here." He turned to Grandpa Butch. "Do you recognize me, Mr. Donovan?"

Grandpa studied his face and raised his eyebrows. "Wait a minute. Sonny Amaral? You gotta be kidding me! I didn't know you back at Crandall. I thought you were working over at Powers Catholic."

Mr. Amaral laughed. "Been back for three years. Sometimes I wish I was still over at Powers. But I feel like I can make a difference here. The kids really aren't much different than when Timmy and I roamed the halls."

Timmy? My father?

"Sonny was one of your Dad's best friends in high school, Kyle. Sonny here was one of the best catchers ever to come out of Crandall. Your dad pitched to him from Little League all the way through high school. You caught at Fordham, right Sonny?"

Mr. Amaral laughed again and nodded. "Long time ago, Butch. Long time ago."

So the principal had been best friends with my father. Hard to believe. They just seemed so different.

"I know the story, Kyle. I've done my research, spoke to your old man. Just know that you have a friend in the principal's office. It's not going to easy...but you know that." Mr. Amaral leaned forward and peered over his oak desk. He folded his hands and said, "Crandall's not Fairview, Kyle. You're going to have to adjust to that. But there's a ton of great kids here, especially on the football team. Be patient, keep your eyes open and be yourself. That's the most important thing. These kids can spot a phony a mile away." He cleared his throat. "I heard you're quite a running back, Kyle." He shot a glance at Grandpa Butch. "Like father, like son, I guess. Anyway, Coach Bonfiglio is here today and would love to meet with you. Do you know how to get to the athletic director's office?" Neither of us had any idea so Mr. Amaral gave us quick directions.

As we left the office, Mr. Amaral shook my hand warmly and said, "Good luck, Kyle. My door is always open. I'm sure everything will go great." He and Grandpa Butch embraced which surprised me because I don't recall ever getting a hug from my grandfather.

The athletic office was located downstairs near the locker rooms and gym. I knocked on the door and Grandpa Butch said, "You want me to wait out here?"

I shrugged but I really did want him to come with me for some reason. "No, you should come in case I miss anything."

Coach Tony Bonfiglio was a huge man with jet black hair, dark brown eyes and a seemingly automatic smile. He wore a white Crandall Hawks Football polo shirt and cargo shorts. For some reason, there was a whistle around his neck even though there would be no football for another four days. Just getting a head start, I guess.

"Kyle, it's great to finally meet you. I've heard nothing but good things,." Coach Bonfiglio turned to Butch and punched the old man on the arm. "How are you, Butchie?"

Grandpa Butch smiled and said, "Semper Fi, Tony. Semper Fi."

Coach Bonfiglio nodded solemnly and said, "You said it, Butch. You said it."

We followed Coach to his office. I noticed that he walked with a pronounced limp although it appeared that he was trying awfully hard not to limp. The Coach's office, like that of Mr. Amaral, was small, cramped and crowded. I began to think that everything in Crandall was cramped and crowded.

"So you want to play football here at Crandall, Kyle?" Coach Bonfiglio asked.

I nodded. Of course, I wanted to play football. It's the only thing that could possibly make this whole ordeal bearable.

"I talked with Coach Pearson a couple of times so I think I have an idea of what's going on. You know, I remember that freshman game between us and Fairview. You must have run for 150 yards that day. We can really use you this year, Kyle but it's gonna be tough. These kids been together for a long time. They grew up here, played Pop Warner together, had a decent season last year. They're really looking forward to their senior season. I told a couple of them you were coming and they weren't real impressed. I'm just warning you, Kyle. They're good kids but they're city kids, you know? Trust me, though, I'm gonna help your transition as much as I can. Okay?"

I wasn't sure about any of this. These kids were going to hate me. And why shouldn't they? I was a rich kid from Fairview who threatened to screw up their senior season. Maybe I should just go to school, keep my head down and not play football. I've seen a few prison movies. I know I could keep a low profile.

"I don't know, Coach. Maybe your kids are right. Maybe I shouldn't play football this year. You guys don't need me. Anyway, thanks for your help." I stood and started for the door. I felt so sorry for myself but Coach Bonfiglio and Grandpa Butch weren't the types of guys you wanted to be wimpy in front of. I felt Grandpa Butch grab my arm.

"Sit down, Kyle. Come on, son."

I really didn't want to leave the office so I turned and returned to my seat.

"Listen, Kyle, this isn't going to be easy. These kids aren't going to welcome you with open arms. You're a threat; you played for a school they hate, for God's sake. You're going to have to earn their trust...and it could take all season." Grandpa put his hand on my left arm. "You just be yourself and treat everyone they way you want to be treated. And you run that ball like you always run the ball, especially against Davis Prep, you hear me? It's going to be okay."

The second reference to the Davis Prep game. Dad must have told Grandpa Butch about my performance because I don't ever remember seeing Grandpa at any of my games.

"Your grandfather's right, Kyle. No one said it was gonna be easy. But it will all be worth it when we're in that championship game, buddy. I promise you that."

How could I not play football? It was late August...it was time for football whether at Crandall or wherever.

"Okay, Coach. I'm in."

Coach Bonfiglio clapped his hands and smiled broadly. "Alright then. Equipment is Thursday morning...we start double sessions on Friday." He stood and winced noticeably. "Come on, I'll show you the weight room."

I was surprised by the size and quality of the weight room. Coach Bonfiglio explained that a wealthy alumnus who owned a bunch of fitness centers had donated almost all of the equipment. I was actually pretty excited because I had become a weight room warrior during the past year and this room compared favorably to the Fairview exercise center.

There were four kids, obviously football players, pumping iron. Two of them were speaking to each other in a foreign language, although it definitely wasn't Spanish.

Coach Bonfiglio cleared his throat loudly to be heard above the eardrum shattering hip hop blasting on the old stereo in the corner. A large white board proclaimed the names of all those students who had bench pressed over 200 pounds. Judging by the number of names on the list, there were plenty of strong kids at Crandall High.

When the lifters noticed Coach, one of them immediately rushed to turn off the radio. Pretty impressive. We would have done the same thing at Fairview if Coach Pearson walked into the room.

"Boys, this is Kyle Donovan. I'm sure a couple of you know all about him. He's gonna be playing for us this year. I want you to make him feel welcome."

The responses ranged from indifference to glares of outright hostility from two of the players. There was an awkward silence and one of the kids, kind of short and well-built with a black crew cut, stepped forward and grudgingly offered a hand.

"I'm Sal LoGrasso," he said. "Quarterback." He shot a glance at Coach Bonfiglio. "Hope to be the quarterback anyway."

I shook Sal's hand and said, "Kyle. Hope we have a great year."

Sal nodded. "Yeah...I heard you're pretty good."

I smiled slightly and said, "Well, I've done okay. You guys are supposed to be good this year, huh?"

Before Sal could respond, a very large Hispanic looking kid with a small black mustache and wearing an Under Armor doo rag approached me and said, "How you doing, Kyle? I'm Eduardo Alves and *eu protegerei seu burro este ano!*"

I had no idea what Eduardo had just said but Sal burst out laughing and whacked Eduardo on the back of his head. I shrugged my shoulders and looked to Sal for help.

"He said he was going to protect your butt this year. Eddie's our starting right tackle," Sal said.

The other two kids continued their work on the bench as if I wasn't even there.

"Hey guys, come on, introduce yourself to Kyle," Coach Bonfiglio barked.

The two toweled off and walked very slowly. The bigger one (and obviously the leader) offered his hand and said, "I'm Marco...starting tailback." He emphasized the word starting. His black eyed glare made me uncomfortable and I wasn't sure how to react. This hadn't happened much at Fairview. I averted my eyes even though I know Grandpa Butch would tell me this was the wrong reaction.

When I looked again at Marco, his unblinking glower hadn't changed. "I'm Kyle...look forward to the season."

I tried to pull my hand away but Marco wouldn't let go. "I gained over 800 yards last year. Some division two schools are real interested in me but I need a big year this year, you know what I mean?"

It was difficult to return his angry stare. I glanced at Sal and Eduardo but it seemed like they were waiting for my next move. "Well, I hope you'll gain a thousand this year. I heard Bentley has a real good program. I know a couple of kids playing up there."

Marco's grip softened slightly. He moved closer, almost nose to nose and whispered, "Don't screw up my senior year, I'm warning you. Eu estou indo faze-lo muito peraroso...you'll be very sorry."

Marco finally released my hand and returned to the bench. The other kid, and Eduardo and Sal, followed.

Coach Bonfiglio walked us to the door and repeated how excited he was that I would be playing for Crandall this year.

We headed for home in silence. Finally, Grandpa Butch said, "That Marco seems like the friendly type." He looked at me and chuckled.

"Yeah, what a winning personality. Hey, Grandpa, what language was Eduardo and Marco speaking anyway?"

Grandpa smiled and said, "Portuguese. Those boys are Brazilian. Better get used to hearing that language. Hell, even I know a few lines."

I nodded. I guess I better get to know a few lines myself.

Chapter Four

Equipment distribution was pretty uneventful even though I kind of felt like a freak with most of the guys constantly staring at me. Except for Marco Almeida and his sidekick, Antonio (whom everyone called Ricky for some reason...I didn't call him anything as of yet). They glared, not stared. I basically avoided their gazes and concentrated on getting through this as soon as possible.

I was the second in line and Coach Bonfiglio and Andy Brennan (running backs coach) spent a lot of time making sure my helmet and shoulder pads fit perfectly. I felt a little self-conscious because these hardguy coaches were definitely being extra nice.

Coach Bonfiglio asked what number I wanted and I almost said "28". I had worn this number since I was eleven (it was Curtis Martin's number). Luckily, I had been scanning last year's yearbook while waiting for the coaches to show up (Grandpa Butch had gotten me to the school 40 minutes early) and I noticed that Marco wore number 28. So I guess I wouldn't be wearing Curtis Martin's number this year. Coach Bonfiglio offered me number 35 and I said that would be fine.

Sal and Eduardo gave me the insider's tour of the school after we received our equipment. The cheerleading team was practicing in the gym and we stopped to evaluate their new routines. Their summer practice outfits encouraged us to extend the observation period longer than we should have. We could have stayed even longer if Eduardo hadn't yelled out "Ooh, Mama!!" The cheerleader coach saw us and ordered us out of the gym. As I was leaving, I noticed a cheerleader with reddish brown hair and perfect teeth smiling in my direction. For some reason, I felt a little embarrassed and turned away. Eduardo noticed and immediately began busting my chops.

"Oh, little preppie boy's face is redder than usual. Boy, that's Katie O'Brien. What do you think, huh? She's Irish, too. You Irish, ain't you, Kyle? Donovan, that's an Irish name, man."

That was actually a good question. I knew I was at least half Irish but my dad never made a big deal out of it. I don't know...it seemed like no one in Fairview had a nationality except American. It was kind of weird, though. I'd only been living with Grandpa Butch for a few days but he appeared much more ethnic than almost anyone in Fairview. And I hadn't even discussed the issue of ethnicity with him.

"Yeah, I'm Irish. Half Irish anyway. I don't really know what my mother is...a mix of a lot of stuff. And, yeah, that cheerleader is cute," I said with a shrug.

Eduardo started cackling. "Ha, ha, ha. You better act fast, man. Ain't too many Irish girls at Crandall, man." He put his arm around me. "And no Brazilian girl gonna touch you, man. Their papas will kill them." He nodded towards Sal who was laughing softly. "Even Sal, man. He took a Brazilian sister to the movies and her brother came rushing into the place with a switchblade ready to kill him." Eduardo now started laughing hysterically. "You should have seen him, man. Sal runs out of the theater, left his jacket and everything. And Sal's Italian, man. Least he looks more like us than you Irish crackers. You date any more Brazilian girls, Sal?"

Sal shook his head. "No way. Value my life too much."

We walked around the school a little more, checked out the new cafeteria and computer lab. Eduardo seemed to know everyone. When I asked him why all the custodians knew him by name, he said, "Man, I had detention so much, I'm like an honorary member of the janitors union or something. Plus, my Uncle Fuzzy used to work at the school until they caught him selling football cards to the seniors."

Sal was a little more distant although, he too seemed to know virtually everyone by name.

We walked outside and Sal offered to drive me home. I had decided earlier to take the bus home so I could get a handle on how to get around. Before they left, Sal said, "Don't worry about Marco, Kyle. He's just a little mad, that's all. You're a threat, you know? Just help us win and everything will be fine. We got a real chance this year. A real good chance to win it all. You can help us do it...everyone knows that, even Marco and Ricky. See you tomorrow."

I shook hands with both and tried to find the right bus stop. I didn't know much about city life but I did know that getting on the wrong bus could result me ending up in downtown Boston. So I really had to concentrate although it was difficult with the six foot tall transvestite trying to make eye contact.

Bus number 94 came rolling down Main Street. This bus would take me to Hubbard Square and from there I figured I could walk the half mile to Grandpa Butch's house. This may sound pathetic but I could recall only one other time that I had actually been on a bus. Paul and I had gone into Boston and his car broke down so we took a bus to his father's office. That's it.

I was one of a few white people on the bus but I really didn't feel threatened. Most of the white passengers were elderly...the rest were workers finishing their day or mothers with baby carriages. Oh yeah, there was one large transvestite.

I spent the rest of the day setting up my new room. Grandpa had already set up a Wifi (although he called it "Wisefive") connection for me so I was online within a few minutes.

My phone vibrated, and I noticed a text from Ashley.

"Hey, what's up?" read her message.

"Nm..u?"

"How's Crandall? Did u get my phone message?"

Now what do I say? I could just turn off my phone and pretend that my Fairview world never really existed, that my real destiny was to be sitting in my grandfather's house in Crandall, worrying about a bunch of Brazilian kids attempting to take my head off in about fourteen hours.

"Crandall's ok. Not as bad as I thought. Got your message...been pretty busy," I typed.

"When can I see u?? Miss u!"

When could Ashley see me? Maybe she could meet me in Hubbard Square and we'd take bus number 94 down to Kiley's Tavern then maybe grab a bowl of *feijoada* at Little Brazil's.

"Don't know. Doubles start tomorrow."

"U mad at me?"

Mad at Ashley? I guess I was kind of mad at Ashley and anyone else who lived in my old world. What could I really say to her? Gee, things are great...wish you were here!! My new high school has metal detectors, half the team already hates me and my grandfather's car smells like a bingo hall. Oh yeah, and my mother's going crazy and my dad's in New York. Sure, let's get together and reminisce about old times.

"Really tired...gotta go. Good luck this year, Ash."

I shook my head, sighed, and went downstairs. Grandpa Butch was just walking through the front door.

"Well, look at himself. How you doing, Boyo?" he said.

I shrugged and helped him with a couple of the bags he was carrying.

"You get your equipment?" Grandpa asked.

"Yeah, coaches were really cool."

"How were the kids?"

"Some friendly, some not so friendly. Just like the weight room the other day."

"That kid Marco there?" I nodded.

"How was he?" Grandpa asked.

"Same as the other day except this time he didn't talk at all. He just stared, you know what I mean?"

We put the groceries away and I saw my father's initials again inside a cabinet door. I felt myself getting angry at my dad again.

"You gotta be hungry, right?" Grandpa asked. He took some Hot Pockets and French fries out of the freezer. "These okay?"

I'm pretty sure that my answer would be of no consequence so I said nothing and Grandpa went ahead and stuck the Hot Pockets in the microwave.

We ate the meal quickly and quietly. Grandpa brought out some cookie dough ice cream, scooped out a huge amount, handed me the bowl and said, "Go ahead into the parlor. I'll be right in."

I sat on the couch and began to demolish the bowl of ice

cream. I was half done when Grandpa entered, holding a videotape. He silently walked over to the television and inserted the cassette into the VCR. He looked at me and sat down in his recliner.

It was a football game, specifically the Fairview Prep vs. Davis Prep game played last October. A slight drizzle interfered with the video slightly but the picture was pretty clear. I could see number 28 for Fairview running sweeps and picks, the ball lodged tightly under the fundamentally correct arm each time. Number 28 eluded would be tacklers with his speed and balance and sometimes simply met them head on, inflicting more punishment on the defenders then they bargained for from a tailback.

We watched in silence for about a half hour. It seemed that number 28 carried the ball about a hundred times. I have to admit...I was real good in that game. Davis Prep was a solid team. Two of their defensive linemen got Division One scholarships. Our offensive line was smaller but quick and tough. We ended up winning 21-14 and Coach Pearson gave me the game ball. Although I was sore for at least three days after the game, it was most definitely the high point in my football career...so far, anyway.

The game ended and Grandpa rose and ejected the tape. He looked at me and smiled that grin that I was becoming more used to. "You can play with anyone, Kyle. City kids, prep school kids...don't matter. It's still football. And you can play football. Remember that tomorrow. Now go up and get some sleep. Big day tomorrow."

I nodded.

"You know, I've caused some real pain in my life, Kyle. It

wasn't that I quit drinking and started praying for real that things began to change," Grandpa said.

"What do you mean, pray for real?" I asked.

Grandpa Butch smiled. "Oh, you know. I was like a lot of Catholics...went to Mass every once in a while, didn't eat meat on Fridays during Lent...you know, all the regular stuff. But then..." Grandpa's voice faded and he looked down at his callused hands. "I guess I got religion. Started meeting with this priest, Father Gambel, a French Canadian. He was an alcoholic, too. Met him at an AA meeting, believe it or not. Things started making sense. He said that God has a plan for everyone...we all have a purpose. I sure wasn't fulfilling my purpose drinking all the time." Grandpa shook his head and almost shivered. "I try not to think about those drinking days...I don't remember much, anyway, I guess. So I started reading the Bible...mainly the New Testament. Every time I read it, I seem to learn something new." Grandpa laughed. "Wish I could quote verses, but I can't. The Protestants are much better at that stuff." He smiled. "Kind of wished I was always a Protestant but...too late for that now."

I stood, walked over to Grandpa Butch and hugged him. I'm not sure why I did this but it felt right and Grandpa returned my embrace.

"Go ahead now. I'll wake you up at six thirty."

I lay on the bed with my Ipod and chuckled when Kanye's song, "Power" came on. It reminded me of Paul and I wondered what he was doing right now. Probably lying in his bed, thinking about double sessions. I thought of giving him a call but that would take way too much effort.

Surprisingly, I woke up before Grandpa Butch had a chance to harass me out of the bed. He was cooking some eggs when I entered the kitchen. I cleared my throat and he turned and chuckled. "Well, well...you sure you got enough beauty sleep?"

"Someday I'll be up before you, Grandpa. You wait and see."

Grandpa scoffed. "Unless you join the Corps, you'll never beat me."

After breakfast, Grandpa offered to drive me to school but I wanted to get used to taking the bus. It was already pretty humid and it was only seven thirty in the morning. The heat never really bothers me like some guys though. Coach Pearson at Fairview was an old school type coach but he definitely took an enlightened view of the importance of being hydrated. We always had plenty of water and could head over to the water table for a drink anytime during practice. Double sessions were supposed to take place in unbearably hot weather and as long as there was plenty of water, it really wasn't that bad.

The morning session involved a lot of administrative stuff. We were tested on the bench and the 40 yard dash and the coaches timed us in the quarter mile. I was in great shape and drew some impressive eyebrow raising when I pushed 265 lbs up on the bench. My forty time was 4.7 seconds which wasn't bad although Marco ran his in 4.65 seconds. He also benched 290 lbs. So I start off a little behind.

Football finally started in the afternoon session. The pads felt heavy like they always did at the beginning. We did some light hitting drills to get used to the contact. I was with the running backs and Coach Brennan lined up the "gauntlet" drill. There was one runner and two rows of backs that would whack the runner as he ran through the "gauntlet."

"Okay, boys, gauntlet drill. Half speed, guys. Get used to feeling the pads again. Kyle, you go first." He flipped me the football.

I gripped the ball under my right arm. "Remember, half speed," Coach Brennan said.

I began to run through the gauntlet and the first couple of rows stuck out their shoulders and made light contact. I felt pretty comfortable until Marco wound up and, with full force, flung his right forearm into my facemask. The hit surprised me (I was running half speed) and I stumbled backwards and fell on my back with a thud. I looked up and saw Marco standing over me, snickering loudly. Coach Brennan pushed him aside and said, "You alright, Kyle?"

I gathered myself and tried to get up as quickly as possible. "I'm fine," I said. I slapped Marco on the helmet and said, "Nice pop, Marco. I'll go again."

The rest of the running backs had quizzical looks on their faces as if they knew that this story hadn't ended yet.

I grabbed the ball and raced through the gauntlet at full speed. When I reached Marco, I could see him bracing himself for the inevitable. I lowered my shoulder and drove my entire body into Marco. He did likewise and there was a collision loud enough for Coach Bonfiglio (who was next to us with his offensive linemen) to turn around.

The collision was a standoff and left both of us shaking the cobwebs out of our helmets.

Later, we ran our first team offense and Coach Bonfiglio had

Marco and I switching at tailback every three plays. Sal directed the offense flawlessly and Eduardo blocked almost as well as he said he could. The offense was pretty sharp for a first day. You could tell that a lot of these kids had played together...the offense was a unit and I just wanted to fit in as well as possible. I just ran the holes and kept my mouth shut. Antonio/Ricky played on the scout defense and tried to tackle me hard a couple of times but he really wasn't quick or physical enough to play the tough guy.

The fullback was a sophomore who seemed a little intimidated by starting for the varsity. Coach Bonfiglio ran a real basic offense with a lot of plays run out of the "I" formation. We also ran a "Power I" where there would be three running backs in the backfield. So the fullback had to block like an agile offensive lineman and get very few carries or glory. Any defense lining up against Coach Bonfiglio better buckle up their chinstraps. It was more important for the quarterback to be a good ball handler than to be an accomplished passer.

Coach Bonfiglio also believed in repetition which meant long practices and a demand for perfection. He wasn't a big screamer but the combination of his imposing physical presence and obvious wealth of football knowledge made yelling unnecessary. A couple of the assistants were screamers but that was par for the course.

I was a bit surprised by how respectful and responsive the Crandall players were. There was definitely more grumbling and general complaining at Fairview. Maybe it was too early to make any comparisons since it was still the first day of football...but it was interesting just the same.

I showered and sat in front of my locker, exhausted but it

was that tiredness that actually felt good, like you had accomplished something. A couple of the other running backs gave me high fives on their way out of the shower and, for a brief moment, I felt almost like I belonged. That feeling was shattered when Marco stopped in front of me and said, "Gonna be tougher tomorrow, preppie. Gonna hit for real tomorrow, man. Today was just a taste, rich boy."

I turned down Sal's offer of a ride and dragged myself on the bus. The same driver drove the 94 every day and he nodded in recognition when I boarded the bus. I nodded back, sat down and tried not to fall asleep or I'd end up lost somewhere in greater Boston. Tomorrow was a new day.

CHAPTER FIVE

The morning session focused on defense which meant that I would have to take some carries against the first defense. Running the ball for the scout offense was a little like being a sparring partner for Mike Tyson. You basically got the crap beaten out of you and then just watched the defense congratulate themselves on how good they are. I ran scout offense a lot for Fairview when I was a sophomore. The only good thing about playing for the scout team is that it gives the coaches a chance to notice you doing something. All coaches like "tough" kids, players who aren't afraid to hit or be hit. On every staff, there's usually one coach who looks out for the "tough" kids and those kids generally earn some playing time, often on special teams. My goal for the morning was to make that coach (whoever he was) notice me.

"Okay first D...let's get an offense out here," Coach Bonfiglio said. Some kids try to hide when it was time to do some real live hitting. Those were the "happy to wear a uniform" players. We had them at Fairview and I could already see that it was the same at Crandall. I glanced around and, sure enough, I saw a bunch of players head for the back of the line, outside of the coaches' view. Like Grandpa Butch said, football is football, no matter where it's played.

I jumped in at tailback and I noticed Coach Brennan nod

approvingly. He would call the offense while Coach Bonfiglio and Coach Kennedy, the linebackers coach, handled the defense. I think that Coach Kennedy was certifiably insane. Eduardo told me that he dented a locker with his head during halftime of a game last year. The guy was at least sixty years old! He seemed like one of those old school coaches that didn't worry about liability lawsuits or public perception. In other words, he could haul off and whack someone at any time. In a strange way, though, he seemed like a really good guy. That's the world of high school football.

Marco started at cornerback for the defense and I could see him slapping fives with Antonio/Ricky who played safety. I looked at the offensive line that was going to block for me and I resigned myself to taking a serious beating. It wasn't that the line wouldn't try...it's just that this line was composed of mostly eager Sophomores and Juniors who weren't big or good enough to start. I saw the fear in their eyes and heard the quarterback's voice break. Ah well, this was the life of the new guy.

Billy Carbone, the backup quarterback, called the play and the offensive line sprinted to the line of scrimmage. That was slightly encouraging although I wish the coaches would let Sal run the scout offense but there was no way they would risk injury to their starting quarterback.

Billy tossed the ball to me, the offside guard pulled like he was supposed to and the fullback, Jimmy Killoran, attempted to block the defensive end like he was taught. Unfortunately, the defensive end, Troy Clark, 240 pounds of aggression and speed with dreadlocks sticking out from under his helmet, threw Killoran aside like a candy wrapper and focused all of his hostility on me. I stopped suddenly and tried to cut back. Troy dived and grabbed my left leg. I attempted to pry it loose but by this time all the blocks failed and at least four defenders threw their bodies at my upright figure. I ducked slightly and as I fell to the ground, I saw Marco put the finishing touch on the tackle by placing his shoulder in my ribs. That hurt.

One of the defenders at the bottom of the pile said quietly, "Welcome to Crandall, preppie." For some reason, I found this funny. I laughed and pushed the defenders off and jumped to my feet. I flipped the ball to Coach Bonfiglio and jogged back to the huddle. I slapped Jimmy Killoran on the back of his shoulder pads and said, "Come on, Jimmy, you gotta at least try to block him."

Jimmy was the sophomore who started at fullback. If he blocked like that, neither Marco nor myself would make it through the first game.

Getting hit never bothered me so I was ready to carry the ball again. Coach Brennan called a "15 Pick" which meant that I would run for the 5 hole between the offensive tackle and defensive end. The offensive tackle and tight end would double team the defensive tackle and the fullback would kick out the defensive end. The other starting defensive end, Deron Willis, was good but not nearly as fast as Troy. Maybe Jimmy would have a shot at blocking this time.

I took the handoff from Billy and the hole opened up momentarily. Jimmy held his block for a couple of seconds but Deron was able to square his body and meet me head on when I reached the hole. I lowered my shoulder and drove Deron back at least a yard. Momentum carried me another two or three yards before the linebackers could make it over and finish the tackle.

"Gain of four, defense!" Coach Brennan screamed.

The offensive line was gaining a bit of confidence. They slapped each other on the helmet and whacked me on the back. "Good job, Jimmy," I said to Killoran who nodded in appreciation.

Coach Bonfiglio was busy reaming out the defense. Coach Brennan smiled in the huddle and said, "Okay, boys, let's really screw them up now. Pro left, torpedo, swing pass left."

When we got to the line of scrimmage, there were nine defenders in the box. They fully expected a running play. A couple of the down linemen grunted and the linebackers always yelled something inaudible. I put everything else out of my mind and focused on the play.

The flanker went in motion and the linebackers screamed for the defensive line to shift. One of the linebackers, Raymond Boursiquot, stepped to the line of scrimmage. He was blitzing. If the guard could get in his way and Billy maintained his composure, this could be a huge play.

The ball was snapped and I flared out to the left. Billy faked the handoff to the fullback. The sophomore guard barely touched Raymond but that gave Billy time to drop three steps. He softly threw the ball just ahead of my forward momentum. Just about the entire defense was in the backfield. I'm sure that Billy got absolutely hammered by Raymond but he got the pass off.

I caught the ball with my fingertips, tucked it and headed for the outside. I had decent speed and the defensive end and linebackers had been sucked in. I turned the corner with a vengeance and there was only one player to beat. Antonio/Ricky stood between me and the goal line.

I had already surmised that Antonio/Ricky wasn't that good. I probably could just outrun him but that wouldn't be satisfying enough. I sought him out, saw him crouch low and lowered my shoulder. Antonio/Ricky had no leverage so he had no shot at stopping me or even slowing me down. I left him on the ground and sprinted into the end zone.

The scout offense mobbed me as if we had just won the Super Bowl. Coach Bonfiglio was furiously blowing his whistle and Coach Brennan was screaming at us to return to the huddle. As I jogged back to the huddle, Antonio/Ricky ran beside me and said, "Hey, good run, preppie."

I glanced at him and said, "Thanks...the name's Kyle."

He smiled and said, "Yeah, yeah, I know. Call me Ricky, man."

"Why Ricky?"

He stopped and laughed. "Cause I look just like Ricky Martin, white boy." He then sprinted over to Coach Bonfiglio who had the entire first defense doing push-ups. You know, he really did look like Ricky Martin.

The rest of the morning session was uneventful. Sal, Eduardo and Raymond Boursiquot were going out to lunch between sessions and I was tempted to join them until I saw my father standing behind the chain link fence that lined the practice field.

I took off my shoulder pads which were soaked with sweat and walked across the track. The cheerleaders were doing calisthenics on the track and I noticed the auburn haired girl again. I tried not to stare too obviously but it was really tough. I quickly looked in her direction and I saw her smile and give the tiniest of waves. I know I blushed a little but at least this time I returned the smile and the wave. Today had been a good day...so far anyway.

I reached my dad and saw that he was dressed very casually in an old polo shirt, khaki shorts and basketball sneakers. I shook my head and tried to concentrate on my father but that cheerleader's smile and wave kept invading my mind.

"How are you son?" Dad asked as I reached the fence.

"Pretty good...not a bad day so far. I'm running with the scout offense but it's okay." I looked over Dad's outfit. "You don't look very Fairview today."

Dad laughed. "Well, I'm not feeling very Fairview today, Kyle. You got time for lunch?"

I jogged inside and changed quickly. I scanned the parking lot for my father's car but couldn't find it. I heard a loud beep and traced it to a black Chevy Malibu. I saw Dad sticking his head out the driver's side window.

"What happened to the Audi?" I asked as I wedged myself into the front seat.

"I wasn't kidding when I said we were starting from scratch," Dad responded.

We drove to the Hubbard Café which I gathered was a high school hangout for Dad and his Crandall High buddies back in the Stone Age.

"This place had the best steak tips and onion rings in the world twenty years ago," Dad said as he pulled into a parking space.

I chuckled. "I never even knew you ate steak tips, Dad."

He put the car in park and looked at me. "I'll be eating them today, Kyle."

We entered through the restaurant side. The place was about half full and I'd bet money that everyone sitting in the Hubbard

Café could be classified as a regular. We waited at the hostess station to be seated.

"Oh my God, you've got to be kidding me. Look who's here!" I turned to find the speaker of those words because it was probably the finest Boston accent I'd ever heard...even better than Grandpa Butch.

I saw a woman about Dad's age with medium length brown hair, a nice tan and unbelievably blue eyes standing behind Dad and me with both hands pressed against her cheeks.

"Timmy Donovan...T-Bone! You remember me, right Timmy?"

Dad's face broke into a broad grin and he looked as happy as I remember him looking in weeks. "MaryAnn...how you doing?"

They hugged and I did notice that both of them held the hug a few seconds longer than necessary. MaryAnn must be one of Dad's old babes, back when he was the big man on campus at Crandall High. I imagined my dad walking around school with his sideburns and letter jacket, girls hanging on each arm. I shook my head and laughed. Just didn't seem possible.

"How have you been doing, Timmy?" MaryAnn asked and it seemed like she did actually care how Dad had been doing.

Dad shrugged a little and said, "Okay, MaryAnn...been better, been worse. How are you? How's Gus?"

MaryAnn's head dropped and she closed her eyes briefly. While her head was still down, she said, "Didn't work out too well, Timmy. Gus never stopped drinking...it seemed like high school never ended for him. So we ended it a couple of years ago. Just as well...I would have wound up in an insane asylum or the morgue if I stayed with him."

There was silence for a couple of moments. Not a real awkward, uncomfortable silence but the type of quiet when you just found out something and you were trying to figure out a response.

Finally, Dad said, "Well, I'm sorry, MaryAnn. You deserve a lot better, believe me."

MaryAnn seemed to perk up a bit when Dad made that statement and smiled warmly. She looked over our shoulders...a line had begun to form at the hostess station. "I almost forgot I was working. Come on, boys, I'll get you a booth."

We sat in an old brown leather booth and MaryAnn handed us our menus. "Kim the waitress will be right over."

"MaryAnn, I never introduced you to my son. This is Kyle. Kyle, this is MaryAnn Kilkenny...or is it Stavros?" Dad said.

I half stood and MaryAnn grabbed my outstretched hand and said, "Don't get up, honey. MaryAnn Kilkenny. It's nice to meet you." She nodded toward Dad. "Your Dad was quite a guy around Crandall back when disco was king. Timmy, make sure you show Kyle the pictures near the bar."

Dad seemed a little embarrassed and his face turned a shade red, probably the same color as mine when I waved to Katie O'Brien.

"Anyway, I gotta get back to work. It was great meeting you, Kyle." She stared at Dad with those sky blue eyes. "I work here five days a week, Tim. Be sure to stop back again, okay?"

Dad opened a menu and held it so I couldn't see his face.

"You gonna show me those pictures, Dad?" I asked.

Dad put the menu down. "Ancient history, Kyle. You ever hear that Springsteen song, 'Glory Days'? That's what MaryAnn's talking about."

Dad and I both ordered the steak tips although I was becoming a little worried about being too full for the afternoon session. I'm not sure Coach Bonfiglio would take kindly to his second team tailback puking his guts out.

Dad took a long sip of his Diet Coke and said, "Things didn't go great in New York, Kyle. A lot of people seem to forget the promises they made."

"So what's that mean?" I asked.

Dad played with the fork on the table. "Not sure right now. There might be something in Hartford. I'm going to check that out tomorrow. If that doesn't work out..."

He didn't finish the sentence so I guess if Hartford didn't work out chances were slim anything would work out.

"Are these banks you're talking to?" I asked.

Dad nodded. "They were willing to anything for me when we were flying high. Now that I hit a rough patch, they act like they've never seen me before. It's tough."

Our steak tips came and they were as delicious as advertised.

"What's going on with Mom?" I asked.

Dad seemed taken aback by the question. He washed down a steak tip with his Diet Coke and looked straight at me. "I'm not completely sure, to tell you the truth. She's been depressed for quite a while and..."

Another unfinished sentence. Come on, Dad, be honest with me.

This time, Dad didn't need my prompt. "She just needs time to get her head together, Kyle. There's a great facility up in Vermont that deals with this stuff." Dad stared blankly past me at the huge painting of Bird, Parish and McHale on the wall. "I ignored it. All we did was fight when I was home and she would just sleep or wouldn't talk at all. So I just didn't come home much. I'm sure you noticed, right?"

Yeah, I knew Dad was hardly ever home but I figured he was at work. Everyone's father in Fairview spent almost every waking hour at the office. I also knew Mom was sleeping a lot and she didn't look right but I guess I didn't care that much. The guilt feelings were returning in a hurry.

"Are you and Mom definitely getting divorced?" I asked.

Dad nodded. "It's for the best, Kyle."

We quietly finished the steak tips and onion rings.

"You want dessert?" Dad asked.

I was stuffed and any further food intake would have dire consequences in about forty five minutes. "No, I'm all set, Dad."

We drove back to the school. As I was getting out of the car, Dad said, "Your grandfather treating you alright?"

I thought of Grandpa Butch. Seemed like he was the only normal one in the whole screwed up family. "Yeah, he's been great. He really cares about me, about school and football. It's been a big surprise."

Dad laughed softly. "I guess he's trying to do it right this time around. Alright, buddy, I'll see you when you get home. I'm staying at Grandpa's house tonight...I have to leave for Hartford early in the morning. You want me to pick you up this afternoon?"

I shook my head. "I've been trying to figure out the bus system. The sooner the better, I think."

I started walking towards the locker room. The track, bleachers and field were empty. No sign of Katie O'Brien. I felt the steak tips settle in my stomach. Maybe it wasn't going to such a great day after all.

Chapter Six

Three generations of Donovan men sat around Grandpa Butch's kitchen table and ate pizza from Cerullo's. I had noticed that Grandpa's demeanor had changed considerably since Dad arrived at the house and it only had been a few hours. He seemed more guarded, quieter. I decided to break the silence mainly because the quieter it was, the more pronounced Grandpa's chewing became.

"What time you heading out?" I asked my father.

Dad swallowed some pizza and said, "Tomorrow morning. I figure I'll leave around 6:30...try to beat some of the traffic."

Grandpa Butch stood and brought his paper plate over to the trash barrel. "You guys want something else to drink?" he asked.

"I'm all set, Grandpa," I said. "Where you sleeping tonight?" I asked my father.

Dad shrugged. "It doesn't matter...I'll sleep on the couch in the parlor."

"You can sleep in your old room...I'll take the couch."

Dad shook his head. "Nah...you're all settled in up there."

And the conversation ended which was kind of strange because my Dad and I always could talk even in bad times. I guess it was just as well because all I really wanted to do was lie down. The hits from the first defense were starting to take their toll...now the adrenaline had died down.

I went upstairs and lay down on the bed and tried to concentrate on Coach Brennan's playbook. Thank God it was pretty uncomplicated...a few basic formations and a bunch of plays run out of each formation. I put on my Ipod and tried to chill.

I woke up with a drool drenched page of the playbook stuck to my cheek. I shook my head and opened my cell phone. It was 9:30...I had been asleep for two hours. I felt a little better but I had that feeling where you think it's much later than it actually is. I yawned and walked towards the staircase.

I heard Dad and Grandpa Butch talking quietly when I reached the top of the staircase. They were in the parlor and the Red Sox game was turned down low. It sounded like a serious conversation so I didn't want to interrupt them. On the other hand, I really wanted to hear what they were saying. So I knelt down beside the handrail and listened.

"He's a great kid, Tim. You gotta think of him. He's already made friends," Grandpa said.

Dad chuckled. "Glad to see you thinking of someone else," he said.

Grandpa's voice remained calm. "Take all the shots you want. I know I deserve them but we're talking about Kyle here."

"Yeah, I know. He's my son. I just don't know about this whole thing...he's not a city kid...I saw a drug deal going down under the bleachers when I was waiting for him today. The kids knew I saw them and they just laughed. Imagine that? They just laughed."

"He's gonna do fine here...trust me. You move him again, what's that do to him? Come on, Tim, he's already playing football, he starts school on Monday. There's still a lot of good kids around here. I see them every day," Grandpa said.

"Did you say 'trust you', Dad? Based on what? What if you start drinking again? I know you found God and all that but..." Dad said.

Grandpa' voice began to rise a bit. "That's not fair, Tim. Haven't had a drop in thirty one years, three months and fifteen days. Don't mock what faith has done for me. Maybe you should try to go to church yourself someday."

Dad chuckled softly. "Haven't seen much of God lately, Dad. I guess you have...wish you had seen him a few years ago."

"I can't rewrite history, Tim. Wish I could, but I can't. But I do know that you have a fine boy there who's been through hell. He needs some stability. You know that. I'll watch out for him."

"To be honest, that's part of what worries me. He's almost seventeen years old, Dad...what are you going to do if he comes home drunk? What if his grades begin to fall?"

"You'll just be in Hartford. It's not like a different time zone. Listen, I live with my mistakes everyday...think it's always easy for me to look in the mirror? I'll do right by him though Tim. I promise you that."

There was silence for a couple of minutes and I imagined it was an uncomfortable silence even though I wasn't in the room. Grandpa Butch cleared his throat and the flem could have knocked the house off the foundation. I gathered that the conversation had ended so I ventured downstairs.

Dad sat on the couch, half reading the Globe and occasionally glancing at the Sox on the television. Grandpa lay on the recliner, almost asleep.

I walked past the parlor and headed for the kitchen. For some reason, I was hungry again. I opened the refrigerator and heard Dad say, "Hey, Kyle... could you come in here for a minute?"

I had a good idea as to the subject matter of this conversation. I tried to decipher what was to come. Hey, I wasn't crazy about living with my grandfather in Crandall but I was almost certain that it would beat moving to Hartford and starting over again. Even though I had only been living in Crandall for a few days, I liked most of the kids on the team and Coach Bonfiglio seemed like a really good guy. And classes started tomorrow...and I might get to see Katie O'Brien again.

I entered the parlor. Dad looked up from the paper and took off his reading glasses. Grandpa Butch's eyes were closed but I don't think that he was really asleep. I had done it enough times to recognize a fake sleep.

"Hey, buddy, let's talk for a few minutes," Dad said in that calm, measured tone that he used when he wanted to be persuasive.

I shrugged and sat down on the couch next to my father.

"You know I'm going down to Hartford tomorrow. I got a call this afternoon...things might work out down there. If they do, I'd have to move...the commute would be much too far."

Even though I knew this was coming, I felt really upset for some reason. "Yeah, how does this involve me?"

Dad cleared his throat. "Well, I'd like you to move down there with me. I called around a little...there's some really good schools...and some really solid football programs."

My anger just increased. I'm not really sure why I was so upset but I felt the heat rising. What the heck? First, they move me to Crandall...now, a week later, he wants me to move to Hartford? Screw that...I wasn't moving again. I'll take my chances in Crandall with Grandpa Butch.

"I'm not moving again, Dad," I said. I think that my tone was respectful but I wasn't sure how much respect my father deserved right now.

Dad seemed a little taken aback. He put down the newspaper. "You want to stay in Crandall? You're not a city kid, Kyle...it's a whole different world down here."

Now he thought I couldn't hack it in Crandall? "I'm fine here. I already made some friends. The kids will be fine...and I'll be playing football."

Dad sighed. "You'll be better off in Hartford with me."

"What about Mom? I miss Mom!" I shouted. I don't know why those words came out of my mouth. But I did miss my mother. All I knew was that she was in Vermont in some facility. I didn't have an address, a phone number, an email...nothing. Here was my father, talking about moving to Hartford. It was like my mother never existed.

"We talked about your mother, Kyle. She's in Vermont...I told you that. You can see her when she's ready. But I want you to come to Hartford with me."

I breathed deeply. "I'm not going to Hartford. I'm staying here. I'm going to school tomorrow at Crandall High and then I'm going to practice after school. That's what I'm doing."

Dad lowered his voice to almost a whisper. "Come on, Kyle...we'll start fresh in Hartford."

I don't know why I decided to take this stand but something inside was pushing me. "I'm staying here, Dad. And I want to talk to Mom."

My father stood up. "Listen, Kyle..."

Grandpa sat up in his recliner and said, "Okay, Tim..."

Dad turned quickly towards Grandpa. "You got nothing to say here, Dad! You understand? Nothing!"

"Come on, Tim. Let the boy stay here. You don't even know if things are going to work out down in Connecticut. Kyle can start school, play football until you're all settled...that's gotta take a few months anyway. You'll have a new job, you know. That's gonna take time. Let the boy stay here, Tim."

Dad stared at Grandpa with a look of disbelief. He was speechless.

"Grandpa's right, Dad. Let me stay here. At the end of the year, we can figure everything out."

I think that Dad heard me but he continued staring at Grandpa Butch.

Grandpa lifted himself out of the recliner and said softly, "You got a lot of reasons to be angry at me, Tim. I can't change any of it, you know? But I promise you that Kyle will be fine here with me. He can see you every weekend. Hartford's not that far...although never been there myself."

Dad nodded and put his face in his hands. My anger at him subsided. He nodded again and said, "Okay." He stood up, started walking towards the kitchen, stopped and looked like he was going to say something but no words came out. He looked kind of confused and just wandered away. I looked at Grandpa Butch who nodded. I nodded back and went upstairs to bed.

As I walked through the massive front door of Crandall High School and stopped obediently at the metal detectors, I began thinking about the way I was dressed. I guess obsessing would be a better word. I knew that I couldn't show up with a doo rag and throwback jersey...no question I would take a beating for that. On the other hand, I just wasn't sure how white kids dressed in Crandall. The football guys all dressed in shorts and tee shirts during double sessions but I didn't know how they dressed for school.

So I was wearing a pair of black Jordan sweatpants and a white Patriots tee shirt. My Nikes were fairly new but not new enough to attract notice...I hoped anyway. My goal was to keep a low profile. Grandpa Butch had encouraged me to avoid eye contact which actually seemed like pretty good advice. If I knew Sal or Eduardo or anyone on the team a little better, I could have asked them but I wasn't that comfortable with everything yet.

The security guard waved his wand down the sides of my body and I stepped into the hallway. It all had been so quiet last week...today; it was an absolute mob scene. The administrators at Fairview always talked about celebrating diversity which struck me as funny because everyone there basically looked the same. What I was witnessing right now was actual diversity. I heard more than a few languages being spoken and skin colors ranged from pale white (like me) to yellow to light brown to the darkest brown you could imagine. I almost felt like turning around and following Dad down to Hartford.

I looked around almost in desperation for a familiar face. Unfortunately, the only person I recognized was Marco who stood with a group of other Brazilian kids near the stairwell. I wanted to follow Grandpa Butch's advice and avoid eye contact but our eyes met across the hall. I braced for the worst but, to my surprise, Marco simply lifted his head in recognition. I did the same and continued down the hallway.

"Hey, look its Justin Bieber."

I didn't recognize the voice so I kept the walking.

"Hey Justin, turn around honey."

Now I knew I had to turn around and face the voice. "The name's not Justin," I said.

The kid laughed and walked closer. He had a black goatee and a tattoo of a tombstone on his neck. "Your name's Justin," he said, glaring into my face with black eyes, the smile still cemented on his face.

We were nose to nose and I came very close to apologizing to him and agreeing that my name was Justin. But I knew I couldn't do that...at least if I wanted to return to this school the next day.

"Look, I don't want any trouble, but my name's not Justin. That's all." I turned around to walk away and took a couple of steps, fully expecting him to grab my shoulder. And that's exactly what happened. I spun around quickly, ready for death or permanent injury.

His fists were up in some type of martial arts pose. The only karate I knew was from old Bruce Lee movies so I'd have to rely on a couple of quick haymakers and then hope for a teacher or security guard to break it up. I put my fists up around my face and quickly noticed that a large crowd had gathered around us. Did this all have to happen this fast?

Before any punches were thrown, I heard a familiar voice say, "D*eixe-o sozinho*, Freddie. *É alright, ele é um amigo*."

I knew no Portuguese and very little Spanish but I heard "*amigo*" and understood that was a good thing. Freddie lowered his fists and simply nodded at me. He walked away and I turned around saw Eduardo grinning at me.

"Man, you can't stay away from trouble with these Brazilians, Justin," he said, wrapping his huge arm around my shoulder.

My shirt was wet with sweat but I think that I may have passed this test, although I wasn't sure. "Thanks, Eddie. Do you really have to call me Justin?"

Eduardo punched me lightly on the arm. "Just kidding, man. Hey, lucky you didn't beef with Freddie. His brother is big with the MS-13, man. He'd cut you up in a minute."

I had no idea what MS-13 meant...I was just happy to be still standing. I had never looked forward more to going to an Algebra class before.

I entered my math class which was located on the second floor. Some greenish yellow drapes covered the windows, the concrete block walls were painted a pale blue and the floor was covered with dark blue commercial tile. I guess it resembled thousands of other classrooms across the country but I was used to Fairview Prep with carpeted floors, designer curtains, smart boards, and about ten kids in a class. I quickly scanned the classroom and figured that at least thirty students were seated in the perfectly aligned rows.

Familiar faces were important to me and I spied Raymond Boursiquot waving to me from the back left corner. I almost sprinted down to the seat next to Raymond before someone else grabbed it. Raymond and I shook hands and as I directed my attention to the front of the room, Katie O'Brien walked through the door. For the first time, I took a really good look at her and discovered that she was as attractive as I thought. It was going to be real tough to concentrate on Algebra with Katie sitting three seats away.

Mr. Bruno was the teacher and I noticed that most of the kids already had their textbooks and notebooks out. Mr. Bruno was about forty years old, seemed like he knew what he was talking about and he spoke with that Boston accent that was becoming much more familiar to me. I concluded that he had a solid reputation because no one was messing around. This was an honors class so maybe things were different in the regular course.

I made it through the rest of the day relatively unscathed. I discovered on my first day that playing on the football team was going to help my transition greatly. I had dreaded lunchtime and even contemplated just going to the library to kill forty minutes. But I took a chance and ventured into the cafeteria. Eduardo, Sal and some other guys were already sitting at a table so I didn't have to eat alone.

I was standing in front of my locker trying to remember my lock combination when I heard a female voice say, "Hi."

I turned and there she was, Katie O'Brien, standing in front of me. "Hi," I responded. It wasn't much of a response but it was better than an awkward silence which was the only other option.

She stuck out her hand and said, "I'm Katie...I think I'm in your Algebra class."

I nodded and tried to think of something witty or at least acceptable to say. Her eyes were as blue as the sky. I shook her hand, trying not to squeeze too tightly and praying that the hand wasn't too sweaty. "I'm Kyle...I saw you in class. You're a cheerleader too, right?"

Katie smiled and I would say that the orthodontist bills were definitely worth it. Her teeth were white as snow and I got this really weird feeling in my throat when she smiled. It was like this lump right below my Adam's apple.

"I try...I'm not as good as the other girls, though. You play football, right?" she said.

I nodded again. "I'm trying, too."

Katie laughed and we just kind of stood there, staring at each other. If I had any confidence at all, I would have continued the conversation but the lump in my throat seemed to be affecting my ability to speak.

"Well, I guess I have to go to practice," Katie said. "It's nice meeting you."

I nodded again for what seemed the fiftieth time and managed to say, "Yeah, me too. I'll see you tomorrow."

Katie smiled again, turned and walked away. I couldn't take my eyes off her as she walked and she turned her head and gave me another smile and little wave. She caught me red handed but I think that was a good thing.

The hall had cleared out and I just stood there, staring vacantly at the stack of books inside my locker. The ringing of my cell phone snapped me back to reality.

"Where are you, boy? Practice starts in ten minutes and that's Coach B. time, man. You just can't be late," Eduardo said.

Oh crap. "Okay, I'll be right there, Eddie."

"Hurry up, man. Don't make me come get you."

I shook my head and hurriedly threw some books into my backpack. I started running to the locker room but it was sure hard thinking of football, Marco or Coach Bonfiglio at this moment.

CHAPTER SEVEN

It had only been a few weeks but it felt strange driving around Fairview again. It was after seven o'clock but it had to be at least 80 degrees out so I opened the passenger window of Paul Elliot's Beamer. We were buzzing around town like we had hundreds of times in the past but it seemed different.

"So what's it like, man? You know, the hood?" Paul asked.

I chuckled, thinking of Grandpa Butch living in the 'hood', strutting around with a throwback jersey and baggy jeans. Whenever I thought of Grandpa now, I laughed or at least smiled. "It's different...no doubt about that. It's really not that bad, though. The school's not like one of those high schools you see in the movies, with gunfights and kids attacking teachers."

Paul took off his sunglasses. "Yeah, sometimes I envy you. It's like you're living in the real world now." He sighed. "Sometimes everything seems so phony around here, you know? Hey, I'm not saying I want to trade places or anything but you're living life, you know what I mean?" Paul looked at me and I was surprised by his sincerity.

"I'm not glamorizing it, buddy. Let's face it; I almost got stabbed on my first day of school. There's gotta be five hundred languages spoken...it's kind of nerve wracking, you know? And I've only been in school for a week...it might get worse. Some kid already broke all of the toilets in the men's room on the first floor. If you gotta pee, you have to walk two flights of stairs," I said.

"How are the kids?" Paul asked.

I shrugged. That was a good question. I guess I had already made a few friends...Sal, Raymond, my man Eduardo. The rest of the kids on the football team were warming up to me, I think. Even Marco would acknowledge me in school, although never on the football field which seemed kind of weird. And then there was Katie O'Brien.

"Hey, you gonna answer me or not?" Paul asked as he punched me on the arm.

"Yeah, sorry. The kids are pretty cool, especially the guys on the team. Some of the kids in the school are pretty scary but being on the football team keeps me out of trouble."

We drove in silence for a couple of minutes and Paul said, "How about the ladies?"

Should I tell him about Katie? But what was there to tell? We had made small talk a few times during the week but that was it. I'm pretty sure she was interested and I knew that I was but the thought of Ashley invaded my mind more than once. She texted me all the time...it sure seemed like she assumed we were still going out. I wasn't as sure.

"You gotta go see Ashley," Paul said as we pulled into a parking space in front of Licata's, an Italian restaurant/lounge located just over the Fairview line in Springville, a middle class suburb that most people in Fairview considered the ghetto. He put the gear in park and said, "She's here, you know."

I nodded. If we were still boyfriend and girlfriend, I guess I would have to see her at some point. But what do I say to her? What could we possibly have in common?

We walked into the lounge side where I immediately saw some graduates from past Fairview teams. I made some small talk and proceeded into the restaurant side where two Fairview buddies and their girlfriends sat in a booth. No sign of Ashley.

"Kyle baby!" Jon Davis yelled as he climbed out of the booth and whacked me on the shoulder. Jon was probably the most talented and strongest linemen at Fairview so the punch to the shoulder hurt a little. "How you doing, buddy? You speaking fluent Spanish now or what?"

He put his arm around me and the smell on his breath indicated that he was about eight beers into the night. Jon was notoriously unpredictable when drinking so it was best to just agree with everything he said. "Like the United Nations there I bet, huh Kyle?"

Actually, it was probably a lot like the United Nations but I had no desire for a political discussion with a hammered 280 pound Jon Davis. "Yeah, just like it, Jonny," I responded.

I glanced over at Paul for help but he was busy trying to pick up the waitress. Jon put his red face close to mine and said, "So when you coming back, Kyle? We need you man." Jon was beginning to slur his words and his breath smelled like the Sam Adams brewery. I made a feeble attempt to break free of Jon's grip but he was holding me as tightly as the beer he held in his left hand.

And then Ashley saved me...like she's saved me so many times before. "Hey, that's my boyfriend, Davis," she said good naturedly.

Jon had a soft spot for Ashley and immediately released me. "Ok...just for you, Ash," he said, spitting out most of the beer in his mouth.

Ashley looked great. She was wearing her black hair a little different...it seemed straighter than before. Her eyes were as big and brown as ever...she was really perfect. I noticed I didn't feel that same lump that I experienced with Katie O'Brien but Ashley was still Ashley.

She hugged me and said, "What's up, stranger?"

I almost felt like I belonged here with Ashley in my arms. I kissed her and said, "Let's go somewhere and talk."

We sat in Ashley's Honda Accord and she said, "You want to drive?"

I hadn't driven since I left Fairview and the prospects of a new car in the near future didn't look too promising. For some strange reason, I didn't really miss driving. "Nah, you drive...you're a better driver than me anyway."

She drove to Lake Harold, which was probably actually a pond located on the west side of town. There was a small beach on the lakeshore frequented mostly by poor families who couldn't afford a place on the Cape. We used to kind of laugh at the families (almost all recent immigrants) who swam in the warm water of the lake and barbequed in the small grassy area adjacent to the beach. The Fairview Board of Selectmen had addressed the issue of so many poor people visiting the town at one time by severely limiting the hours that the beach was open. They took away the grills too. The whole thing didn't seem so funny anymore.

Ashley parked the Accord and we sat on one of the few remaining picnic tables. The evening air was still warm. Ashley had a bag of French fries from Licata's. "You want some?"

"Nah, I'm pretty stuffed. Me and Paul got subs around an hour ago."

Ashley slid over so our bodies touched. "So where are we?" she asked.

That was Ashley. No bull, just right to the point. Sometimes, I had problems with her forthrightness...like now.

"What are you talking about?" I asked, reverting back to my tried and true strategy of avoiding the issue. Ashley wasn't going to let me off the hook this time, though.

"Come on, Kyle. It seems like you're avoiding me...you can't fool me. Remember, I'm going to be a Psych major. Are we still a couple?" I felt her hand softly grip my left arm.

I sighed deeply. "Of course we are, Ash. It's just tough being so far away, you know what I mean? Everything's different, that's all."

"We can make it work. I have a car and Crandall's not that far. I know you feel bad about what happened but you shouldn't. I'm still here for you."

I honestly wish there was some way to escape but I was trapped on the picnic table with Ashley's arm wrapped around mine. I was starting to sweat way more than I usually do. Ashley was beautiful; she was kind, gentle, all that good stuff. But she was Fairview...all Fairview. I just wanted to find Paul and head back to Crandall.

"I know you are, Ash. I just feel kinda weird about the whole thing, you know what I mean? I guess I'm asking you to be patient with me." I lifted my arms and stretched. "I'm really tired for some reason."

"You staying at Paul's tonight?"

That was the original plan but now I just wanted to get back to Crandall. "I don't know. I just don't feel that good."

Something had changed between Ashley and me and, as I

spoke, I was angry at myself. She didn't deserve whatever I was doing although I'm not real clear on just what I was doing.

"I'll drive you to Crandall...I don't mind," Ashley said. Her voice sounded almost sad.

"I just gotta check with Paul...who knows where he is now."

I called Paul's cell phone and had to listen to his annoying "Power" ringtone.

"What's up?" he said.

"Listen, I'm going home. Ashley said she'd drive me if you're busy."

I heard a female voice in the background. "Well, I'm kind of busy, if you know what I mean."

"The waitress?" I asked.

"Yeah...but that's okay. I can come get you."

I looked at Ashley sitting in the front seat of her Accord. She just stared straight ahead...it could be an uncomfortable ride back to Crandall but I couldn't bother Paul now. "Nah...I'll go with Ashley. Talk to you later, man."

"You guys cool?" Paul asked.

I sighed. "Not sure. See you later."

I climbed into the passenger side. "You're a lucky girl, Ash. You get to drive me back to God's country." It was a really lame attempt at cheerfulness and Ashley was way too smart to fall for it. So she said nothing...just as I expected.

We were both quiet on the way to Crandall. I stared out the open window and felt what was probably the last warm breeze we'll have for months. Ashley focused stoically on the road. Thankfully, there was virtually no traffic so the drive took less time than usual.

Ashley pulled the Accord in front of Grandpa Butch's house.

"It's quiet here," she said as she put the car into park.

"Yeah, it's funny...this street's really not much noisier than my street in Fairview. A lot different than I thought when I moved here. Then again, I've only been here a few weeks but...I don't know...it's just not that different in some ways."

Ashley took the key out of the ignition. "How's your grandfather?"

I smiled. Most people ask question like that just to be nice. The sincerity is usually lacking. Not Ashley, though. I think she really wanted to know about my grandfather.

I reached for her hand and said, "You know, he's great. Like I said, a lot of things have been much different than I expected."

"Are you embarrassed by everything that's happened?" Ashley asked earnestly.

I wasn't about to get touchy feely with anyone, even Ashley. Embarrassed? That's a strong word. Messed up? Angry? Those were probably more accurate.

"Hey, when did you become Oprah?" I said.

Ashley shook her head. "Can't we talk about this? It involves us, Kyle."

"I really don't want to talk about it...what's there to say anyway? My dad's in Hartford, my mom's in a nuthouse and I'm living with my grandfather in Crandall. Doesn't that sum it all up for you?"

We sat in silence for another minute or two but it seemed much longer. "I'm sorry, Ash but this is going nowhere. Like I said, I don't feel that good." I reached for the door handle and, somewhat to my surprise, Ashley let me go. Before I shut the door, I said, "Hey, thanks for the ride. Sorry."

"Sorry for what?" Ashley asked. "I'll see you later."

With that, Ashley Novack headed back to her manmade pond and great room and advanced placement classes. I shrugged and tried not to get too philosophical about the situation. I almost felt relieved to be climbing Grandpa Butch's brick stairs.

It was after eleven, about three hours later than Grandpa's bed time. I entered the kitchen and all of a sudden, I was hungry. Should-a taken those fries from Ashley, I said to myself.

Grandpa Butch kept the fridge pretty well stocked and I spied half a cheesecake on the bottom shelf. "Money," I said as I reached down and carefully pulled the cake out of the refrigerator.

I was about to take my first bite when I heard a scream.

"*洞窟から出なさい!*" I know that I hadn't heard that language spoken before, even at Crandall High. Then I heard Grandpa Butch scream in English, "Get out of the cave! Now!"

Grandpa sounded like he was in pain so I ran up the stairs to his room. I found him sitting up in his bed, drenched in sweat and gasping for air. I rushed to his bed and said, "Grandpa, you alright?"

He looked directly at me and yelled, "Get out of the cave! It's about to blow!"

Get out of the cave? "What cave, Grandpa?"

And then he lay down and was snoring within seconds.

I had no idea what was happening but figured it wouldn't be good to wake him up so I sat in the armchair in Grandpa's room. I just sat there for about a half hour until I was sure that Grandpa was okay. I walked over to his bed and he seemed to be sleeping soundly.

I kept his door open and walked downstairs into the dining room. For some reason, I opened the credenza drawer and shuffled through piles of old paper. At the bottom of the drawer, I found a small book entitled 'My Diary-1943-1945.'

Inside the diary, I found a Purple Heart and three commendations for bravery from his commanding officer. I opened up the diary and began to read.

14 May 1945

Another screwed up day in a completely screwed up place. Tried to take Sugar Loaf again today. They gave me flame throwing duty and I torched everything I could. In front of one spider hole, there was a Jap mother and two children. I yelled at her to put her hands up and get away from the cave. She was holding a big rock. She was screaming real loud in Japanese and the kids were crying their eyes out. She took the rock and started banging it off the older kid's head. He was about three, I guess. Blood squirting everywhere, mother screaming at the top of her lungs. She lay the baby down on the ground, raised the rock over head and smashed the poor kid's skull. I'm standing there the whole time just watching, not knowing what to do. She took a knife from her pouch and pointed it at me, still screaming like crazy. I released the flame and burnt her to a goddamn crisp. I couldn't stand looking at the two dead kids so I flamed both of them too. That was today.

19 May 1945

The Japs left Sugar Loaf last night and I'm on death detail. There are bodies everywhere, soldiers, men, women, children, Japs, Marines. Some of the bodies have been out here for a while and the gas was rising off their bodies. I had to cover my face with a towel because of the smell. These white maggots were eating away at the bodies and we tried the best we could to shoo them away but they were persistent little bastards. I still can't get that buzzing sound they made out of my head. I don't know why but I just got pissed off at the Japs and I went on a souvenir hunt. I took my knife and cut off two ears and two fingers off dead Japs and put them in my bag. I don't know what I'll do with them but they're mine.

After reading a few more pages, I closed the diary and placed it back in the drawer. I found a couple of Grandpa Butch's Sixth Marine Division patches, studied them and placed them carefully in the drawer.

I grabbed a blanket and my pillows, placed them on the floor in Grandpa Butch's room, lay down and went to sleep.

Chapter Eight

The Crandall Hawks had a major problem. Jimmy Killoran could not block. He tried hard enough but a 185 Sophomore fullback attempting to block 240 pound defensive ends that were also mean and fast just wasn't working.

We played our first game scrimmage against Prentice High School, a neighboring city that was very similar to Crandall. Our defense was far ahead of their offense but our offense really sputtered. We ended up only gaining around 60 yards rushing which didn't please Coach Bonfiglio one bit. I carried the ball seven times for around thirty yards. We won the scrimmage 8-0 but everyone on the team realized that our effort wasn't good enough to win our conference, let alone the state championship.

I sat in front of my locker after the scrimmage and thought about what just happened. I never hurried out of the locker room like some guys. There are generally two locker room types: those that get changed like maniacs and fly out of the locker room and those who took forever to leave. I was the latter type. Marco was slow also...he sat across from me, digging dirt out of his cleats and bobbing his head to the beat of the music inside his Ipod.

I glanced at him and he surprisingly returned my look with a shrug of his shoulders. Usually, Marco glared at me like I had kidnapped a member of his family. It was as if we both knew something had to be done.

I rose and knocked on Coach Bonfiglio's door. He growled "Come in!" and I thought about fleeing the locker room immediately.

I entered his tiny office and saw him standing at the white board with bloodshot eyes. Coach Brennan sat slumped in an office chair. I almost felt like reminding them that it was only a high school football scrimmage, but I decided against that course of action.

"What is it, Kyle?" Coach Bonfiglio asked.

"Well, Coach, I've been thinking..."

Coach Brennan sat up and chuckled. "Uh, oh...this sounds dangerous."

I smiled and continued. "Nothing against Jimmy but he's young and kind of small. I was thinking that maybe...that maybe I could play fullback."

Coach Bonfiglio looked at Coach Brennan and they both laughed. "This is unbelievable, Kyle. We were just talking about how we needed a change at fullback...and we were thinking about switching Marco over."

No, no, no! That's all I need...I'd have to have Eduardo start testing my food if that happened. I HAD to play fullback...that was all there was to it.

"I'm a better blocker than Marco, Coach. Coach Brennan can back me up...right Coach?" Coach Brennan nodded his agreement.

Coach Bonfiglio sat down. "Yeah, but you're a better runner too, Kyle."

I'm not sure if that were true but it felt good to hear it anyway. "Coach, you know how important team chemistry is.

I'm not sure that would be best for the team, if you know what I mean."

Coach Bonfiglio crossed his arms and appeared to be in deep thought. Finally, he glanced at Coach Brennan who simply nodded again.

"Okay, Kyle...tomorrow you start working with the fullbacks."

"I'm ready, Coach," I said and turned to leave the office.

"Hey Kyle," Coach Brennan said. I turned around and he said, "You would have gained a thousand at Fairview this year, wouldn't you?"

Yeah, maybe fifteen hundred yards, I thought.

"You're a team guy, Kyle...a team player all the way. See you tomorrow."

I walked out the office with a certain amount of self-satisfaction. I was a Junior, Marco was a Senior and football was supposed to be the ultimate team sport, wasn't it?

Marco still sat in front of his locker, headphones hanging around his neck. I stopped at his locker and said, "I'm with the fullbacks tomorrow."

He looked at me and nodded but there was a different look on his face, a look that indicated respect but not quite affection.

I nodded and said, "Yeah, it's best for the team."

Marco left and I was the only straggler left in the locker room. It was too late to take a shower so I just finished dressing. The coaches were still scheming in Coach Bonfiglio's office.

As I walked out into the dramatically cooler September evening air, my legs and body felt tired all of a sudden. It would take a Herculean effort to finish the quarter mile walk home from the bus stop. Sal had stopped asking me if I needed a ride because I took the bus every day. Today, his 1998 Pontiac Grand Am would seem like a stretch limo.

I began to make my way to the bus stop which was located in front of Emilio's Barber Shop. I had gotten my haircut from Emilio two days before. As usual, the elderly barber was smoking what was probably his fiftieth cigarette of the day and reading Sports Illustrated.

I leaned against a streetlight and waited for the number 94 to rumble in. The transvestite made eye contact with me and I just sighed and nodded my head. It must have been fatigue because today he looked vaguely like Jennifer Lopez on steroids.

I closed my eyes for a brief moment and was awakened by a horn. I opened my eyes and there was an old hunter green Ford Taurus parked illegally in front of the bus stop.

The passenger window was down and Katie O'Brien said "You look tired. Want a lift?"

Maybe going to Mass every week with Grandpa Butch was starting to pay off.

"If you can stand the smell. No shower today."

Katie laughed. I liked her laugh. "Just bought a new air freshener."

It might have been caused by being overtired but my humor was clicking today. "You want to give Howard a ride too?" I said as I climbed into the front seat.

"Who's Howard?" Katie asked. I pointed to the transvestite blowing kisses at us and Katie laughed again. It was a hearty, sincere laugh, the type that you just can't fake. I was becoming more attracted to her by the second.

We pulled away and I stole a quick look at Katie. Man, she was gorgeous in that urban Irish-American sort of way. She had a different look than Ashley. Even though Ashley's personality and interests seemed to contradict the stereotype of the typical Fairview student, she definitely looked the part. Preppie designer clothes, perfect color coordination...everything put together right out of the Abercrombie and Fitch catalogue. Her parents may have been from Dorchester and she may have been the save the whales type, but Ashley dressed according to the rules established by Fairview tradition.

And then there was Katie O'Brien. More gel in the hair, a little more hip hop in the clothing selection although not to the point of imitation. Her reddish hair was also a bit bigger than Ashley's and the makeup and lipstick were a little heavier. But she carried it off well...actually, in a sort of classy way.

"So how you doing?" Katie asked.

"Pretty good...considering. How about you?"

Katie laughed again. "How's the team? How you doing in classes, adjusting to a new school, you know, all that?"

Girls were so much better at this than guys.

"Ah, I think the team's gonna be okay. We have a lot of talent, guys been playing together for a while. That always helps." I stared out the window as Katie pulled away. "I'm trying to fit in...it's tough, you know?"

Katie smiled. "To go from Fairview Prep to Crandall...that's not easy. You seem to be doing okay in classes and at lunch. I guess it's good to be on the football team."

I nodded. "Yeah, that's helped a lot. It's just...I don't know." No sense spilling my guts to a girl that I hardly knew.

Katie laughed softly. "Oh, you're one of those Irish guys that have trouble expressing his feelings. Haven't you heard that it's the 21st century?"

I smiled. "So what about you? Not many Irish girls hanging around Crandall any more. My dad says they all moved to Prentice and Medford."

Katie drove the Taurus into Hubbard Square. "You want to get something to eat or drink?"

As tired as I was, there was no way that I was going to blow this opportunity. "Sure...I just gotta call my grandfather."

Grandpa Butch was disappointed that I would miss out on the Hungry Man instant meal he had cooked but he understood. He also asked if Katie were related to Kenny O'Brien.

"Hey, my grandfather wanted to know if you're related to Kenny O'Brien," I said to Katie.

I noticed a slight grimace on Katie's face as she said, "Yeah...he's my grandfather."

I shrugged. "I guess they know each other. Where you want to eat?"

"Have you been to Palermo's yet?" Katie asked, stealing a quick glance at me. Thank God I wasn't picking my nose at that moment.

Katie pulled the Malibu into the parking lot of a small, white stucco restaurant with a big map of Sicily on the wall next to the front door. We were greeted at the door by Mario, a middle age Italian American wearing a white apron and black pants.

"Katie, how are you doing?" Mario asked as he sat us in a booth with a window view of Hubbard Square Auto Body across the street.

"I'm good, Mario...thanks," Katie responded.

Mario nodded. "That's good, that's good." He paused. "How's your grandfather, Katie?"

"He's good, Mario. I'll tell him you were asking for him."

Katie and I scanned the menus. "Everyone seems to know your grandfather, huh?" I asked.

Katie smiled. "Yeah...he was Mayor of Crandall back in the 60's and 70's. He helped Mario get his liquor license. Mario thinks he was the greatest guy in the world."

"That's cool," I said.

Katie shrugged. "The veal is unbelievable here," she said.

I closed the menu. "Sounds good to me then."

I ate about six rolls and smothered each one with butter which, according to Mario, is a true Irish American tradition. Katie and I talked like we were old friends. She was a real down to earth regular girl who also happened to be gorgeous.

It was quiet for about three minutes, the time it took for me to down my veal parmiagana. I noticed how Katie was digging into her meal and I was impressed by her ability to eat.

"So I told you my sad story. What's your family like?" I asked.

Katie made a weird face and I thought that she was simply going to avoid my question but she took a deep breath and said, "Pretty dysfunctional...like most American families, I guess."

She stopped speaking. So that's it? Wasn't she just giving me crap for being unresponsive? I was never one to pry, though, and this was our first real conversation so I just dropped the subject. I was really interested in Katie's story, which sort of surprised me.

So we talked about the teachers at high school and football and the differences between Fairview and Crandall. Overall, it was a pretty pleasant conversation and the veal was definitely worth a return trip.

Katie glanced at her watch and said, "Well, I guess we both

have homework to do."

I chuckled and said, "It's kind of weird but I think that I get more homework at Crandall High than I did at Fairview Prep."

Katie smiled broadly which again elicited that strange lump in my throat. "You're one of those smart nerds taking all the honors courses."

"That makes you one of the nerds then because I seem to remember you in my Algebra class." And then I reached across the table and held her hand. This bold action shocked me and I wasn't quite sure why I did it. It was a completely spontaneous move and I'm not a real spontaneous guy.

Katie let me hold her hand and again smiled that smile. "This has been real nice, Kyle."

I just nodded because that's what I always did when I couldn't conjure up a response.

"No girlfriends back in Fairview, huh?" Katie asked, still softly gripping my hand.

Ashley's face suddenly interrupted my dreamy vision of me blowing a kiss to cheerleader Katie after scoring the winning touchdown in the state championship game. I almost instinctively pulled my hand away from Katie, but some part of my brain prevented that action.

I cleared my throat. I could just lie to her. What were the chances of Katie ever actually meeting Ashley? I hadn't known Katie for long but I think that it would be really difficult to lie to her. She was a city girl who was both book and street smart. There would be no telling fibs to Katie O'Brien.

"Well, there is one girl but it's real complicated and screwed up right now."

Katie gently removed her hand from my mine. "I don't play

games, Kyle. If there's someone else, that's okay, but I'm not getting involved. I wouldn't want that to happen to me, you know what I mean?"

"Like I said, it's complicated. It's one of those things where I'm not sure whether we're still going out or not. Tough to understand, I know, but that's the way it is. With everything that happened to me the last few weeks, it's..." And I stopped talking and studied the autographed photo on the wall of Mario shaking hands with Roger Clemens. What did she want me to say?

"You haven't told me much, Kyle, but I heard some stories about what happened to your parents. It stinks...I know it stinks because stuff has happened to me, too. But maybe you need to straighten things out with your Fairview girl before anything happens with us."

Both Ashley and Katie were way too mature for me. Maybe I could just become a priest...after all, I was officially a regular communicant at St. Teresa's now. I even held the basket at the collection last Sunday.

"Her name is Ashley and I think it's over. Fairview just seems like a whole other lifetime, you know? And she's part of that other life I used to have," I said.

Katie patted my hand. "Like I said, that's okay. I need more than 'I think it's over.' I know you're not a player, Kyle but you have to get things straightened out. Can we leave it at that?"

I nodded although I wanted to say more but didn't know exactly what to say.

Katie drove me home. At Grandpa Butch's house, she leaned over and kissed me on the cheek. "I'll see you tomorrow, okay?"

I got out and watched Katie navigate the Taurus down

Lodge Avenue.

I entered the house and heard Grandpa snoring in the parlor. The Herald sports section lay across his chest and the Red Sox post game show blared on the television. There couldn't be anyone who turned up the volume louder than Grandpa Butch. I quietly turned off the television and went into the kitchen. I gulped down some Tropicana orange juice out of the carton, closed the fridge door and trudged upstairs to my room.

I turned on my laptop and checked my Facebook page. Eduardo was online. His screen name remained Brazil Stud despite all the crap we had given him.

"U there, white boy?"

I typed a response, stood and flipped on the radio. As I would have predicted, the station was playing a Kanye song. All of a sudden, a nostalgic feeling overcame me and I thought of Paul...and Ashley.

I returned to the computer and saw another message from Eduardo. I was about to type when a message from Ashley appeared.

"Kyle, how u doing?"

I thought about responding for a brief moment but instead I logged off, shut down the laptop and went to bed.

Chapter Nine

At Fairview, I didn't block much. I was the featured tailback and, unless I was helping out with pass blocking, I either rushed the ball or ran short pass patterns. And pass blocking differed greatly from run blocking.

Coach Bonfiglio was fanatical about repetition so I staggered through blocking drill after blocking drill. Blocking is a lot like rebounding in basketball: effort was much more important than skill.

I crashed into blocking dummy after blocking dummy, constantly reminding myself (and being reminded by Coach Brennan) to stay low and keep my legs moving. There were only three fullbacks and Jimmy Killoran seemed very relieved to have lost the starting position.

Our offense was beginning to click in practice. I'm not trying to sound cocky but I was a much better blocker than Jimmy. I was older, stronger, more experienced and wouldn't hesitate to hit someone. That was a key to football success...even if you hit the wrong guy...just hit someone every play. I think that every player is a little scared but you have to block the fear out of your mind and just do it. You can't hesitate. And Jimmy hesitated too often. It might have been because he was just a sophomore but that didn't matter. If you hesitated in football, you lost. It was that simple. The same rules applied to tackling, running the ball, catching the ball or blocking. That's why I admire Tom Brady so much. He makes his decision and that's it.

The scout defense couldn't stop our offense. Whatever play we ran, we gained a minimum of eight yards. Marco was running with a confidence that I hadn't seen before. It was as if this huge burden had been lifted off his shoulders. He even slapped me on the helmet a couple of times after I helped open a hole.

For some reason, I really bought into the whole notion of football being the ultimate team game. It wasn't like baseball where everyone seemed obsessed with individual statistics. Linemen blocked, running backs ran, quarterbacks threw and…fullbacks blocked. I probably wouldn't get forty carries the entire season but that was okay. You had a sense of accomplishment every play that worked and you didn't have to stand around in the outfield waiting for the stray fly ball. I just really liked to hit people on the football field. Off the field, I was pretty laid back. I think I had been in two real fights my entire life. Most of the football players I knew were like that. Something just happened once they put on the pads.

After practice, I finally accepted Sal's offer of a ride. As we climbed into his Grand Am, Sal said, "Hey, why don't you come over to my house for supper? My mother's making gnocchi's and eggplant parm."

I had never heard of "gnocchi's" but I liked Italian food and I liked Sal so I accepted the offer immediately. I also had deducted that Sal may be the type that got insulted and there was no need for that.

Sal's house was located on the west side of Crandall which was clearly the nicest section in the city. It was located near

Prentice University, a prestigious college on the Crandall-Medford line. The neighborhood was composed of mainly very well kept "Philadelphia" style two family houses.

We arrived at Sal's cream colored stucco house with a small brick wall surrounding the tiny front yard. A statute of Saint Francis of Assisi stood in the yard watching over an assortment of flowers and shrubs. Black wrought iron covered the wall and guarded each side of the perfect red brick stairs leading to the concrete front porch.

The interior of Sal's house was bright and welcoming. Grey marble covered the hallway and kitchen while the rest of the house had gleaming hardwood floors. I quickly figured that Mrs. LoGrasso spent a lot of time keeping this house clean.

The house smelled sort of like Palermo's, Katie O'Brien's favorite restaurant. Sal led me into the kitchen where I met Mrs. LoGrasso. She stood in the kitchen, dressed in a stylish black sweat suit, an obviously Italian woman on the younger side of middle age with big brown eyes, straight jet black hair pulled back and a huge smile showing white pearly teeth.

"Nice to meet you, Mrs. LoGrasso," I said.

Mrs. LoGrasso took my hand enthusiastically and said to Sal, "What a handsome boy. You're an Irishman, aren't you? You look like Brad Pitt in Ocean's Eleven!"

Two things struck me. First, everyone in Crandall seemed aware of everyone else's ethnicity. Second, no one had ever compared me to Brad Pitt. I decided right then that I really liked Mrs. Lo Grasso.

"Sit down, boys," she commanded and I was immediately presented with bread and a plate of stuffed mushrooms. I tried to eat only one mushroom but I couldn't help myself. Sal laughed and said, "My mother loves to watch Irish people eat."

Mr. LoGrasso, short and well-built and dressed in dusty work clothes, came home midway through out meal. He shook my hand and had the same kind of death grip as Grandpa Butch. I was almost mesmerized by his thick, callused hands, the kind of hands you just never saw in Fairview.

Mr. LoGrasso didn't say much which was okay because Mrs. LoGrasso literally never stopped talking through the entire meal. Sal's father sat at the head of the table chewing softly with a bemused look on his face.

I guess about ten potato filled gnocchi's would satisfy the average person but both of Sal's parents were impressed with my ability to completely gorge myself. Mrs. LoGrasso even offered to make some more but I politely declined as I inhaled my third bowl. Sal's mother sat beaming.

Sal drove me home and as I opened the door to exit the car, he said, "Hey, everyone knows that you volunteered to play fullback. That's pretty cool, Kyle."

I shrugged nonchalantly but I felt a sense of acceptance that hadn't really been there before. I climbed Grandpa Butch's brick front stairs feeling more satisfied than I had felt in a long time.

"What's going on, Grandpa?" I shouted as I entered the hallway.

"In the kitchen, Boyo," Grandpa responded. I don't know why we yelled from room to room, but I think it was a Donovan family tradition.

I told Grandpa about eating at the LoGrassos, playing fullback and feeling acceptance from teammates. I could tell that Grandpa Butch sensed my happiness because he sat there eating his frozen pizza with a big smile on his face.

"Guillermo Billy LoGrasso... nice guy and a better bricklayer. I worked a couple of jobs with him years ago when he was just a kid. You work for him in the summer and you'd stay in shape, sonny," Grandpa said between bites.

Grandpa stood up and walked over to the refrigerator. He took a yellow memo note from under a magnet and silently handed it to me.

I stared at the note for a few seconds and then looked up at Grandpa Butch.

"She called around five o'clock. Had a nice conversation with her...probably the best in ten or fifteen years. She sounded good, Kyle and she really wants to speak with you."

A wave of guilt swept over me. I hadn't thought much about my mother in about a week. Everything had just been so crazy that I had almost forgotten about my own mother. Playing fullback and being told I looked like Brad Pitt didn't seem too important anymore.

"She says to call her anytime, Kyle."

"Can I go see her?" I asked.

Grandpa Butch sat down and said, "From what she said, she's not ready for visitors just yet, but she'll be all set soon, I guess."

I nodded and continued staring at the note.

"When you call, you'll get the main number but just dial that extension. That's your mom's room."

"Thanks Grandpa," I said as I rose from the chair.

Grandpa Butch put his plate in the sink and grabbed his blue American Legion jacket. "I'm playing bingo tonight, Kyle. I'll be home around ten. Don't wait up for me."

"Okay, Grandpa," I said absently.

I sat down again at the kitchen table and dialed the number written on the yellow note.

"Castlegate Health Facility," the male voice on the other end of the line said.

"Hi, could I have extension 8708 please."

"Could I have your name, sir?"

"Kyle Donovan."

"Putting you through now, sir."

The phone rang once and Mom picked up. My eyes welled up at the sound of her voice but I tried to hold it together.

"Kyle?" Mom asked, the voice sounding a little weaker than I remembered. But it was definitely Mom.

For a brief moment, I didn't know what to say.

"You there, honey?" Mom asked.

I shook my head although Mom couldn't see that through the telephone. Finally, I said, "Yeah, Mom. How're you doing?"

Now it was Mom's turn to hesitate.

"I'm doing better, Kyle. It takes time, you know? It takes time but the people here...the people here are wonderful. I'm starting to feel better, starting to feel like my old self, like when you were little. Remember those days, Kyle?"

I remembered them well. In fact, I thought about them every day. I felt guilty when I forgot to think about them. "When can I see you, Mom?" I asked.

"Soon, honey, very soon. You know none of this is your fault, right Kyle?"

That's what Grandpa and Dad said, too. But this little part of me didn't believe them. When I lay in bed awake at night, this little part of me told me over and over that I screwed up, that if I had paid more attention to Mom, she wouldn't be living at the

Castlegate Health Facility. Maybe if I had read the desperation in Dad's face for the past few months, I could've helped, maybe I could have done something, anything to help keep us together. Instead, I spent so much time with Ashley and Paul and looking at my biceps in the mirror that everything fell apart around me and I was the last to know. What a selfish clown I am.

"Yeah, Mom, I know it's not my fault."

There was silence for a moment and then I said, "What's wrong with you, Mom? You know, what's specifically wrong with you?"

"Depression, Kyle. The doctors here call it major depression. They're helping me deal with my thoughts...to sort out all my different thoughts. Dr. Ellis tells me not to believe everything I think. And I'm starting to do that. Piece by piece, I can feel myself being put back together."

"What about you and Dad?"

I heard Mom sigh through the phone. "Sometimes, things just don't work out. Your dad's not a bad person and I don't think I'm a bad person but it's just not realistic that we live together anymore. Emotionally, we left each other quite a while ago. But your father loves you, Kyle, and would do anything for you. Remember that."

"I really want to see you, Mom."

"Very soon, Kyle, very soon."

Mom would change the subject a lot when she was getting upset and that's just what she did now.

"How's your grandfather treating you?"

I smiled. "He's great, Mom. Like nothing I remember. He's my best friend right now."

We talked for a few minutes more about high school and

football and I lied about how well Ashley and I were doing. Mom promised that I could visit her within a week or two.

After I hung up the phone, I felt this strange mixture of anger, guilt and sadness. I wished that I could strap on my helmet and shoulder pads and just hit someone. I looked around the kitchen for something to run into. The refrigerator would probably get the best of me and if I broke any of the cabinets, Grandpa Butch would put me before a firing squad.

So I went downstairs to the cellar and dragged out an old punching bag that Grandpa used in his boxing days. I leaned it against the wooden shop table and I flailed away at the bag until my arms felt like two pieces of cooked spaghetti. I sat down on Grandpa's work bench and tried to catch my breath. I stared at a Knights of Columbus calendar on the wall above Grandpa's shop table. A picture of Jesus standing with his hands out spread looked at me directly in the eyes.

"Okay, Jesus. Can you take this burden, too?" I stood up and walked towards the picture. He continued to stare at me. "I wish you could talk to me, Lord." I closed my eyes, and I could feel His presence. "I know you're listening. I have to stop feeling sorry for myself. This is my cross, right?" I thought of the Stations of the Cross in St. Teresa's, and Jesus falling down, but always getting up...always carrying that Cross. "Yeah...this is my cross, this is what I have to deal with." I blessed myself, and stood, leaning against the shop table.

After a couple of minutes, I walked upstairs to the parlor, turned on the television and waited for Monday Night Football to begin.

Chapter Ten

In all of my years playing football, I had never attended a real pep rally. Things like pep rallies were frowned upon at Fairview and even if one had been held, it was doubtful how many kids would actually show up.

But here I was, in the Crandall High gymnasium with the huge painting of a menacing hawk's head on the far west wall, standing in front of the entire student body, waiting for Mr. Amaral and Coach Bonfiglio to call my name.

I heard Coach shout out "At fullback, Kyle Donovan!" and I ran through the two lines of cheerleaders furiously waving their pom poms and took my place next to Marco who stuck out his fist and almost smiled. I tapped his fist and scanned the bleachers filled with teenagers of all races and ethnicities screaming in a variety of languages. Freddie, the kid who almost killed me on the first day of school, flashed some kind of gang sign at me. I smiled and waved and he cracked up laughing. I think he liked me.

I caught Katie's eye and smiled. She winked and waved the pom poms in my direction. That lump in my throat quickly returned and swallowing became difficult.

Eduardo performed some ridiculous freestyle rap about the team (and his starring role on the squad) and the entire gymnasium erupted in laughter. Mr. Amaral was almost crying he was laughing so hard. You know, Eduardo may be president someday. Of course, he had to pass Government class first.

As I left the gym after the rally, I felt someone push me gently on the shoulder. I turned and saw Katie O'Brien smiling at me with those pearly white, perfectly straight teeth.

"Hey, what's going on?" I said.

"You guys ready for Walsh tomorrow?" she asked as we walked out of the gym together.

Archbishop Walsh was our first game of the season. They were a Catholic, all boys' school located in Boston. The school was a mix of tough Irish and Italian city kids and less tough but very big kids from Boston's south shore suburbs. We scrimmaged them my Freshman year at Fairview and they kicked our butts off the field. For a Catholic school, they didn't give us much mercy. I think the final score was 38-12.

So Saturday promised to be a very tough game.

"I guess we're ready...you never really know until you put on the pads," I answered.

Katie laughed. "You sound like Bill Belichick. You'll make a great coach someday."

Clichés and coach speak would never work with Katie O'Brien. You'd have to be smart to be in a relationship with her. Sometimes I worried I wasn't that smart. Maybe not smart enough for Katie anyway.

"Well, Katie, they put on their pants one leg at a time, just like us. On any given Sunday, anything can happen. And also..."

Katie cut me off before I could continue. "Please stop before I have to hurt you."

I chuckled. "Hey, you like being a cheerleader?" I asked for no apparent reason. But I was kind of interested in why girls became cheerleaders.

Katie actually frowned a little and I immediately worried that I had raised a sore subject. "I'm sorry...it's none of my business," I said.

She shook her head. "No, it's okay. It's just that I never saw myself as a cheerleader type growing up. But I was never an athlete either. To tell you the truth, I just liked to read a lot."

"Nothing wrong with reading."

Katie smiled. "When I got to high school though...well, look around. There aren't many kids here who look like me. I wanted to fit in somehow so I tried out for cheerleading my freshman year. And I made it. I belonged, you know? The girls, black, Brazilian, Spanish, they accepted me and that's a good feeling when you're fourteen. And we're not cheerleaders like you see in the movies. It's dancing, gymnastics...it's pretty cool, actually."

"Well, I'm glad you're on the squad," I said, feeling that annoying lump return to its home inside my throat. The gym was empty except for us.

Katie took both of my hands in hers and said, "We're not that different, Kyle."

"Hey, I'm developing some Irish pride," I said.

Katie sighed and looked away. "No, I mean, my family. My grandfather was the mayor of Crandall. My dad was a city councilor until..."

I guided Katie over the bleachers and we both sat down.

"Until the FBI burst into our house one day and arrested him. I guess there was some misuse of money coming from the federal government. It involved concrete or paving contracts or something like that. I read in the newspaper that the FBI had a sting operation that lasted for over a year. The whole thing reached my grandfather somehow and he...he ended up with a suspended sentence." She shook her head. "After all those years of service. Then the government went through all of his assets...they left him with his pension and not much else."

"God, I'm sorry, Katie."

She kind of waved her left hand, reached inside her pocketbook for a tissue and managed a small smile. "I was in sixth grade when it all happened. My father pleaded guilty and ended up serving eighteen months in Danbury. When he was released, he just up and moved to Florida with his girlfriend. Said he wanted a fresh start. Left my mother, my sister and I stuck in Crandall with nothing. My mother was a dental hygienist before she had kids so she went back to work. So there it is, my story." Katie looked up at me, her blue eyes focused directly on mine.

I put my arms around her and held her tight for a couple of moments. I looked at Katie and said, "You gonna be okay?"

She nodded and hugged me again. "Yeah... it's not a new story but I know what you're going through, Kyle. I really do. You can't do it alone...you think you can, I bet. But you can't."

I didn't really have a pre game ritual. Some guys had to get taped at a specific time before every game, some guys ate three eggs sunny side up on game day and some guys just sat on the floor, listened to their Ipods and chilled.

I woke up early on that Saturday but then again I always woke up early, particularly since I moved in with Staff Sergeant

Donovan. Grandpa Butch heated up some frozen waffles and French toast which I swallowed down with a couple of glasses of orange juice. Neither of us said much at breakfast. Grandpa worked furiously at a crossword puzzle and I pretended to be interested in the back of a cereal box. To be truthful, I didn't feel like talking, even to Grandpa Butch. He seemed to understand completely.

At around 8:15, I heard the front door open and Dad walked into the kitchen. I stood and we hugged each other. I hadn't seen him in a week and I was real glad that he was going to make the game.

"How you doing, son?" Dad asked. There were dark circles and bags under his eyes that I hadn't noticed before. Suddenly, he looked a lot older than he did when we lived in Fairview. Or maybe I was just more observant.

Dad leaned over the kitchen table and shook hands with Grandpa Butch. "How's it going, Dad?"

Grandpa Butch grasped Dad's hand eagerly and said, "Sit down, Timmy. Let me get you some breakfast."

"Anything new in Hartford, Dad?" I asked.

Dad shrugged his shoulders. "Kinda tough, Kyle. I'm working on it, though. Actually have a couple of possibilities. Keep your fingers crossed."

"That's cool," I said. As much as I wanted Dad to have success in Hartford, I couldn't keep my mind off Archbishop Walsh. Coach Bonfiglio and Coach Brennan had them scouted down to the quarterback's cadence and the middle linebacker's favorite kind of ice cream. As I listened to Dad, I couldn't help thinking of Andrew Delvecchio, the all-state Walsh middle linebacker who would be looking to take my head off every play.

Dad gently punched me on the shoulder. "So you ready for Walsh today?"

I nodded absently. For some reason, this game seemed to have so much more meaning than any other regular season game I could remember. Before, I always wanted to have a good game. Today, I felt like I needed to have a really good game.

I finished another glass of orange juice and excused myself. I lay down on my bed and turned on my Ipod. During Music class at school, I had downloaded a pretty extensive Pearl Jam greatest hits collection. It was old stuff, but I actually liked it a lot better than new music. At least it was rock music. I fast forwarded to track seven and closed my eyes:

He could've tuned in, tuned in

But he tuned out

A bad time, nothing could save him

Alone in a corridor, waiting, locked out

He got up outta there, ran for hundreds of miles

He made it to the ocean, had a smoke in a tree

The wind rose up, set him down on his knee

A wave came crashing like a fist to the jaw

Delivered him wings, hey, look at me now

Arms wide open with the sea as his floor

The blaring of Sal's horn interrupted the boys from Seattle. It was time to go.

Like me, Sal liked to get to the locker room early. When we arrived, only Marco and the coaches were there. Marco nodded at me as he slowly taped his right ankle. The coaches were pretty clear in directing that only the school trainers were allowed to tape but Marco, and nobody but Marco, taped his own ankles. I'm pretty sure that Coach Bonfiglio knew but I guess he couldn't fight every battle.

I heard Coach Brennan shout my name and I hurried to the coach's office. "What's up, Coach?" I asked.

"You all set for today, Kyle?" Coach asked, a wide smile plastered to his sunburned face.

I nodded vigorously. "Yeah, I'm psyched Coach. Really psyched."

Coach Brennan stood up and stuck out his hand. "Alright buddy. We need you today...we really need you. That Delvecchio kid is a home wrecker. Stay low on him. You try to block him on the shoulder pads and you'll have a lot of cleat marks on your butt. You know what I mean?"

I nodded again. I had watched so much film of Archbishop Walsh, I felt like I was related to Andrew Delvecchio. Six two, two hundred thirty pounds of anger and speed. Boston College bound Andrew Delvecchio. Coach Bonfiglio wanted to isolate Delvecchhio, which was the opposite of most teams' game plan. Coach wanted to challenge the linebacker...Coach B was that kind of coach. That meant that I would be leading Marco through the hole a lot today. That also meant many collisions with Mr. Delvecchio.

I put some eye black under my eyes although it was cloudy

outside. I had brought all my gear to the cleaners yesterday so my uniform had that fresh out of the laundry clean smell. Steve the trainer checked my helmet and tightened my facemask. With an unsharpened pencil, I cleaned the bottom of my cleats, clapped them together a couple of times and laced them up. I was ready to go.

Coach Bonfiglio called the team together. He stood in the middle of the circle and said, "This is it, boys. This is your year. It all starts today. I don't have to tell you again how important this game is. Right now, this is the most important game of your life. Seniors, step it up. Give it your all every down, every play. Don't leave that field thinking that you could have done more. Sidelines, I want you loud, going crazy every play. Alright, boys, everyone up here."

Coach Bonfiglio then led a prayer which ended with "Mary, Queen of Victory, Pray for Us!" I learned from my Government class that the Supreme Court had ruled that we couldn't pray like that but evidently no one sent Coach B. the memo. And no one on the team seemed to mind. We then ran through the locker room door like we were escaping from a mental asylum.

The stands were almost full. Archbishop Walsh brought a pretty good crowd and both sides were very loud as the teams gathered on the sidelines. Much louder than Fairview. We won the toss and Coach B. elected to receive the ball. I was glad to be on the kickoff return team because it would give me the chance to hit someone early and get my pads loose.

My job was to help provide a wedge for Marco and Sammy Griffin who were lined up at about the ten yard line for the kickoff. I wasn't supposed to turn my back until I knew the ball had gone over my head.

The kick was short and headed in my direction. I tried to focus on the football and not the sea of maroon uniforms sprinting towards me with the singular goal of separating limbs from my body.

I caught the kick and ran directly up the middle of the field, just as Coach Brennan had designed. I eluded one tackler and then lowered my shoulder at the two defenders lined up to bring me down. I kept my balance for about another five or six yards until someone caught my ankle and I fell to the turf.

I heard the crowd screaming and Eduardo was slapping me on my shoulder pads so I guess it was a pretty good return. I glanced over at the sideline and noticed Coach Brennan clapping wildly. I saw the kid holding the yard marker standing at the Archbishop Walsh forty yard line. I had returned the kick almost thirty yards. The adrenaline was flowing now.

Sal took charge of the huddle and said, "Alright, here we go. I right, thirty two iso, I right thirty two iso, on one, on one, ready!"

We clapped hands in unison. As I bent down in my three point stance, I tried not to think about Andrew Delvecchio, although I know I heard him grunting and shouting out defensive signals. At the snap of the ball, the center and right guard nicely double teamed the nose guard and I ran towards the hole unimpeded. I felt Marco's hand on my back and I launched myself at Delvecchio. It was like throwing myself against the Prudential building. He didn't try to avoid my block. Instead, he raised his forearm and lowered his shoulder and met my block with all of his strength. I kept my legs moving and Marco breezed by my right side. Delvecchio eventually threw off my block and dragged down Marco but not until he had gained five yards. I tumbled to the ground, feeling the full effect of Delvecchio's massive forearm to the helmet. Thank God I had the facemask tightened before the game.

Marco grabbed the back of my shoulder pads and helped me to my feet. He had sort of this crazy grin on his face. *"Aproximado, homem. Você retrocedeu seu burro!"*

I think he was paying me a compliment although my Portuguese was still pretty poor, despite Eduardo's attempts at educating me. I shook my head to clear the cobwebs and jogged back to the huddle.

Coach Bonfiglio stayed with his strategy and we were gaining three to six yards a play. After the eighth play of the drive, we got to about the nine yard line. It was first and goal.

Sal leaned forward in the huddle and said, "Okay, Kyle, it's your turn. I left thirty three ride, I left thirty three ride, on one, on one, ready!"

I took the handoff from Sal and followed Peter Sousa, the left guard and Eduardo the left tackle. I was barely touched as I darted through the hole and attempted to turn the corner to the sideline. A cornerback knocked me out of bounds at the three yard line. Gain of six. Eduardo grabbed my facemask and yelled, "See how good I am to you, white boy!" I slapped him on the helmet and returned to the huddle.

Two plays later, Marco scored from the one yard line. Coach Bonfiglio elected to try for the two point conversion even though Ricky was a pretty good kicker. This was called going for the kill. And Coach Bonfiglio definitely possessed the killer instinct. Sal called for a play action pass and easily hit a wide open Marco in the end zone. The score was 8-0.

That first drive set the tone for the entire game. By the fourth quarter, we were winning 35-6 and Coach B. cleared the bench with a couple of minutes left. The final score was 35-14.

I felt exhilarated but very tired after the game as I walked off the field. I only carried the ball six times but I couldn't remember feeling more satisfied. I knew that tomorrow morning my body would experience the full effect of at least twenty collisions with Andrew Delvecchio but right now, things couldn't be better.

As I left the field, I saw Paul standing with Grandpa and Dad behind the fence. He's a good friend.

"You guys are good but I don't know if you're ready for Fairview," Paul said, smiling through the fence.

I stopped and said, "Hey, thanks for coming, man."

Dad said, "I'm proud of you, son. You blocked like a maniac out there."

"And thirty yards on six carries. Pretty good, if you asked me," Grandpa added. Dad looked at Grandpa Butch and smiled. I think it was the first time I ever saw Dad smile at Grandpa.

"We'll let you two guys talk. Come on, Dad," my father said and he and Grandpa Butch walked towards the parking lot.

"I mean it, you guys are good, man," Paul said.

"Yeah, I think we're gonna be okay. Walsh wasn't as good as I thought, though." As I finished the sentence, Katie walked by and punched me gently on the arm with a pom pom. "Nice game, Irish boy," she said.

"Thanks Katie."

She continued walking and I looked at Paul who stared at me with his eyebrows raised and mouth open. "You're making friends fast here, huh 'Irish boy'?"

I shook my head. "It's not what you think."

"How you know what I'm thinking?" Paul asked with a grin.

I chuckled. "How are things in Fairview? You guys ready for next week?" The private schools usually started their football season a week after the public and Catholic schools.

"We'll be good. We miss you, though. Zach Tyler is playing tailback. I mean he's okay but...you know."

We stood in silence for a moment and Paul said, "Ashley says hi. I think she's a little confused."

"Well, I'm a lot confused," I said.

Paul nodded. "Yeah, I understand. Hey, big party tonight at the Sternbergs. The parents are in the Bahamas and Lily has the place all to herself. Come on up for it...I'll even wait around and give you a ride. You can stay at my house tonight."

I had already been invited to a 'victory party' at Peter Sousa's house in Crandall. And I knew that Katie would be there. "Thanks man. But I can't go tonight. I'm gonna go home and probably fall asleep watching the Notre Dame game. Maybe next week after your game."

Paul shrugged. "Okay. Listen, I'll talk to you this week. Anything you want to say to Ashley?"

I thought for a moment. "Nah. Hey thanks for coming today."

"Okay, Irish boy." Paul started to walk away and then turned around. "You gotta straighten things out with Ash. One way or another, Kyle. She deserves that."

I nodded. Paul was right but I wasn't going to straighten anything out today.

Sal gave me a ride to Peter Sousa's house which was located not far out of Hubbard Square. It was actually within walking distance but my legs hurt so much walking from my room to the shower seemed like a marathon.

Paul was the youngest child and lived with his mother, who worked nights at a big hotel in Boston. So there was no adult supervision which meant that there would be plenty of alcohol and probably plenty of other assorted behavior enhancers.

Eduardo greeted Sal and me at the front door and he was already slurring his words. "Come on down the cellar for a bong hit, white boy. You deserve it, man. Kicking Delvecchio's butt like that, man." Eduardo had his huge arm draped around my shoulders and I think that he was actually holding himself up. His eyes were glassy, his shirt reeked of that unique marijuana smell and his breath smelled like he had dived into a swimming pool of beer.

I laughed. "No thanks, Eddy. I don't want to pass out that fast."

Jay Z was on the stereo and the living room was full of kids bumping and grinding. There were so many people standing in the hallway, I could barely make my way to the kitchen.

I saw Peter and Raymond who both congratulated me on my performance against Delvecchio. It was about a hundred degrees in the small apartment and I needed something to drink. I looked in the fridge and grabbed a Mountain Dew. I tried to make small talk above the music and crowd noise, finished my soda and looked around for Katie. I didn't see her anywhere.

Most people were either high or drunk by this time. I didn't smoke weed and I didn't drink much. These factors and the absence of Katie severely lessened my motivation to stay at the party.

I decided to slip out the back door unnoticed. My legs ached but I figured the refreshing night air would help me make it back to Grandpa's house.

I walked up Peter's street to Main Street and headed in the direction of Lodge Avenue. As I passed the Hollywood Video, I heard a voice call, "Hey, Kyle!"

I turned and saw Katie O'Brien, dressed in a pink, zippered hooded sweatshirt, jeans and white Skechers standing beside her car. "Where you going?" she asked.

"Home," I said.

"Come on, I'll give you a ride."

Chapter Eleven

As I leaned against the fence outside of the track surrounding the Fairview Prep football field, one thought dominated my mind. These guys were good. Paul was just being nice to me when he emphasized how much I was missed by the team. The kid who was playing tailback, Zach Tyler, was a strong, straight ahead runner, a north south running back who was helped by that massive offensive line. The Fairview line must have averaged 270 pounds. They just looked so much bigger than they did last season. Maybe some steroid testing was in order.

Fairview defeated Ashby Hill Academy by a score of 24-3. And Ashby Hill was considered a challenger for the Independent School Conference title. Fairview toyed with them the entire game. It seemed that the Fairview offense could run any play it wanted and the Ashby Hill defense couldn't do a thing about it. Fairview could have scored at least fifty points but Coach Pearson was an old school coach. A lot like Coach Bonfiglio actually. Those guys just didn't run up the score.

Paul played well. He's a tight end and caught a few passes because Coach Pearson loosened up the offense a bit this year. I keyed on Paul for quite a few plays and noticed that he went full go every play.

I also realized that I really missed playing for Fairview. I had a chance to speak to a bunch of the guys and Coach Pearson before the game. Speaking to Coach in particular made me want to suit up immediately. I really missed him...and I understood how much I really missed my friends on the team.

As I waited around for Paul after the game, a lot of parents shook my hand and made small talk. I watched as they strolled to the parking lot full of Land Rovers and Infinities. I thought of Grandpa Butch's Buick and I felt bad. I didn't feel bad for Grandpa though. I felt bad for myself for some reason.

Like me, Paul was a straggler so I just sat down on one of the benches outside the locker room and tried to remain patient. Finally, Paul emerged, his hair soaking wet.

"Nice game, buddy," I said, shaking his hand.

Paul shrugged. "It's like you guys against Walsh. Ashby Hill wasn't as good as I thought."

"Or you guys are better than you thought," I added.

"Yeah, you might be right. We'll see," he said as we walked to his BMW.

Neither of Paul's parents attended the game. In fact, they rarely did. I don't know if this bothered Paul or not because we never really discussed the subject.

As we drove to Paul's house, I rolled down the window and took in the sights and sounds of Fairview, Massachusetts. I felt differently than the last time I had visited the town. Last time, I was uncomfortable and couldn't wait to get back to Crandall and Grandpa Butch. During this visit, I was feeling pretty nostalgic and maybe even a little homesick.

Paul's mother wasn't home so we called Dominoes for a couple of pizzas. There must have been four thousand pizza/sandwich shops in Crandall. If you wanted pizza in

Fairview, however, you had to call the Dominoes in Springville.

For a kid who basically fended for himself, Paul was pretty well grounded. He was an early riser and he wasn't a big partier. Paul drank a little but didn't smoke weed or take ecstasy or any of the crap that many of other kids did. In other words, we had a lot in common.

Paul, however, was a ladies man. There was no lack of Fairview girls that were attracted to Paul. And he took full advantage of the situation.

It was seven o'clock by the time Paul took a little nap; we ate our pizza and watched some college football.

"Hey, let's go down to the Ambrose. Everyone's gonna be there," Paul said.

"Definitely...I want to see everyone. Sounds good," I responded. There was a huge parking lot behind the old Ambrose warehouse where kids congregated most every weekend. Opposing groups in the town had been fighting for years over what to do with the site but it just sat there, this huge rectangular concrete block building surrounded by weeds and, of course, the massive parking lot. As long as there was no booze or drugs or general mayhem, the Fairview cops were pretty lenient about letting us hang out there. A police car would drive around once every couple of hours or so.

And then I thought of Ashley. She hadn't been at the game and I hadn't even told her I was coming to Fairview for the weekend.

"You think Ashley will be there?" I asked.

Paul chuckled. "What's the matter Irish boy? You nervous?"

"Of course I'm nervous. I didn't even tell her I was coming up this weekend."

Paul stood up, searching for a last piece of pizza crust. "Well, call her now. When was the last time you talked to her?"

I breathed deeply. "I don't know...Monday, maybe Tuesday."

"That's not too bad. Go ahead, call her. You want to call her, right?"

Actually, I did want to speak with Ashley. I was feeling really homesick about Fairview and no one represented my memories more than Ashley. "Yeah, I'm gonna call her now."

"Good boy. I'll go get changed."

I felt a little weird as I dialed Ashley's cell number. I guess part of me hoped that I would reach her voice mail. No such luck, however.

"What's up?" Ashley said, answering the phone.

"Hey, I'm in Fairview. I just got back from the football game."

"Didn't you have a game this weekend?" she asked.

"Yeah, we played last night."

"How'd you do?"

"Beat Medford 12-0." Tough, tough game. Defensive struggle. One of our touchdowns came on a punt return by Marco. Our defense was incredible. Our offense? Not so incredible. We'd be hearing about that from Coach Bonfiglio plenty this week.

"You going over to the Ambrose tonight?" I asked.

There was a brief silence. "Are you going to go?"

"Yeah, me and Paul are heading over in a little while. Why don't we pick you up?"

Another silent pause. "Are we going to able to talk?" Ashley asked.

I glanced at the stairs leading to Paul's room. He better not have said anything about Katie and the Irish boy comment. "Sure, Ash. I want to talk."

"No, I mean really talk."

I sighed quietly so Ashley couldn't hear it. "Yeah, I want to really talk, too."

"Okay then. I'll see you in a little while."

We picked Ashley up at about 8:00. I got out of the car so she could sit in the front passenger seat. We kissed briefly and I immediately noticed how great she smelled. It was that fresh out of the shower fragrance.

By the time we arrived at the Ambrose, there were about twenty Fairview kids already milling around. As I entered the group, I was mobbed. Two hundred eighty pounds of Jon Davis gripped me in a bear hug and I felt various other slaps on the back and shoulder.

"How you doing, Kyle?" Jon asked as he released me. He was sober which made it much easier to carry on some type of civilized conversation.

"Alright, Jonny, alright."

Jon again put his huge arm around my shoulder. "You gotta come back, Kyle. We're almost there, you know? With you, state champs this year, man."

That was the general sentiment on this evening. Tonight, the guys were treating me like I was returning after five years in a POW camp. I glanced over at Ashley who was sitting on the hood of Paul's car with a bemused look on her face. I smiled and winked and she did the same.

Jon and a couple of other linemen, Todd Gardner and Jeremy Stein, were going out to buy a couple of cases of beer.

They asked if I wanted to come along. Even though I didn't feel like drinking, I was tempted to go for the ride. I spied Ashley again and decided against going.

I walked over to Paul's car and gave Ashley a long kiss. Paul threw me the keys to the BMW. It still had that new car smell and the grey leather was immaculate. I turned on the radio and Pearl Jam's "Evenflow" blared out from the classic rock station. Good omen.

We drove down to Lake Harold. I parked near the beach, turned off the car and put my arm around Ashley. She looked at me and said, "What's going on tonight? You seem like a different person."

I laughed softly. "I don't know. I just miss this place so much...I guess I just kind of realized it." I ran my hand through her black hair. "And I miss you, Ash."

"I miss you, too, Kyle." She looked out the passenger window. "I just don't know what's going on. You seem so different lately. I mean, I know about everything that's happened to you but you always seem so distant, like you don't really want to talk to me. I'm here for you, Kyle. I don't want you to go through this whole thing alone."

My mind turned to Katie O'Brien and her words that day of the pep rally. I hadn't talked to her much this past week. I knew that I was coming out to Fairview; I knew that I'd probably see Ashley, and, for some reason, I felt guilty about it all. So I basically tried to avoid Katie for the entire week and I did possess a skill for avoiding people.

I cleared my throat and Ashley said, "Here we go with the throat clearing. You don't have to say anything if you don't want to, Kyle."

"Hey, I'm really sorry, Ash. It's just tough for you to understand. My life is completely changed." I patted the dashboard of the BMW. "I mean, look at this car. My grandfather drives an old Buick. Paul is seventeen years old...you know what I mean? And he's driving a brand new Beamer? Are you kidding me? The guys I play with mostly live in apartments the size of your living room. A kid at my school held a teacher at knife point last Wednesday. I sit next to a transvestite on the bus every day. My mother calls me from the nuthouse. Believe me, Ash, it's a different world so...yeah, I guess I was bound to change."

Ashley held my hand and we sat quietly for a few minutes, the only noise coming from the crickets around the trees surrounding the beach.

"Is it that bad?" she finally asked.

I shook my head. "Nah, it's really not that bad. It's just so different and then I come out here and I see how different. I think everything will be okay and then I see you and all the guys and I know nothing is the same, you know? And it will probably never be the same. And it pisses me off and I just wish I could be pissed at someone."

"You still upset at your father?"

I shrugged. "I don't know. He's living in Hartford and I barely see him. He screwed up bad, I know that. I'm madder about my mother. I don't know why he couldn't have done something for her, you know? And I don't know why I couldn't have done something either. So I guess I'm pissed at both of us."

"It's not your fault, Kyle."

I smiled. "Everything keeps saying that so it must be true."

But I knew deep in my heart that it was at least partly my fault.

"How's your grandfather?"

I smiled again. "He's awesome. Thank God for Grandpa Butch."

And then we sat quietly for a while. I rolled down the window and felt that crisp fall air. I could smell that smoky odor of burning leaves and the sky was full of stars. I held Ashley and had this peaceful feeling that I wish I could just save and break out every once in a while when things got crazy.

"Just always remember that I'm here for you, Kyle. Always," Ashley said as she placed her head on my shoulder.

Paul had given me a hard time for returning his car so late but he never really stayed mad at anyone, particularly me. I slept until ten thirty the next morning and felt a pang of guilt that I missed Mass.

Ashley was going to give me a ride back to Crandall and I heard the beep of the horn at around noon time.

I thanked Paul, promised to see him next weekend and climbed into Ashley's Honda Accord. She pulled out of the driveway and we began the trip to Crandall, the other side of the galaxy.

We were both pretty quiet during the drive although it wasn't an uneasy quiet. We held hands for much of the ride...until we exited Route 93 and headed towards Crandall.

The bars, Laundromats, check cashing stores...all of them seemed so much more noticeable and numerous on this trip. Ashley seemed kind of nervous, her hands gripping the steering wheel tightly and her teeth furiously (and loudly) chewing a piece of gum.

"Hey, don't worry, Ash. I walk around here everyday. Never been bothered." She smiled weakly.

She turned the Accord onto Lodge Avenue. Grandpa Butch was sitting on his brick front steps, reading the Sunday Tribune sports page. At our approach, he stood and walked to the car.

"Grandpa, this is Ashley. Ash this is my grandfather Butch."

"Pleased to meet you, Ashley." Grandpa Butch stuck his hand through the window. I noticed Ashley shook the hand with some hesitation. That seemed a little strange.

"You want to come in and have something to eat or some coffee?" Grandpa asked.

Ashley shook her head quickly. "No... thanks anyway. I really have to get home. I have three tests tomorrow. It was nice to meet you."

After Ashley drove away, Grandpa and I walked up the stairs and into the house.

"Good time?" Grandpa asked.

I nodded. "Yeah, it was good, Grandpa. I saw a lot of my friends."

We both lingered in the hallway for a moment. Part of me wanted to open up a little to Grandpa Butch, tell him how much I missed Fairview, my friends and football but the words just wouldn't come out. I think Grandpa was waiting for me to say something but when I didn't, he patted me on the shoulder and walked back outside.

I checked my cell phone and noticed that Eduardo had left a voice message. I turned off the phone and went upstairs to do some homework.

Chapter Twelve

Monday morning. No game at the end of the week. I really had to drag myself out of bed and go to school today. On the way to school, everything and everyone annoyed me. The bus driver was too cheery, a couple of riders hadn't worn deodorant and we must have hit every red light on Main Street. And, to top it off, I couldn't get a seat. Bad start to the week.

I was comatose through most of the school day. I even skipped lunch and just chilled in the library. I attempted not to make eye contact with Katie in Algebra class with some success. My goal was to just put my time in and get out of this hellhole as soon as possible.

Coach Bonfiglio had given us the day off from practice since there's no game this week. I was planning to travel straight home after school but Eduardo and Sal asked if I wanted to shoot some hoops in the gym with a few of the basketball players.

We arrived at the gym and there were about ten kids either shooting around or playing half court games of three on three. Except for one kid whose ethnicity was unclear, every player on the court was African American.

Eduardo called next game at one end of the court. I was a decent hoop player...I even started at the small forward for the freshman squad at Fairview. However, I decided to devote myself to football after freshman year and had only played sporadically since then.

Naturally, Eduardo began talking trash to the six players on the court. Most of them just smirked or, more effectively, ignored him.

The game ended and Eduardo immediately strolled onto the court and began shooting practice three pointers. He actually shot the ball pretty well. I worked on a bank shot from about ten feet.

"You're so white, man," Eduardo said as our three black opponents all chuckled.

"Fundamentals, buddy, it's all about fundamentals," I responded as I took turnaround eight footer.

"Okay, man, we ain't got all day. This practice ain't gonna help you anyway," Jabreel, one of the black kids, said.

We'd play defense first and I matched up with a stocky kid named Earl who wore earrings in both ears and a real serious expression on his face.

It was actually a pretty close game. These kids were real basketball players with very quick first steps and nasty crossover dribbles. But we were stronger than they were and all three of us pretty much had our way down low on the post.

Our opponents were getting frustrated and they began fouling us almost every play. Of course, you call your fouls in playground basketball and no one really wanted to appear weak.

On game point, Sal looped the ball down to me on the post and as I turned and pump faked, Earl jumped in the air and then slammed his forearm on my shoulder as I attempted to shoot.

"Hey, what's that?" I shouted as I rose from the floor.

"Can't take it, preppie boy?" Earl said, laughing and wiping his face with his shirt.

"That's a foul," I said, bounce passing the ball back to Sal at the free throw line.

"This cracker needs a diaper. Your mommy ain't here, is she?" Earl said.

I took a step towards Earl. "My name's Kyle."

Earl's face began to show some rage. "Don't step to me, punk. You understand? Now back off, and get yourself back in the game." Earl turned his back.

I pushed him in the back. "Hey, I'm not done talking to you."

I'm not really sure why I did this. I could have let it go and gone back to the game. But I wasn't happy anyway and I didn't appreciate this kid calling me a punk and talking about my mother.

Earl charged me and rammed his shoulder into my midsection. I fell to the floor, trying to grab his shirt. Eduardo and Sal jumped in and pulled Earl off my body.

"Who you think you fronting, preppie?" Earl yelled as he was being restrained by Sal and Eddy. Earl's two buddies stood on the side, laughing hysterically.

"Take it easy, man," Sal said.

Earl pushed Sal away. "Get your hands off me!" He pointed at me. "Me and this rich boy ain't done."

This was another test and I was getting tired of tests. "Bring it...whatever you want," I said.

"Look, man, everyone calm down," Eduardo said, stepping between us.

"No, screw this...you want to go outside, that's fine with me," I said.

Earl took his shirt off and both of us stormed out the side door into a little alleyway that separated the gym from the cafeteria.

I barely set foot on the pavement when Earl came at me with a roundhouse right. I stuck up my left arm and deflected the punch but he came again with another wild right hand. This punch caught me square on left eye and I fell to the ground. I couldn't see anything out of the eye but I instinctively put my forearms up in front of my face.

I knew that Earl would attempt to dive on top of me and I was able to grab his neck and use his momentum to pull him to the ground beside me. I quickly rolled over and dived on top of him and just started swinging wildly.

I know that I landed a couple of punches but then Earl took his right foot to my chest and I fell backward. Earl wasn't in the best condition because he got up real slowly as if he was hoping someone would step in and break up the fight.

I rose warily and noticed that just about every kid in the gym had congregated around us in the narrow alleyway. I sure didn't want to fight anymore and both of our prayers were answered when Coach Reilly, the JV basketball coach, pushed his way through the crowd, frantically blowing his whistle.

"Both of you, in the office, NOW! Everyone else: back in the gym!" he shouted.

"Nice going, *meninobranco*!" Eduardo said to me, patting my back as I trudged off to Mr. Amaral's office.

Earl and I took our seats in the two chairs located against the wall outside Mr. Amaral's office. He looked at me and shrugged and I did the same while Coach Reilly filled him in on the details of the battle inside the office.

Mr. Amaral poked his head out the door and said, "Earl, Kyle...come on in." His voice didn't sound angry. It sounded more tired than anything else.

Mr. Amaral gave a loud sigh and said, "Sit down, guys." He took a quick look at some notes on a legal pad and said, "So who wants to talk first? What happened?

We both sat there in silence and Mr. Amaral smiled. "Come on, guys. What happened?"

I stole a quick look at Earl who simply shrugged his shoulders again. I took a deep breath and said, "We were just playing basketball and things got out of hand. One thing led to another and we went outside. It was really over by the time Coach Reilly got there."

"Is that your story, Earl?" Mr. Amaral asked.

Earl nodded.

Mr. Amaral leaned back in his chair and put his hands behind his head. "Okay, one day suspension for both of you. Stay home tomorrow. Earl, I'm going to call your mother...she won't be happy about this. Kyle, I know your grandfather will also be upset when I tell him what happened." He leaned forward and folded his hands on his desk. "Now listen, this ends here. I don't want any more of this crap. You both have athletic careers to think about. Don't let something stupid screw it all up. Now shake hands."

I offered my hand to Earl who shook it and again shrugged his shoulders which I was beginning to believe was his main mode of communication when he wasn't playing basketball.

We both rose to leave and Mr. Amaral said, "Kyle, you stay

here." I sat back in the chair."

Mr. Amaral got up and sat on the desk in front of my chair. "How's everything going, Kyle?" he asked.

I felt like Earl when I shrugged my shoulders. "Okay, I guess."

He pointed to my left eye. "You're going to have a nice shiner in the morning."

I put my hand to my eye. It felt puffy and was sore to the touch.

"It's not easy, Kyle, I know that. Coach Bonfiglio says you've been great with the team. In fact, he says you're becoming a team leader. He also told me about you switching to fullback. Your teachers also have good things to say."

I nodded. "Football's been great and Coach B. is cool...so are most of my teachers. It's just that..."

"What?"

I looked out the window. "I don't know. It's just so different. When it was just football and no school, it was better. Now...I don't know."

Mr. Amaral nodded. "It has to be hard, Kyle. But you have to talk about things. My door is always open. I'm sure Coach Bonfiglio would be happy to talk any time. He says you seem to doing fine socially."

"Okay, I guess. I really can't explain it. The guys on the team are great. But even with them, I feel, I don't know, kind of like an outsider, you know? Eduardo and Sal are probably my best friends in Crandall but it's still not like it was at Fairview."

Mr. Amaral got up and sat back at his desk. "Give it more time, Kyle. It takes a while for a lot of these kids. Remember, you're white and most of them think you're still rich. That's two strikes right there. Hang in there...maybe this will turn out to be one the best experiences of your life."

I touched my eye, chuckled and said, "Doesn't feel that way right now."

"Yeah, you have to take care of that eye. Well, we won't see you tomorrow... get some rest and try to stay positive. You want me to call Butch now?"

I shook my head. "No, if that's okay. I'd like to talk to him first and then you can call him tonight, if that's alright with you."

"That's fine. Don't worry about Earl. He's no gang banger. His mother's going to kill him."

"Thanks, Mr. Amaral," I said as I shook the principal's hand.

"Be careful, Kyle. And come on in and talk again soon."

I walked upstairs to my locker. The school was basically empty. I heard a voice say, "From Fairview, weighing 190 pounds, Kyle 'the killer' Donovan!"

I turned and saw Sal and Eduardo at the other end of the hallway, laughing loudly. I just waved and continued putting books in my bag.

"Hey, come on, I'll give you a ride," Sal said.

"Nah, it's alright."

"You sure?"

"Yeah, I'll be fine. Thanks anyway," I said.

When Sal and Eddy left, I sat down on the floor in front of my locker. My head was pounding and my eye felt like someone had taken a sledgehammer to it. How did my life ever turn out like this, I wondered. As I looked around through my one good eye at the dark hallway, the chipping paint on the concrete block walls and the indecipherable graffiti on many of the lockers, I began to feel sorry for myself in a big way. I thought of Paul's BMW and hanging at the Ambrose and Ashley. I thought of my mother in white hospital clothes sitting in some room in Vermont talking to a psychiatrist. I thought of my father, driving around Hartford, Connecticut, begging banks to lend him money. I began to pray to Jesus for help but then I stopped. I just didn't feel like praying.

The conversation with Grandpa Butch went better than expected. I didn't tell him too much but he seemed to understand that sometimes you had to fight. Once a Marine, always a Marine, I guess.

I wanted to tell Grandpa Butch about how much I missed Fairview but I think that would only make him feel bad. I didn't want him to feel responsible because he (and football) were the only factors making life in Crandall tolerable.

I went upstairs and turned on my laptop. Once I logged in, I was barraged with messages concerning the afternoon fisticuffs. I ignored the Crandall instant messages and instead contacted Paul.

"What's up?" he typed.

"Horrible. Big fight today."

"U fighting?"

"Ya."

"U win?"

"Tie. It sucks here."

"Come back. F-view has plenty of financial aid."

"Stuck here in this hole. Lata."

"Talk soon. Lata."

I sat at my father's old desk and opened up my US History-Advanced Placement book. Usually, I kind of enjoyed reading about Washington, Jefferson and King George, but I just couldn't focus using only one eye.

I got up and looked in the mirror. Mr. Amaral was right. The whole area around my left eye had grown darker. It still stung to the touch and I stared at myself for a couple of minutes. I actually looked kind of tough which wouldn't hurt walking around Crandall High. Although I wasn't sure I ever wanted to go back to that nightmare.

After I opened my eyes on Tuesday morning, I rolled over and checked the clock radio. 12:15. I don't remember ever sleeping that late. More remarkably, Grandpa Butch hadn't awakened me.

I checked myself in the mirror and the eye looked worse than the day before. I sighed and walked downstairs to the kitchen where Grandpa was sitting at the table, eating lunch.

"The prince has arisen," he said as I entered the kitchen.

"Can't believe it. You didn't wake me up?"

Grandpa Butch smiled. "Ah, I figured you might need the rest."

I poured some Frosted Flakes and milk into a cereal bowl and grabbed the Tribune sports page from the kitchen wastebasket.

"I don't want to go back, Grandpa," I said. I'm not sure why I chose this particular point to make this statement.

Grandpa continued chomping away at his ham and cheese Hot Pocket. After what seemed to be an eternity, he said, "I know it stinks, Boyo, I know it does. Like I said, life dealt you this hand...it's not your fault. Is it that bad?"

"Not here at the house. Not you...this is the only sanity in my life right now...this and football. But I miss my friends and my school and everything the way it used to be. It just really hit me."

Grandpa took another bite of the croissant. "You know, Kyle, when I was in the Marine Corps in the Pacific...

I interrupted him. "Believe me; I'm not comparing my situation with yours, Grandpa."

Grandpa Butch shook his head. "No, no, that's not what I'm saying. I was nineteen years old when I crossed the Hagushi Beach on Okinawa. Sixth Marine Division. Didn't know my butt from my elbow and here I was knee deep in bodies and blood. You know what kept me going, kept me from going crazy?"

I shook my head.

"That when I got home, everything would be better. Anything that reminded me of home did the trick. The Red Sox, the old movie theater in Hubbard Square, an old girlfriend Rosie McManus who used to write me every once in a while...anything at all. I tried not to dwell on the heap of crap that the US government stuck me in...instead I thought about the future, how good things would be. It got me through, Boyo. You wouldn't believe what I saw on that island." Grandpa Butch rubbed his hands through his bristly snow white hair. "And then I came home. Got married eventually, had three kids, your dad's the youngest. Proud of all of them, even though they weren't proud of me sometimes."

I sat at the table, looking at my grandfather, at his tanned face, the shamrock and Marine Corps tattoos showing under the neatly pressed white pocket t-shirt and I thought about the diary I read. How do you go through that and then carry on a normal life? I wonder if Dad ever read that diary.

Grandpa Butch rose from the table and shuffled to the dining room. He returned holding his Sixth Marine Division patch. He put his hand on my shoulder and handed me the patch. "This is my division patch from the war. I want you to have it." He winked at me. "Help you remember this old man when he's dead and buried. No matter how bad things seem, they'll get better. They always do. It's different here...but this whole thing will make you a better person. Tough to see that now but it will. Remember to pray. Talk to God...he's listening all the time, even if it doesn't always seem that way. So my unsolicited advice is to hang in there."

I squeezed the patch tightly and then carefully placed it in my pocket with the prayer card. We finished out respective meals quietly until Grandpa Butch said, "You bowl, Boyo?"

Bowling. I bowled once for laughs with Paul and Trevor Smith when we were freshmen. Of course, there were no bowling alleys in Fairview.

"Not really, Grandpa."

Grandpa Butch clapped his hands. "Go get ready, son. We're bowling at 1:00."

I laughed. Bowling with my grandfather? Yeah, let's go bowling.

Chapter Thirteen

I saw Earl when I returned to school and we basically just ignored each other. His two buddies now say hi to me in the hall which is sort of confusing.

I'm already tired of some of my classes. English class is a joke. The teacher, Mr. Anderson, is retiring at the end of the year and he just doesn't care. Kids literally throw notebooks at each other in class. He can barely be heard above the constant noise so basically he doesn't even bother trying to teach. So we do grammar worksheets every day and sometimes Mr. Anderson lets us read our own novels in class. Grandpa Butch gave me "Lonesome Dove" by Larry McMurtry to read and I'm almost done with all 945 pages. It shows you how much we accomplish in class. Great preparation for taking the SAT's in the spring.

My Algebra teacher, Mr. Bruno, and my US AP teacher, Mr. Irwin, are outstanding. I would say they're better than any teacher at Fairview especially considering the size and diversity of their classes. At Fairview, a class of eighteen kids is considered huge. These guys have to deal with thirty students whose parents haven't paid twenty grand to send them to school.

I've been making small talk with Katie every once in a while and she doesn't seem to be surprised or upset. I'm terrible at small talk. I wish I could talk at length about the Kardashians or Jersey Shore but I just don't care. I don't think Katie cares much either which makes the meaningless conversations even more pathetic.

Ashley's coming down on Saturday. I'm actually pretty psyched about it. I figure she can meet Eddy and Sal and a few of the guys and I can show her around Crandall a little bit.

Football practice during an off week can be torturous. There's no game to anticipate so the week becomes an endless series of drills and conditioning. Coach Bonfiglio and Coach Brennan have been busy getting back to basics with the offense so that means more hitting and more repetition. Thank God there's a game next week.

After Sal dropped me off at Grandpa Butch's house, I had to pee so bad I almost broke an ankle rushing to the bathroom. As I washed my hands, I noticed small drops of blood on the tan tile floor.

"Hey Grandpa," I yelled in no particular direction. "What's with the blood on the floor?"

I heard a couple of grunts emanating from his bedroom. Grandpa emerged from the room and said, "Cut myself shaving," he said, rubbing his face. "Getting old...sometimes I can't see too good in the mirror."

I walked closer to Grandpa. "I don't see any cuts on your face."

Grandpa Butch laughed. "What are you, a doctor? Come on...let's see what's for supper."

Grandpa made some hot dogs and beans which he said was a regular meal for most Irish Americans on Saturday nights back in the day.

As I bit into my third hot dog, I heard a key open the front door.

"Anyone home?" Dad called.

I got up and greeted Dad in the hallway. "Hey Dad, what's going on? You home for the whole weekend?"

Dad shot a look past me. I turned and saw Grandpa standing in the kitchen with his hands in his pockets. "Yeah...how you doing? What happened to your eye?" he asked, placing his hand gently on my face.

I shrugged. "I took an elbow playing basketball after school. It doesn't hurt anymore."

Dad nodded. "How you doing, Dad?"

"Not bad for an old man," Grandpa said. "I got franks and beans all made. Come on and eat."

"Now here are some memories," Dad said as he sat down.

"Memories can be good, Timmy," Grandpa said as he spooned some beans onto Dad's plate.

Dad looked up. "Some memories, Dad...memories can be bad too."

Grandpa shrugged but I could see him close his eyes and his face became kind of contorted. As he reached for the plate of hot dogs, he knocked the pan of beans off the counter. I immediately grabbed a roll of paper towels and began cleaning up the mess.

Grandpa appeared shaken and he sat down at the table, using his hands to guide himself into the chair. He seemed more tired and worn out than usual.

"You okay, Grandpa?" I asked.

He sat just staring at Dad. "I'd take it back if I could, Timmy. I've told you that a thousand times. I don't know what else to say, I really don't. If you can't forgive me, you can't forgive me," Grandpa said, his voice rising with emotion.

Dad continued to shovel the beans into his mouth.

Grandpa Butch put his hands on the kitchen table in front of Dad and said, "You hear me, Tim? What can I possibly do...huh, tell me what to do?"

Dad stared at Grandpa for a long moment. I wasn't sure whether he was going to say anything but then he blurted, "Why'd you do it, Dad?" Dad banged his fist on the table. "Why'd you do it?"

I stopped cleaning up the beans and rose to my feet. Grandpa Butch turned and looked at me and let go a deep sigh.

Grandpa Butch sighed again and then looked at both of us. "I guess you should know this about your grandfather, Kyle. I'm an alcoholic, Boyo. I got my discharge from the Corps, got drunk and then drank every day for over thirty years."

Grandpa shook his head. "I'm not talking a beer or two either. I was a mean drunk, too, you might know the type. I'm sure most people didn't like me because I didn't like myself much in those days."

He glanced at Dad who was staring at his plate. "I wasn't much of a father, I'm afraid. Always worrying about my next drink...no time for anything else." There was a look of pain on the old man's face.

"Anyway, one day I got home and the empty trash barrels were still out front. Your dad had forgotten to take them around back. I had been drinking up at O'Tooles' in the square and I could barely walk. I got inside and your grandma, Dad and your two aunts were just sitting in the parlor watching TV." He stopped again to compose himself.

"Then I just lost it. I knocked over chairs, pulled pictures off the walls...just out of control." Grandpa's gruff voice became barely a whisper. "And then I turned on your father. Beat him up bad. He was only thirteen years old. Thirteen years old. I dragged him outside and threw him into the barrels. Broke his right arm when I pushed him down...it was April; he missed half the baseball season. I gave him a worse shiner than you have right now."

There must have been a look of horror on my face because the pain in Grandpa's face became more pronounced as he looked at me. "You gotta know everything, Kyle. Made marks and welts all over your dad's back. And then I just went back inside and fell asleep on the couch. Next thing I knew, your grandmother was standing over me with two cops who hauled me into jail for the night. No charges were ever pressed but your grandma threw me out of the house. I lived in Bingo Lonergan's basement for a month and then Teresa took me back as long as I promised to stop drinking. I kept my promise but that couldn't undo the damage and pain I caused. Your aunts were older...they both moved out of the house by the time they were twenty. Maybe to get away from me."

Dad had turned his chair around so that he faced the front door. I couldn't see his face. Grandpa stood and placed his hands on Dad's shoulders. "Strange thing is that I forgot so much of what I did when I was drunk. But I remember that night thirty years ago so clearly. Timmy, I know you can never forgive me but you have to know that I think about it every day. I'm so sorry, son."

I felt like I should do something but I just sat at the table, frozen to my chair, speechless. Dad reached back and put his hands on top of Grandpa's hands. They held hands for a minute or so and then Dad stood and hugged Grandpa. The old man's body seemed to collapse while receiving the hug and Dad struggled to hold him up.

"You okay, Dad?" he asked, helping Grandpa Butch into a chair.

"Yeah, I'm fine, I just...I'm just old," Grandpa said, his voice cracking. He turned to me and said, "I'm sorry you had to hear this about your grandfather, Kyle. I can't hide the truth from you. I hope you can forgive me."

I reached into my pocket and grasped the Sixth Marine Division patch. I wasn't really angry at Grandpa Butch...I was more sad about it all. I was sad for my father who had seen his father turn into a monster. I was sad for Grandpa Butch who had to live with this for his whole adult life. For the first time in two months, I didn't feel too bad for myself.

I thought about Grandpa Butch's diaries from World War II and I began to connect the dots. How do you cope with living after seeing all that crap? I guess you start drinking and you don't stop until you can't remember anything. I wasn't sure if Dad had read the diaries. Not that it would heal any wounds or anything. But it seemed like Dad should read them.

"I read your diaries, Grandpa," I said.

Grandpa Butch winced as if someone had closed a door on his finger.

"What diaries, Kyle?" Dad asked.

I breathed heavily through my nose. "Grandpa?"

Grandpa Butch nodded and I retrieved the diaries from the credenza drawer in the dining room. I handed them to Dad who had a perplexed look on his face.

"I don't get it," he said, turning towards Grandpa.

"A lot of war stuff, son. Not sure why I even saved them. I should have burned them a long time ago. More bad memories."

Dad leafed through a few pages. "Were these written to Mom?"

Grandpa shook his head. "No. I just needed to write stuff down. Like I needed some record of what happened on that island. I figured no one would ever believe the stories so I wrote it down so I'd remember exactly." He nodded towards the diaries. "It's all a hundred percent truth...unfortunately." He looked at me. "You're the first person other than me to read them. Even my wife never read them."

Dad rose from the table, clutching the diaries. "I'm going upstairs."

After Dad left, Grandpa said, "I'm sorry, Kyle."

I studied Grandpa Butch's tanned, lined face, the clear blue eyes, the sharp features, the neatly trimmed eyebrows and I saw my father and I think I saw myself. Life dealt Grandpa and Dad some crappy hands. I guess I wasn't alone.

Grandpa went into the parlor to watch an <u>Everybody Loves Raymond</u> rerun and I finished cleaning up the kitchen. Within fifteen minutes, I heard him snoring.

I sat at the kitchen table and attempted to finish my Algebra homework without cheating and checking the answers in the back of the book.

Dad came downstairs about a half hour later. He put the diaries on the table and said, "These are yours, Kyle. This is your grandfather's life." He sat down and placed his right hand on the small book. "Unbelievable. I never knew. I mean I knew that Grandpa served in the Marines and that he had a few medals but...this." Dad raised his eyebrows. "This is mind boggling."

"Do you hate him, Dad?"

Dad shook his head. "I did for a long time. All the way through high school and even college. After your mother and I got married, a lot of stuff began to fade. You came along, Dad was sober and went to Mass all the time, and I still loved my mother so I tried to bury some of the bad. I guess I never completely buried it because I got a little angry every time I saw your grandfather. And after Grandma Teresa died, well, there wasn't much reason to visit here much anymore. It's weird, though, now I feel closer to him than I ever have before." He picked up the diary. "And this...well, like I said, I never knew any of this. It explains a few things...doesn't justify anything but I understand him a little better, I guess."

I took the Sixth Marine Division patch from my pocket. "He gave me this, Dad."

Dad examined the patch and smiled. "He loves you, Kyle, probably more than he's loved anyone. Never lose this."

"I carry it everywhere, except on the football field...I'm not sure why but it makes me feel better. Weird, huh?"

I looked down absently at my Algebra book. "There's something else, Dad. I found drops of blood all over the bathroom floor. Grandpa said he cut himself shaving but his face looked pretty clear."

Dad tapped his fingers on the table, the way he always did when he was nervous. "Your grandfather has never cut himself shaving."

"There were just little drops but it seemed kind of strange.

And then when I asked Grandpa about it, he just kind of shrugged it off but his face looked different, you know?"

Dad grimaced and got up from the table. He waved to me to follow him into the parlor.

Grandpa lay in his recliner, still snoring loudly. Dad stood close and examined Grandpa's face. Grandpa woke up suddenly and let out a loud grunt. This startled Dad who jumped back a couple of feet.

"What the hell is going on?" Grandpa asked.

"What's with the blood on the bathroom floor, Dad?"

"I told Kyle...I cut myself shaving."

"You've never cut yourself shaving, Dad."

"I'm getting old, Timmy. Things change when you get old. You'll see," Grandpa said as he pushed down the recliner.

"Come on, Dad, what's going on?"

Grandpa Butch looked at me and winced like he had at the kitchen table. "Colorectal cancer, Timmy. Found out last week. I'd been seeing a little blood in my stool so Dr. Patel, the GI doctor, ordered a colonoscopy. He took a biopsy and, sure enough, cancer. The good news is that it's real early...stage I they call it."

"What's the treatment?" Dad asked.

"Hasn't spread but they want to use radiation to zap the tumor. Dr. Patel said this makes more sense than surgery. He calls it endocavitary radiation therapy, I think."

"How often is the radiation?"

"Pretty sure it'll be three or four days a week for a couple of weeks. Dr. Patel thinks this will do the trick and the tumor will be gone. If not, who knows," Grandpa Butch said, holding his hands out in front of him. "I don't want either of you worrying.

Bingo's gonna take me to treatment. He's got nothing better to do, believe me. Don't get any stupid ideas about rearranging your schedules over this. Five weeks and it'll be all over. The doc says there may be some minor diarrhea or nausea. He also says I may have problems performing sexually." Grandpa chuckled and I had to laugh, too. "So I'll have to take it easy for a few weeks." Grandpa rose from the chair. "Now, all this talk about my colon has made me sleepy. Good night, gentlemen."

After Grandpa went upstairs to bed, Dad and I sat in the parlor and looked at each other in silence.

"You think he'll be okay?" I finally asked.

Dad nodded. "There's not a man alive tougher than your grandfather, Kyle."

I tried to use my father's words to feel better but they didn't work.

Chapter Fourteen

"So, are we ever going to have a normal conversation again?"

I looked up from my Algebra book and saw Katie standing over me in the library, softly chewing a piece of gum and it struck me. She closely resembled one of Grandpa Butch's favorite actresses. We had watched an old John Wayne movie, "The Quiet Man", last night and the actress, Maureen O'Hara, looked so familiar. She looked just like Katie O'Brien. I was going tell Katie but I quickly thought better of that idea.

"Yeah, of course. I've just been real busy, you know." Pathetic. Ridiculous. And lame. I honestly don't think I'll ever get the hang of the talking to women thing.

Katie chuckled. "Busy, huh?"

I cleared my throat. "This is the quiet area of the library," I said.

Katie nodded and smiled. "So, are we ever going to have a normal conversation again?"

I sighed and that lump began to grow in my throat again. "Yeah, Katie. It's complicated right now."

"I know we're not married, Kyle. But how long do you think you can avoid me? It's not like everyone else around here looks just like us. This isn't Fairview, you know."

"I know it's not Fairview, Katie."

She sat down in the chair across from mine. "There's no commitment here, Kyle, I know that. But you've been sneaking around, avoiding eye contact. You won't even look at me in class."

"I know, I know. It's just weird right now. I feel funny because..."

Katie stood. "It's okay to feel funny, Kyle. But try to have some maturity. No matter who you go out with, no girl wants to be treated like an idiot."

I watched Katie walk out of the library. A couple of Freshmen sitting at the same table were laughing. I just looked at them, shrugged and packed up my books.

I was pretty fired up for our game against Muldoon High School. Their record was 2-1; ours was 3-0 so it was a big conference game. Ashley and Paul were at the game, sitting with Dad and Grandpa Butch.

As I ran on to the field. I glanced over at Katie, who stood on the track with the other cheerleaders screaming wildly. Now it was her turn to avoid eye contact.

Muldoon was a pretty rough city and their coach was known for encouraging "aggressive" play. I found this to be the truth on our first play from scrimmage when I felt a fist pound against my ribs at the bottom of the pile. Luckily, I was wearing a rib protector because the punch could have done some damage.

Marco ran like Barry Sanders on this particular Saturday. A couple of Division 2 college coaches from Bentley and Assumption were in the stands and Marco played as if his ticket to college was riding on this game. There were supposedly some Division I coaches from big time schools scouting an offensive lineman playing for Muldoon.

It was a nasty, pretty dirty game. Ultimately, we won by the score of 18-7. The Muldoon coaches and players didn't even line up to shake hands after the game which was a first in my football career.

In the locker room after the game, Coach Bonfiglio was as emotional as I have seen him.

"Gentlemen, I can't tell you how proud I am of you. They threw punches, kicks, everything at you but you guys...you guys kept your heads. You never stooped to their level...and you just kicked their ass on the field. You make me proud to coach Crandall High School." Coach Brennan whispered something in Coach B's ear. "Oh yeah, Marco and Raymond, there's a couple of gentlemen who would like to see you after you shower up."

As I peeled off my uniform, Marco came over to my locker and just stared at me. By now, I was kind of used to Marco's confusing personality traits, so I just ignored him and continued undressing.

I looked up again and Marco still stood there, holding out his hand. "Amigo."

I accepted Marco's handshake. He smiled and said, "I was wrong about you, Irish boy. I'm happy you're on our team."

I nodded and smiled. "Good luck with those coaches, man."

Marco continued to grip my hand and said, "I couldn't have done this without you blocking the way you do. *Você é um jogador da equipe. Agradece o amigo.*"

I knew enough Portuguese by now to understand that

Marco was thanking me and calling me his friend. *"É meu prazer,"* I said. I think I said 'it's my pleasure', but I'm not sure.

Marco laughed out loud, nodded his head and returned to his locker.

After I showered and changed, I headed out of the locker room. I walked by Katie, who congregated with a few players and some girls from school. She flashed me an incredibly fake, insincere smile. She ignored my wave and went back to talking and laughing with the group.

Dad, Grandpa Butch, Bingo Lonergan, Paul and Ashley were standing around Paul's car.

"Muldoon's always the same," Grandpa said. He looked tired and pale from his treatments which had started on Thursday.

Bingo took a sip of coffee and said, "Yeah, their fans used to show up with brass knuckles and bats. Something in the water over there, I guess." Bingo was almost completely bald, his face that rosy tinge that afflicted many elderly Irish American males. He usually stated the obvious but he was Grandpa's best friend, a fellow former Marine who was pathologically loyal, probably to a fault.

"Wow, I've never seen a game like that," Ashley said. She wore a slightly oversized beige Calvin Klein sweater and jeans. Her black hair was pulled back and, as usual, her makeup and mascara were perfect.

"The Fairview cops would be arresting most of those Muldoon kids after the game...probably the coaches, too," Paul added.

It was a rough game but a pretty fun game to play, to be truthful. For me, cheap shots only served as motivation.

Nothing better than pointing to the scoreboard after a kid talks trash or jumps on a pile late.

"Well, you kids have fun. Good game, Kyle," Dad said, as he guided Grandpa and Bingo away from the BMW.

"Thanks, Dad. You going to back to Hartford tonight?"

Dad frowned and nodded. "Unfortunately. Although I should be happy, I guess. It looks good right now."

We climbed into Paul's car and he said, "So, where do you want to go?"

"Let's go to the Hubbard Café. Its real close and Sal and Eddy want to meet you guys," I said. I noticed some slight tension in Ashley's face.

"You alright?" I asked, taking hold of her hand.

"Oh yeah. The Hubbard Café sounds good. I'm hungry."

We drove through Hubbard Square and I pointed out the various landmarks which seemed to really interest Paul but Ashley appeared a little uncomfortable.

As we walked into the Hubbard Café, we were immediately greeted by a group of long time Crandall High boosters who patted me on the back and told me they wished I was old enough for them to buy me a beer. All five of them wore their Hawks Nest jackets and Crandall High baseball hats.

Eddy, Sal, Peter Sousa and Raymond Boursiquot sat in a booth in the back of the restaurant, eating rolls and waiting for their pizza.

Eddy stood up and hugged me, pointed menacingly to Paul and Ashley and said, "So, these more rich kids from Fairview?"

I don't think that Ashley and Paul knew he was joking because they seemed a little startled by the 260 pound Brazilian left tackle wearing a doo rag, baggy jeans, massive gold chain and a Kaka Brazilian team soccer jersey.

"Hey, we love Fairview here in Crandall," Eddy smiled and said, offering his hand to Paul, who shook it enthusiastically. Eddy than turned to Ashley who took a step back. "I won't bite, menina. How you doing?"

Ashley seemed a little embarrassed by her nervousness and shook Eddy's hand. "I'm Eduardo, the next mayor of Crandall." He gestured to Sal, Peter and Raymond and said, "Don't bother meeting these guys. They're unimportant."

Paul and Ashley met the rest of the guys and we all sat down and waited for the pizza. Within minutes, Paul had entered into an animated football discussion with Sal and Peter and all three were actually diagramming plays on the placemat.

"So, how you like Crandall, *Menina*?" Eddy asked Ashley, his huge arm draped around my neck. "Little different than Fairview, I guess, huh?"

"It's very nice," Ashley said, cleaning her empty glass with a napkin. She then looked to the kitchen, as if the pizza would save her from further conversation with Eduardo.

Eddy looked at me and raised his eyebrows a little.

"Ashley works in Dorchester sometimes. Don't you have cousins over there, Eddy?" I said.

"Yeah, yeah...the Oliveiras. Let's see, there's Alfredo, Amancio, Branca, Elisa and Henrique. You know them?"

Ashley shook her head. "No. I really don't know many people there. My father works at a clinic sometimes and I help out."

"What's your father do?" Eduardo asked.

"He's a cardiologist. There's a health clinic in Fields Corner in Dorchester that he works at every month. It's right next to a food bank. I help him."

Eduardo whistled softly. "Sounds like a good homem."

Ashley smiled and again glanced towards the kitchen. She seemed nervous and uncomfortable.

Eddy hated silence but it became apparent that Ashley had little interest in conversation. So, Eddy turned and joined in the rock vs. hip hop debate that was raging between Paul and the Crandall guys.

I turned to Ashley and said, "You okay? You seem really different today."

Ashley shrugged. "I don't know. I'm just not feeling that well."

"You want to go back to Grandpa's house?" I asked.

"I hate to take you away from your friends," she said.

"It's okay." I asked Paul to borrow his car. He flipped me the keys without looking at me, too engrossed in the loud but very friendly debate to verbally respond.

Ashley told everyone she was glad to meet them and we left the restaurant.

She was really quiet on the way back to Grandpa's house. Ashley sat there, alone in her thoughts as she stared out the passenger window.

"Hey, you can lie down at Grandpa's if you don't feel good," I said.

Ashley shook her head. "I think I better just go home, Kyle. I have a really bad headache."

We pulled into Grandpa Butch's small driveway and parked behind Grandpa's Buick. Ashley got out of the car and immediately walked towards her Honda Accord.

"You sure you don't want to come inside?" I asked.

"No, I just have to go home and lay down," she said, opening the driver side door.

"Well, okay. Thanks for coming down today."

Ashley reached out the window and I leaned in and gently kissed her on the lips. "I'll call you tonight," she said and the Accord sped down Lodge Avenue, in the direction of Fairview.

By the time I returned to the Hubbard Café, the pizza had been served and Paul and the Crandall guys were making plans for next weekend. Paul said his goodbyes to his new friends and Eddy walked us to the door.

Paul exited the restaurant and as I was about to leave, Eddy grabbed me and said, "Amigo, Ashley didn't like me much."

Eddy's usually happy face looked hurt and I realized this was a sensitive 260 pound tackle. "Hey, she just didn't feel good, Ed. I'm sure she loved you," I said.

Eddy shook his head. "Nah. She don't like me and she don't like her boyfriend's new home. Mark my words."

I opened the door. "Come on, Eddy, don't say that...she's a great girl, she just didn't feel good."

The smile returned to Eduardo's face. "Okay, Irish boy...whatever you say."

On the drive back to Grandpa's house, Paul said, "Those are good guys, buddy, real good guys." He turned to me and said, "I never thought I'd say this but you're kind of lucky. I mean, when would you ever get to meet guys like Sal and Eduardo if all this crap hadn't happened? And what would you have thought of them if you hadn't met them?" He nodded vigorously. "Yeah, now I'm glad that I met them."

I laughed softly. "Yeah, well, I don't feel lucky most of the time, Dr. Phil. I'm not driving around in a beamer. It's kind of easy to say how lucky I am when you'll be driving back to Fairview."

"Hey, screw that. You think I'm really lucky? I got a father I never see and I'm not sure my mother even likes me, let alone love me. You think she knows where I am right now? You think she cares? Give me a break. I'll trade this car for your grandfather any day of the week." Paul's face got red, a sure sign of his anger. I thought about apologizing but I didn't think there was really anything to apologize for.

As he parked in front of Grandpa's house, I said, "Hey, thanks for the ride. I'll talk to you this week, okay?"

Paul sighed. "Yeah, okay, man. I'll see ya."

As I entered the house, I heard a loud, wrenching cough coming from the downstairs bathroom. "Grandpa?" I shouted.

I hurried to the bathroom and saw Grandpa Butch kneeling in front of the toilet, his body heaving. I put a towel under the faucet and then held it against his head. Grandpa's veins popped out of his hands as he gripped the edge of the toilet bowl.

"You okay, Grandpa?" I asked.

"Doc Patel said this might happen," Grandpa said, his voice barely audible. "Can you help me up, son?"

I put my hands under Grandpa's shoulders and hoisted him to his feet. He slung his left arm around my neck and I helped him out of the bathroom and into the parlor. He collapsed into his recliner. I turned on the television and draped a blanket over Grandpa Butch's legs.

"Thanks, Boyo," he whispered.

I sat on the couch and watched as Grandpa quickly fell asleep. I went into the bathroom, cleaned up the mess and checked Grandpa's medication which was color coded by day and time. I set the timer on my cell phone to remind myself to wake him up at seven o'clock for a pill.

Almost seventeen years old and its six o'clock on a Saturday night and I'd rather watch college football with my grandfather than go out. My body ached from the game against Muldoon and I couldn't stop thinking about Paul and Eduardo's words. I also thought about Katie O'Brien and reflected that the lump in my throat only occurred when I spoke to her and no one else, not even Ashley.

As all these thoughts rattled around in my mind, the ringing of the phone shocked me back to reality. I answered the phone and immediately recognized the voice on the other end. "Hey, Coach Pearson."

Chapter Fifteen

I couldn't believe it. Coach Pearson from Fairview Prep was on the other end of the phone line.

"How you doing, Kyle?" he asked in that gruff voice.

"Good, thanks. I was at your game last week...you guys look real good."

There was a momentary silence and then Coach said, "Not good enough, Kyle but we'll get better."

Many people compared Coach Pearson to Lou Holtz, the old Notre Dame coach who always downplayed his own team's chances and over hyped the opponent. Come to think of it, Coach Bonfiglio did the same thing. Maybe it was a trait of good football coaches.

"Anyway, I'm calling for a reason, Kyle. I've felt real bad about everything that's happened to you. You know, your parents, having to leave your friends and school, you know. So, I've been doing a little research and I have some good news. At least I think its good news."

Good news? There hasn't been a heckuva a lot of that being passed around the Donovan clan lately.

"You there, Kyle?" Coach asked.

"Yeah, I'm here, Coach."

"Well, there was this family, the Millers, which sponsor a scholarship to Fairview each year. It's for one kid who has...let me read it to you. It says 'The Miller family has established the Goodwin Miller Scholarship for a student who demonstrates substantial financial need, above average academic achievement, and a thorough commitment to the values and ideals of the Fairview Preparatory School. The Goodwin Miller Scholarship will cover the cost of tuition, books, and room and board for the academic year. Students must maintain a record of service to the school and a grade point average of at least 2.8. The student's record will be evaluated at the conclusion of the school year.' Well, what do you think?"

I was stunned. A full scholarship to go back to Fairview?

"I know this is a shock, son. But the kid who got this scholarship got homesick and went back home to Brooklyn. I checked with the Admission Office who checked with the Miller family and they all agreed that you would be a perfect recipient. Dick Crocker, the history teacher, is a nephew of the Millers and he had you last year in US History. He gave you his highest recommendation." Coach Pearson paused and then said, "There is a catch, though. You have to live at the school. The scholarship says that 'the student must reside on the Fairview campus during the academic year.' I guess they want the kid to experience everything that the school has to offer."

I quickly thought of Grandpa Butch leaning over the toilet bowl. "This is a big surprise, Coach. I mean, I really appreciate it, believe me...I just might need a couple of days to figure things out. There's some stuff at home I have to take care of."

"I understand completely, Kyle. The Millers promised to hold the scholarship for you for two weeks. After that, they'll open it up again."

And now, the important question. "Can I play football for

you if get the scholarship or do I have to wait until next year?"

Coach Pearson laughed softly. "I figured you'd ask that question. No, you can play immediately. We're not subject to the state rules on this anyway but I checked to be on the safe side. You'd be eligible on a hardship basis no matter what." Coach cleared his throat. "But I want to be clear, Kyle. I would have done this for you if you were in the band or the drama club or whatever. This is for you the person, not the football player."

I believed that Coach Pearson meant what he said. "I don't know what to say, Coach."

"That's alright. You got two weeks, Kyle. Talk to your father, grandfather...it's not an easy decision. But you only have two weeks."

"Thanks a lot, Coach."

I hung up the phone and walked back into the living room. Grandpa Butch was sleeping and Miami was playing Virginia Tech on the television. I sat on the couch and watched as Grandpa snored peacefully on his recliner. His face was a little paler since the treatments had started but, in my heart, I knew that he would make it through this. He had faced down the Japanese army, alcoholism, and fifty years of hauling plywood and sheetrock. He'd pull through. But would he need my help?

I was standing at my locker after practice on Friday and soon found myself in a headlock. "Time for you to get some Brazilian culture, amigo!"

Sao Paulo was playing the Corinthians in the Brazilian soccer championship and Eduardo insisted that I come to his house for a soccer party.

"This is big, amigo. My whole family will be there rooting for Sao Paulo. That's our team. Sal and Raymond are coming so you won't be the only *estrangeiro* there." He laughed that loud Eduardo laugh. "You'll be the whitest though." He paused and said, "Maybe I'll invite Katie so you'll be more comfortable." Eduardo laughed loudly again. "It's a joke, Irish boy."

Watching a soccer game with about a hundred Brazilians screaming in Portuguese made me a little nervous but I knew that refusing would be considered a really big insult. "Yeah, I'll come, Eddy. I'm not much of a soccer fan, though."

Eddy smiled and hit me on the shoulder. "This ain't soccer, Irish boy. This is futbol, man!"

Eduardo got serious. "Now listen, man. Make sure you bring some sort of gift for my mother. Doesn't have to be anything big...just something nice. Don't spend a lot of money."

"A gift? I don't know how to buy gifts."

Eddy frowned. "I'm serious, man. Just a small gift." The frown only lasted an instant. "Okay, homey. So come Saturday, after the game...around two o'clock. Game starts at three."

I was going to ask more questions about the gift but Eduardo's cell phone rang and soon he was yelling in Portuguese. I sighed, took my cell phone out of my locker and dialed Grandpa Butch.

"Hey Grandpa...how you doing?"

Grandpa Butch grunted which usually meant that he felt pretty good. "Not bad for an old man, Boyo."

"I'm going to this soccer party at Eduardo's house on Sunday and Eddy says I should bring a gift. What should I bring?"

Grandpa chuckled. "They go crazy for soccer. Don't understand it...lucky if there's two goals in a game."

"Yeah, but what about the gift, Grandpa?"

"Well, I used to work with Brazilians in the union. Helluva good workers, I'll tell you that. Anyway, they loved coffee...not Dunkin Donuts coffee, their own coffee. Why not bring some coffee? Stop and Shop has that international section...it's about three aisles now."

Coffee...that sounded perfect. Even the young guys like Marco, Eddy, and Ricky drank coffee every morning. "Yeah, that's good, Grandpa. I'm gonna grab a can on the way home."

Sal dropped me off at the Stop and Shop just outside Hubbard Square. I entered the store and headed directly for the international aisles. There was a Jewish Kosher section, a Haitian area and even an Irish section. Finally, I found the Brazilian segment which took up almost an entire aisle.

There were quite a few different types of coffee but I chose a bag of Caffe' Ferrero. I had no rational reason for choosing this coffee but the bag looked really cool and it was priced mid way between the highest and lowest brands. My mother always said that you wouldn't go wrong if you chose something priced in the middle.

After I bought the coffee, I walked the half mile or so to Grandpa's house on Lodge Avenue. When I reached the house, I saw Grandpa climbing into his Buick. I looked at my cell phone and saw that it was almost seven o'clock. For Grandpa Butch, it might as well been midnight because he almost never left the house after six o'clock, unless it was bowling night.

"Where you going, Grandpa?" I yelled.

"I got some errands to run," he responded.

Errands? "Hold on," I said.

I jogged over to the car and opened the front door. "What's going on?"

Grandpa sighed. "I ran out of Excedrin Migraine and my head is killing me."

"Come on, Grandpa. I'll go."

Grandpa slowly climbed out of the car and said, "Thanks, Kyle. I'm sorry that you're running around for me. You got enough on your mind."

I drove the Buick to the CVS in Hubbard Square and contemplated telling Grandpa Butch about Coach Pearson's offer. I just couldn't bring myself to do it.

As I pulled into the parking lot, I saw Katie's Ford Taurus parked in the employee section. I almost decided to leave and go back to the Stop and Shop across the street but, for some strange reason, I wanted to see Katie. Glutton for punishment, I guess.

I didn't see Katie when I first entered the CVS. I wandered around a few aisles searching for the aspirin for Grandpa Butch. Finally, I found the correct area, grabbed the Excedrin and headed for the front register. It was slow at the CVS this evening and there was only one cashier standing there, looking professional and neatly attired in her red smock.

When Katie spotted me, I noticed a nervous look on her face. It only lasted a moment but it was there nonetheless. If she didn't still like me, why would she seem a little flustered? Hey, I'm probably wrong but it made me feel better.

"Hey, Katie," I said as I approached the register.

Her face had stiffened into a mask of boredom. "Kyle," she responded.

I placed the Excedrin on the counter. Katie scanned the aspirin and said, "You have a headache or something?"

I shook my head. "Nah...it's for my grandfather."

Now a genuine look of concern appeared. "Is he okay?" Katie asked.

I hadn't planned on telling anyone (even Sal, Paul or Eduardo) about Grandpa's condition but for some reason, I almost told Katie but I decided against it at the last moment.

"He's got a real bad headache and he swears by these things."

"Nothing serious then?" Katie asked as she accepted the ten dollar bill.

I glanced at the fresh stack of snow shovels arranged near the front door. "No, he's pretty good. He's been getting these headaches all his life."

I looked back at Katie and saw her staring at me with slightly narrowed eyes. She handed me the bag and change and said, "I'm glad it's nothing serious."

"Thanks, Katie. I'll see you at the game tomorrow."

Katie nodded, still with the squinty eyes. "Okay, Kyle."

I went to bed early because our game on Saturday was being played at 10:00. Coach B wanted us at the school at 7:45. Sometimes, it was tough being surrounded by former Marines.

We played our most complete game of the season and absolutely hammered Springville High School on Saturday. I barely played in the second half and it was fun standing on the sidelines, rooting on the kids who hadn't played much in the first four games. We were winning 24-0 at halftime and Coach

Brennan lectured us on the importance of supporting the backups when they got in there. I only carried the ball four times but I scored a touchdown on a twenty five yard run so my rushing average was pretty good.

The whole city was starting to rally behind the team. The bleachers were almost completely full and the crowd was crazy. It was a cold day but a bunch of students were running around shirtless, their faces painted Hawk red with numbers painted on their chests. One kid had a big, red number 35 on his chest and back and that made me feel pretty good about me.

Students and adults had begun tailgating before the games. This was an early game so the Hawks Nest was serving muffins, donuts and coffee in the parking lot. All of the older guys in the club cheered Sal and me as we walked to the locker room from the student parking lot. It's a really cool atmosphere. Unfortunately, someone broke into Peter Sousa's car the night before so not everyone felt the same level of school spirit.

After showering, I dialed Ashley's cell phone and was sent to voice mail. Again. I really didn't feel much like a long conversation anyway but I had called her a few times during the week and only spoken to her once. She seemed a little distant since her trip to Crandall last weekend.

I really didn't have time to worry about Ashley. I couldn't stop thinking about Coach Pearson's offer. I hadn't spoken to anyone about the phone call, not even Dad or Grandpa Butch. I just needed some more time to sort out my thoughts.

Grandpa Butch let me take the Buick over to Eduardo's party although I had to make a solemn promise not to consume any alcohol. Sal had offered to drive me but he had a new girlfriend and I didn't want to be the third wheel.

Eduardo lived on Hillside Street, about a mile south of Hubbard Square, in the part of Crandall known locally as Bricktown. Grandpa Butch had told me that the largest masonry yard and gravel pit in New England had once been located near Eduardo's house. The section used to be populated mainly by Irish, Italian, and Greek working families but now Bricktown was inhabited almost solely by Brazilian families.

Hillside Street was jam packed with cars. I had to park a couple of streets away and I wasn't crazy about doing much walking in this neighborhood.

I followed Grandpa's instructions and walked quickly, looking straight ahead. My grip on the bag of coffee was so tight that I became worried that I would bust it open.

As I reached Eduardo's street, I heard a somewhat familiar voice call, "Oi, amigo!"

I turned around and saw Freddie Andrade (the kid from school who almost killed me on my first day) standing in front of a convenience store across the street with a group of five or six guys, all of whom looked as tough as Freddie.

"Hi, Freddie," I said nervously.

"You lost, amigo?" he asked while his friends laughed.

I cleared my throat. "Nah. I'm going to a party over Eduardo's."

"Sao Paolo and Corinthians?"

I nodded so fast that I almost pinched a nerve in my neck.

"Alright, man. I might see you over there later," Freddie said.

"Cool," I said. I looked down at my hands and they were shaking and soaking wet. I tried to dry them off on my jacket so the coffee bag wouldn't be damp.

I reached Eduardo's house, a blue vinyl sided three family with new front porches and windows. A huge white banner with black and red stripes hung over each of the three porches. The second floor porch was already full of people, none of whom were speaking English.

I rang the doorbell but there was so much noise that no one answered. I gently pushed open the front door and climbed the stairs to Eduardo's second floor apartment.

As I reached the top of the stairs, I spied Sal and his girlfriend, Angela. Sal's face was stuffed with food.

"What are you eating?" I asked, looking at his plateful of what looked like rice, black beans, bacon, and boiled eggs.

"I don't what they call this, man, but it's good." He pointed to a long table the length of the small dining room. The table was absolutely full of food.

I heard a loud voice bellow over the crowd. "Irish boy is here!" It was Eduardo, wearing what I assumed was the Sao Paolo soccer jersey. "Come on, amigo. You have to meet my mother." He lowered his voice. "Did you bring a gift?" I nodded and showed him the bag of coffee. Eduardo smiled widely and said, "*Perfeito!*"

There was a group of women in the large kitchen, all of whom seemed incredibly busy cooking, washing dishes and placing immense amounts of food on plates. Everyone also seemed to be talking. One woman appeared to be in charge, though. She stood over by the kitchen sink, wearing the women's version of the white Sao Paolo soccer shirt, her frosted hair pulled back tightly.

"Mama, this is Kyle. *Menino* Irish," Eduardo said.

Eduardo's mom quickly wiped her hands with a dish towel.

She hugged me and kissed me on the cheek.

"Handsome boy!" She shouted to the other women in the kitchen. "*Olha como o* Brad Pitt! You call me Maria."

"Hey, my mama thinks you look like Brad Pitt, homey," Eduardo said. "I always thought you were ugly, man." At least two women in the universe thought I looked like Brad Pitt. Not bad.

I gave Maria the coffee and said, "This is for you."

She hugged me again. "Ah, Caffe Ferrero! What a nice *menino.*" All of a sudden, she looked at me very seriously. "Did you eat yet?"

"Ah, no. I just got here."

"Eduardo, you take Kyle and feed him. Pressa!"

Eddy took me over to the long table. "Okay, Irish boy. You start with this...*feijoada*. You gotta eat this." He continued to survey the table. "Yeah, and you want some barbeque. *Churrascaria*. Better than the Salisbury steak you always buy at lunch." Eddy piled so much food on my plate that it actually began to get heavy.

There were two television sets ready for the game. I noticed that some elderly relative or friends of Eduardo had already secured the best seats on the two couches near the TVs. And they weren't budging.

Once the game started, all other activities ceased. Some women continued to clean up and cook, although I couldn't imagine anyone being hungry. I kind of hung with Sal and Angela, eating until I felt like unbuttoning the top button of my jeans.

Sal actually liked soccer and he constantly reminded anyone that understood English of the superiority of Italian futbol.

There was a lot of good natured kidding and I was quickly impressed how passionate everyone was about the sport. It was like a whole nation rooting for one team the way that Boston rooted for the Red Sox.

I never had much interest in soccer so I stayed in the back and let the real fans get a good view of the televisions.

I felt a tap on my shoulder. I turned and Eduardo's mother said, "Come. Follow me." This was an order so I followed Maria into the kitchen.

"Okay, we make some *quadrados de leite*, you call them milk squares." She motioned for me to roll up my sleeves. "Okay, let's go."

We poured about three cups of sugar into a quart of milk and Maria instructed me to stir the pan constantly. Eventually, we poured the finished product into a cookie sheet.

"We let cool for a while," Maria said. "Eduardo, he likes you a lot. I agree, you're a *menino agradável,* a nice boy. You Catholic?" I nodded. "You go to church?" I nodded affirmatively again.

She sat down at the kitchen table and motioned for me to do the same. "Eduardo, he needs to go to college, right?"

I nodded.

"You help him?" she asked.

I wasn't really sure how to answer the question so I said, "Ah, yeah. I'm not sure I know what you mean."

Maria laughed softly. "He looks up to you...you are, how do you say it...a role model. That's it, a role model. No drugs?" I shook my head. "Grades are good?" I nodded. She folded her arms and a look of resignation came over her face. "Many boys around here, they get screwed up, *parafusado acima.* Gangs, drugs, stupid stuff. Eduardo, he play football...American football. He's good?"

I nodded enthusiastically. "Very good. One of the best I've seen."

Maria smiled. "*Ajudar-lhe por favor*. Please help him. *Dar um jeito.*"

I still wasn't quite sure how I could help Eduardo go to college but I think I knew what Maria was talking about. She was asking me to look out for her 260 pound son who terrorized defensive linemen on a weekly basis. Kind of strange but I think I understood.

Maria clapped her hands together. "Okay, now we cut the milk squares."

I left the party around nine o'clock, having consumed more food than any human ever should. I kept my word to Grandpa Butch about the booze, even though there were some interesting looking bowls of punch on the table after coffee and dessert.

Eduardo walked me over to Grandpa's Buick. "Don't want you to be scared, little white boy."

When we reached the car, I said, "Hey, thanks, Eduardo. The party was awesome, you family's great and the food...forget about it."

Eduardo laughed. "And Sao Paulo won."

We shook hands and I watched Eduardo walk to Hillside Street, still wearing his soccer jersey, baggy jeans and massive gold chain. I took a look around the neighborhood before climbing into the Buick. It didn't seem so scary this time.

Chapter Sixteen

I rolled over and checked the alarm clock. Three thirty. I've slept about fifteen minutes. I rose, walked over to my desk, and turned on the light. I ripped out a sheet of paper from a notebook. I was never much of a list maker, but I needed to resolve this thing in my mind.

I made a pro and con column under the title 'Going back to Fairview', drew a line down the middle and started writing.

If I went back to Fairview, I could honestly see myself eventually playing football for Harvard or some other Ivy League school. Coach Pearson had a ton of contacts and each year a couple of his players ended up at Harvard or Yale or Princeton. It could be me next year. Of course, I'd have to finish up my Junior year strong and have a great Senior year and not get injured. All big ifs but why not?

If I stayed at Crandall...I'm not sure Harvard even knew Crandall High School existed even though it was located about fifteen minutes from the Harvard campus in Cambridge. I wasn't good enough to play for Boston College or another division I college so I had to set my sights realistically on a division 1A or II school with a top flight academic reputation. Could Crandall High help get me into one of those schools?

If I went back to Fairview, I'd have to live there and that might be tough. There were only a few kids on athletic scholarship at the school, mainly African American basketball players. No one ever said much about those guys but I don't ever recall them being invited to any parties at the Sternberg mansion. All those weird feelings about my family's financial situation would probably get worse.

What about Grandpa Butch? He acted like the cancer was no worse than poison ivy, but I've seen him when he returned from his radiation treatments. Even he couldn't fake feeling good. And I couldn't stop thinking about what Eduardo's mother had said.

I sighed and tossed my list into the wastebasket. I needed help with this decision. Who could help me? I guess I'd start with an elderly former Marine who ate too much frozen food.

As usual, Grandpa was up at the crack of dawn. I had never gone back to sleep and I wandered down to the kitchen at around 5:45. I think I startled Grandpa who wasn't used to company that early in the morning. He sat at the table, drinking his coffee and eating his English muffin. As always, he was studying the box scores in the sports page.

"Jesus, Mary and Joseph, you surprised me, Boyo," he said, rising from the table. "Let me fix you some breakfast."

"No, no, Grandpa...sit down. I have to talk to you about something," I said.

A quizzical look appeared on Grandpa Butch's face as he slowly sat down.

"Okay, what's going on?" he asked.

I took a deep breath and said, "Coach Pearson from Fairview called me the other day and..." I had trouble finishing the sentence.

"And?" Grandpa asked.

"Well, he says I can go back to Fairview. There's this scholarship and Coach says it's mine if I want it."

Grandpa leaned back in his chair and I noticed a slight grimace on his face. "What do you want to do?"

I discussed my list with Grandpa and he listened quietly. After a few moments, he said, "It sounds like there's no choice, Kyle. If you think about your future, you gotta go back to Fairview. Imagine playing ball at Harvard or Yale or somewhere like that." He shook his head and laughed. "Your great grandmother would get the biggest kick out of that. My mother, she came over from Ireland, County Cork, when she was nineteen. She got a job working in the student dining room at Harvard." He laughed again. "Worked there off and on for forty years. She used to make sure John F. Kennedy got his rice pudding. Every day at 4:30, she would get up and take the bus down to Harvard Square. Kept the family above water all through the Depression. I was the oldest so I'd get the rest of the kids up and off to school."

I never even knew that Dad had any aunts or uncles. "What about your father?"

Grandpa shrugged. "Took off when I was nine. He was from Cork, too...all I really remember was him sleeping on the couch in the parlor. Left when I was nine and I never saw him again." He sighed deeply." Enough about the Donovan family history. The point is you can't pass up an opportunity like this. You go back to Fairview and the world's your oyster. You stay here and...who knows? Not many future Ivy Leaguers would be graduating with you, Boyo. You know that, right?"

I nodded.

"That's not putting anyone down or anything. Hell, I've lived here my whole life...wouldn't live anywhere else. But you, Kyle...you got it, you know what I mean?"

I nodded again, although I wasn't quite sure what Grandpa meant.

"Listen, Boyo. This is about your future. Okay?"

"Yeah, what about Coach B and Eduardo and Sal and the rest of the guys? And...what about...you?"

Grandpa waved his hand. "Me? Come on, Kyle. Bingo will take me to radiation...heck, I'm almost done. Dr. Patel said I'm doing great. Don't worry about me. As for your teammates, they'll understand. Believe me, they'll understand. And so will Coach Bonfiglio."

I looked at the wall cabinet above the sink and noticed the small "T.W.D" and "F.X.D" initials carved on the inside of the open cabinet door. "This isn't easy, Grandpa," I said. "I don't know...I'm starting to feel like I belong here, you know? And the team...we could really go places this year." I glanced again at the initials on the cabinet door. "I don't want to leave you, Grandpa. This is home now."

We sat in silence, each avoiding eye contact and Grandpa pretending to read the newspaper. Finally, Grandpa Butch broke the quiet. "Going back to Fairview is best for you, Kyle. I don't want you to leave...I feel like God's given me this second chance to make things right. I'll miss you, Boyo, but I'll be there at the games and you can come down and stay over on weekends after the season's over...if you want. But it's your decision, son. Just think what's right for you...don't think about anyone else. Okay?"

Grandpa brought his dishes over to the sink and said, "And

now, I have to relieve Bingo, Jimmy Devlin and Ralphie Greco of their social security checks." He checked his watch. "We play poker at the Legion at 7:00. Imagine that...card playing at seven in the morning. We must be old, huh?"

Grandpa shuffled out of the room at a slower pace than I had remembered. I poured some Apple Jacks and stared absently at the sports page on the table in front of me.

Sal gave me a ride to school this morning and I wanted to tell him all about Fairview and Coach Pearson's phone call but it just wasn't the right time.

I had a free third period and I decided to venture down to Coach Bonfiglio's office. The light was on in the office and I heard Coach B talking on the phone to another athletic director. I waited until he was done with the call and then knocked softly on the door.

"Come in," Coach B. barked. He sounded angry but I knew that this was just his regular speaking voice.

"Hey Coach," I said as I walked into the small office.

Coach B. turned around in his office chair and took off his glasses. "Hey Kyle...what's going on?"

I cleared my throat. "Can I talk to you for a couple of minutes, Coach?"

"Yeah, sure. Here, sit down." Coach stood and removed some Crandall High track sweatshirts from the metal folding chair beside his desk. "There you go."

Coach sat down and said, "Okay, fire away, Kyle."

I glanced around the office at the various pictures of the Crandall High football team from years past. There was a signed football from Bill Parcells and, hanging on the wall above his desk, a big glass picture with a Crandall High football shirt inside reading, "Coach B. No. 1." It was a gift from the class of 1991.

"Well, Coach, I got a call from Coach Pearson from Fairview. And he...and he..." This was tough...I didn't think it would be this tough but I really didn't want to disappoint Coach B.

I was struggling for words when Coach said gently, "And what did he say, Kyle?"

"He wants me to come back to Fairview, Coach. I guess there's this scholarship that will pay all my tuition and room and board." I looked again at the football shirt above Coach's desk. "I don't know...I'm just real confused."

"Did you talk to your Dad or Mom?"

I shook my head.

"Have you talked to anyone else yet?" Coach asked.

I nodded. "Yeah, I talked to my grandfather this morning."

"What did Butchie have to say?"

"He told me to go back to Fairview." I pulled out my list of pros and cons and handed it to Coach B. "I made up this list. My grandfather wants me to do what's best for me. I don't know, if I go back to Fairview, I could end up at Harvard or another Ivy League school. If I stay here..."

Coach B. smiled. "If you stay here, you probably won't go to Harvard, right?"

I nodded.

"You may be right, Kyle. Let's face it, not many kids from Crandall go on to the Ivy League. Some do but the vast majority don't." Coach B. studied my list. "This list took a lot of thought. You're a mature kid, Kyle. And a talented, polite, intelligent, hard working kid. You're gonna do well no matter where you go to school. Your grandfather's right. You have to do what's best for you. Do I want you to stay? Hell, yes. You've made a huge difference for us this year. We wouldn't be undefeated without you. Coach Brennan and I really appreciate the way you stepped aside for Marco. Like I said, you're a team player, Kyle. You know, you might end up being a Division I player next year...and you'd be our featured back. So, yes, I want you to stay. But is that what's best for you? I don't know, only you can answer that. There's some real good arguments for going back to Fairview, no question about it. Al Pearson is a great coach and a better guy. I think what you have to consider is where you're happiest. This has been a different world for you, I know that. The bottom line is: go where you'll be most happy. I wouldn't worry too much about the college thing because I think you'll be okay no matter where you graduate from. So I say concentrate on what makes you happy, you know what I mean?"

This was the longest conversation I'd ever had with Coach Bonfiglio. And he made a lot of sense. I had been thinking of nothing but the future. Maybe I should consider the present a little.

I rose from the chair and said, "Thanks Coach."

Coach B. shook my hand and held for a moment. "Everything will be alright no matter what, Kyle? You know what I mean? It's a big decision but you've got two good options here."

I left the office more confused than ever. Maybe that's the way it should be.

All through the school day, I replayed Grandpa and Coach's words in my mind. I don't think I listened to a word spoken by any teacher in any class. I even skipped lunch and went to the library and just chilled out in one of the cubicles.

I kind of went through the motions at practice after school. At one point, Marco whacked me on the helmet and said, "Wake up, dreamer do dia!"

Coach B. must have told Coach Brennan about my dilemma because even he didn't hassle me during practice. I just couldn't get into any rhythm at all but that better change because we played St. Patrick's on Saturday and I'm pretty sure those guys weren't all that concerned about my life choices.

I took the bus home after practice but got off before Hubbard Square so I could walk around a little before I got home. It added another half mile onto my journey but the cool, fresh air felt good.

I stopped in at Licata's House of Pizza, bought an eggplant sub, sat down and did some more thinking. If I returned to Fairview, there was no way I'd ever eat an eggplant this good again. Then again, I'm not sure eggplant subs were sold anywhere within the Fairview town borders.

I was going to talk to Eduardo and Sal today but I just couldn't take that step. Grandpa Butch and Coach B. were right. This was a decision I alone had to make.

I finished the sub, waved goodbye to Mrs. Licata and walked up Main Street into Hubbard Square. I passed the CVS and saw Katie's Ford sitting in the parking lot. I thought about stopping in and buying a candy bar or something but I just kept walking.

As I turned onto Lodge Avenue, I heard my cell phone ring. It was Ashley. I hadn't spoken to her all week, although I had tried to call her a couple of times.

"Hey, what's going on?" I asked.

"Long time, no talk," she answered.

"I called you a couple of times," I said.

Ashley sighed. "I know, I know. I've just been so busy all week. We're doing this big service project at school. Kids from my dad's clinic came to visit the school today so it's been crazy all week setting up and everything. I'm sorry I didn't call earlier."

"That's okay. What are you doing this weekend?"

"That's one of the reasons I'm calling. I'm having a party on Saturday night. My parents are in Europe for two weeks, so we should party a little, don't you think?"

I guess so. I know that if I threw a party while Grandpa wasn't home, he'd probably remove my eyeballs. I don't care how old he is...I'm still kind of scared of him. "Yeah, that sounds good. What time?"

"Around eight. I'm trying to keep it pretty small...you know, just the regular crew if possible."

"Hey, is it okay if I bring a couple of the guys from Crandall? You know, Eduardo, Sal, Raymond...the guys you met at Palermo's." I'm not sure why I asked this question. I hadn't planned on it. It just happened. Part of me kind of wanted to test Ashley.

There was silence for a moment or two. "Yeah, that's okay, I guess. You can't bring too many, though."

"No, no. Just me and those three, that's all. I'm not even sure if they'll want to go." In my heart, I knew they'd want to come, though.

"Well, okay. I'll trust your judgment on them. I don't know them too well."

"They don't have to come, Ash. I just thought it would be

cool. Paul knows them...they're always texting each other. But if you're nervous, they don't have to come."

More silence. And then Ashley said, "Okay. I hope nothing happens, though."

I was getting a little irritated. "Like I said, they don't have to come. It's no big deal."

"No, I want them to come. So, eight o'clock, okay?"

"Yeah, sounds good. See you then."

I started up Grandpa Butch's brick stairs and then stopped on the landing and stared at the phone. Nothing about that conversation felt right.

Chapter Seventeen

Seven wins, no losses. First place in the Metro Conference, which means an automatic berth to the state championship tournament. There were six Division One conferences in Massachusetts including the big public schools (like Crandall), the major Catholic schools and the largest private school conference. Fairview was also undefeated setting the stage for a possible Crandall-Fairview playoff game. No matter which side I'm playing for, that would be unbelievable.

At this point, I guess I'm leaning on returning to Fairview. As much as I liked my teammates and Coach Bonfiglio, I think I had my best shot getting a scholarship if I went back there. The funny thing is that I feel as comfortable in Crandall now as I did in Fairview.

Grandpa Butch and Coach B. both said that I should do what's best for me. But that's pretty hard to figure out. Yeah, I probably could go to a better school if I went back to Fairview but should that be the only reason? What about Grandpa Butch? What about all those guys in Crandall depending on me? What about what Eduardo's mother said? It's not easy being me.

I prayed like crazy after Mass on Sunday and I felt a little better. But part of me thinks Jesus would want me to stay in Crandall.

I've decided not to discuss this with my father until after I've made my decision. I know that he would encourage me to return to Fairview and would basically hound me until I actually went back. So I'm not crazy about getting his input at this moment. Plus, he had too much going on without worrying about more of my problems.

I sat in front of my locker in full uniform (except for my helmet) for a few minutes after our game against St. Patrick's. We beat them, 14-10, and if we had played another five minutes, St. Pat's probably would have beaten us.

I felt like every muscle in my body ached. I think even my ears hurt. Marco strained a calf muscle in the third quarter so I ended up carrying the ball more than I had all season. After the game, Coach Brennan told me that I had gained eighty nine yards on twenty one carries. Not one yard was gained easily. I tried to lift myself off the bench and take off my game shirt and shoulder pads but that took too much effort. Deron Lawrence, the other starting offensive tackle, helped me out.

I stayed in the shower for a good twenty minutes. The steaming hot water helped me feel almost human again. As I toweled off and changed, Eduardo came by my locker.

"What's the matter, Irish boy? Not used to carrying the rock, anymore, huh?" he said.

"I don't know, man. It's like a truck ran over me."

Eduardo laughed. "Yo, you gotta feel better, homey. We got a big party tonight!"

I looked up and Eduardo and he stood there, grinning like a little kid. I smiled and said, "I'll be ready, amigo."

"Hey, you tell them to hide the silverware, Irish boy?"

"Nah, just take whatever you want," I said. I hoped Eduardo knew I was joking.

I rode home with Grandpa Butch. I was too tired to talk about the game or anything else for that matter. The cool thing is that Grandpa always seemed to understand when I just wanted to be quiet.

Grandpa pulled the Buick in front of the house. I noticed that he winced slightly as he opened the car door. He'd been doing that pretty consistently since he started his treatments.

"You okay, Grandpa?" I asked.

Grandpa Butch waved me off. "Yeah, I'm fine. Just getting old, that's all."

After he closed the door, he stopped and leaned on the car for a moment. "Goddamn stomach. Dr. Patel says it's normal but I gotta keep running to the head."

I put my arm under his elbow and helped Grandpa up the stairs. When we reached the top step, he looked at me in sort of a different way. He patted me on the face and made his way as quickly as he could to the bathroom.

"Boyo, can you get me that Pepto Bismol in the fridge?" he asked.

I searched the fridge but there was no sign of the Pepto Bismol. "Can't find it, Grandpa."

"Forget about it, Kyle. I'm alright," he called as the toilet flushed.

I knew he'd say that. But if he asked me to find the Pepto Bismol, there's no doubt Grandpa needed it.

I threw on my jacket and grabbed the keys to the Buick. "I'll be right back," I said as I opened the front door.

"Hey, don't be crazy. I'm fine," Grandpa said without conviction.

"You want anything else at the store?" I asked.

Grandpa shrugged and said, "I'll take some Pringles if they got 'em."

I pulled into the CVS parking lot and there was Katie's car. I parked a couple of spaces away and peeked in the Taurus as I walked towards the store. It was immaculate inside...only a couple of CDs and an empty Dunkin Donuts' coffee cup cluttered the interior.

I entered CVS and glanced towards the front but there was no sign of Katie. I found the Pringles in the food aisle and headed down back for the Pepto Bismol.

I saw Katie stocking shelves in the aspirin aisle. She looked as hot as usual, even with the red smock. I walked down the aisle pretending to look for the Pepto Bismol and then said, "Hey, Katie."

She looked up and a brief, fleeting smile appeared on her face. It disappeared quickly but it was there, I swear to God. "Hi Kyle...good game today."

"Thanks. We were lucky, huh?"

This time Katie smiled a bit longer and that lump returned to my throat. "There has to be games like that. That's how you find out if you got what it takes to win it all, you know what I mean?"

I chuckled. "You sound like John Madden."

Katie laughed. "I've been watching a lot of football the last couple of years."

She dropped a box of Tylenol. I hurried to pick it up. "Please note that gentlemanly move," I said.

Katie accepted the box and carefully placed it on the shelf. "I have to admit that you are kind of a gentleman."

"You working a lot of hours here?" I asked.

Katie nodded and sighed. "Yeah. My mom hurt her back last week and she's been out of work. The dentist is still paying her but who knows how long he will? We're still going to have to pay the rent and buy the groceries."

"I'm sorry about your mother," I said.

"She'll get better. It's happened before," Katie said as she moved down the aisle. "Hey, what are you here for anyway?"

I scanned the aisle and said, "Actually, I'm looking for some Pepto Bismol."

Katie narrowed her blue eyes the way she did when she was suspicious. "A few days ago it was Excedrin Migraine and now it's Pepto Bismol? What's happening to you?"

"Nah, not for me. It's for my grandfather."

Katie's face became concerned. "Is everything okay? Don't lie to me."

Now I wanted to tell Katie everything. About Grandpa Butch's cancer, about Coach Pearson and the scholarship offer, about what a jerk I've been. "Do you have a couple of minutes?"

Katie checked the big clock above the pharmacy desk. "I can take an early supper. Give me two minutes, okay?"

I bought the Pepto Bismol and checked the time on my cell phone. It was five thirty. I was supposed to pick up Eduardo and Raymond at six thirty. Sal and his girlfriend would follow us in Sal's car. I really didn't want to go to this party.

Katie emerged from behind the customer service area wearing a red Crandall High School pullover fleece jacket.

"Hey, that matches your smock," I said in what I thought was a pretty effective stab at humor.

Katie actually laughed that sincere laugh. "Company policy. You can only wear red here."

We left the store and the air was becoming noticeably cooler. "You mind if I bring this back to my grandfather?"

"No, not at all," Katie said.

I unlocked the passenger door for Katie and held the door. She looked up and smiled as she climbed onto the seat. She reached across the front seat and unlocked the driver door and I was reminded of that scene in "The Bronx Tale". In the movie, the mobster told a teenager that you could always identify a great girl if she reached across the front seat and unlocked the driver door for you. Katie passed that test. Now I didn't want to go to the party at all.

I ran inside and gave Grandpa Butch his Pepto Bismol and Pringles. "Can I use the car for a few minutes?" I asked.

"Yeah, sure. You going to the party this early?"

"Nah, Katie's in the car and we're just gonna talk a little."

Grandpa raised his eyebrows and said, "Katie, huh?" He smiled. "That's good, that's really good."

I drove back to the CVS parking lot. I turned off the ignition, opened a bag of Doritos, and offered it to Katie.

"So what's going on?" she asked.

I took a deep breath and said, "A lot of crap, Katie. My grandfather's got colorectal cancer. It's at stage one, thank God, so they're treating it with radiation but I know it's still tough on him, you know?"

"I'm so sorry, Kyle. He's such a great guy."

I laughed softly. "Yeah, he is. I just wish I could do more for him. But he doesn't want any help. He always says he feels fine."

"Maybe you just being around helps," she said.

I shrugged my shoulders. "Yeah, maybe, I guess. There's

more." I took another deep breath. "The coach of Fairview called me last week. I qualified for this scholarship...I can go back to Fairview and not pay any tuition. And the scholarship would be renewable for next year. I'd have to live there, though."

We sat in silence for a couple of moments. Then Katie said, "Wow. What are you going to do?"

I closed my eyes. "I don't know, Katie. I really don't know. I don't want to leave Grandpa Butch, I don't want to abandon the team, you know? I'm finally starting to get a little comfortable here. But if I go back, maybe I could end up playing football at Harvard. I'm just not sure I'll get the same opportunities here."

Katie stared at me with those blue eyes. "Have you talked to anyone else?"

I nodded. "Grandpa Butch and Coach Bonfiglio."

"What did they say?"

"They both said I should do what's best for myself, you know, what's best for my future."

"Are you sure going to Fairview is best for you?"

I sighed again. "I don't know, I really don't know. So much has happened. I don't mean to whine, I know things are a lot worse for a lot of people but...there's just been a lot of crap. Now maybe I have a chance to get back what I had."

We sat in silence and I thought about that last sentence. Did I really want what I used to have? I guess Katie was reading my mind because she said, "What did you have, Kyle? I guess you had plenty of material stuff. I bet you had a nice house and everyone drove nice cars. But are you the same person now? Maybe what's been best for you is getting to know your grandfather and Eduardo and Sal and all the rest of those guys. Maybe, just maybe, that's been best for you. You lose all that if you go back to Fairview. And, believe me, if you have a 3.8 and you're a football star at Crandall High, you'll get noticed...even by Harvard." Katie stopped abruptly. "I'm sorry, Kyle. This is your decision, not mine."

I took her hand and pulled her softly towards me and kissed her. Katie didn't flinch or jerk her head away.

"Have you discussed this with your girl in Fairview?" she asked.

Ashley. I shook my head. "You know I wasn't lying when I said that it was complicated. And now it's more complicated than ever."

"I have to get back to work, Kyle," Katie said. She flipped down the mirror and took some lipstick out of her pocketbook. She opened the car door and said, "It's a big decision, Kyle. Either way, I'm sure you'll be fine. But don't just think about where you're going to college. I think there's a lot more to it than that."

"Can I call you tomorrow?" I asked.

Katie stepped out of the Buick and ducked her head in the door. "My phone should be on." She closed the door and walked back to CVS.

I sat in the car and thought about what Katie had said. I'm not the same person I was two months ago. Did I really want what I had? I used to have a mother and a father and a house. I really didn't have that at all anymore and I don't think that was coming back...ever.

I started up the Buick and the clock on the stereo read six thirty. Damn, I thought to myself. I really didn't want to go to this party. But, then again, maybe it would help answer some questions for me. Maybe.

Chapter Eighteen

It was seven fifteen by the time I picked up Eduardo and he wasn't happy.

"Damn, Irish, why you so late?" he asked as he entered the Buick.

I shrugged. "I don't know. Lot of stuff going on." I hesitated and then said, "I talked to Katie for a while."

Eddy's anger disappeared. "That's what I'm talking about. Yo, she's the girl for you, amigo. I mean I'm not talking bad about Ashley or anything but...you and Katie, that works, amigo."

"I don't know, we'll see. Technically, I'm still going out with Ashley so it's complicated, you know."

Eduardo scoffed. "Your things are always complicated. Man, life ain't that complicated if you ask me."

I looked at Eduardo's yellow and green track jacket and huge gold chain and said, "I don't know...your outfit is pretty complicated if you ask me."

He looked down at his jacket. "You kidding? I'm the one who's stylin' here. What do you have on? More Abercrombie? Or is it American Eagle? Come on, menino."

We picked up Raymond, who lived on the outskirts of Bricktown. Raymond was Haitian and as he left the house, his mother was screaming at him in Creole (I think) from the second floor porch. At six two, 230 pounds with a mean streak on the field that would make Ray Lewis proud, Raymond was a scary dude. Off the field, though, he was quiet, polite and almost gentle. And here was his mother, who was barely five foot tall, absolutely terrifying not only Raymond but Eduardo and me. "Okay, maman, okay," Raymond said at least twenty times.

Eduardo leaned out the passenger window and called, "Bonswa, Mrs. Boursiquot." She briefly smiled and waved and then returned to her lecture directed at Raymond.

"Man, those Haitians are strict," Eduardo said. "The Irish like that?"

"Not really...actually, I don't know. I didn't even really know I was Irish until I started living with Grandpa Butch."

Raymond finally made it to the car with a sheepish smile on his face. "What's up, boys?" he said.

Eduardo turned around and said, "Amigo, I am very scared of your mother."

Raymond laughed. "You're not alone, brother. You're not alone."

By the time we made it over to Sal's and hit the road, it was 7:45.

I pulled the car onto Route 93 north. Grandpa had done the brakes a couple of days ago and the Buick really drove nicely.

"Hey, I'm not sure I've ever been to Fairview," Raymond said.

"Well, let's just say that there's not a 'sizeable' Haitian population in that town, unless you start counting maids and house cleaners. Am I correct, Irish boy?" Eduardo asked.

I nodded. "That would be correct."

Eduardo sniffed the air. "Damn, Raymond, your cologne smells like a dead animal."

Raymond immediately became defensive. "You better be joking, man. This is Armani. I smell good. Those Fairview girls be climbing all over me."

There was silence in the Buick for a couple of minutes as we exited Route 93 and drove onto Route 128 south. I sensed that both guys, especially Eduardo were a little nervous because they were way quieter than usual.

"Hey, you guys been talking to Paul a lot lately, huh?" I asked.

"Yeah, yeah. He's a good dude, man," Eduardo said. "Said he was going to bring a bottle of cachaca." He glanced over at me. "It's okay if I have a glass of cachaca, Uncle Kyle?"

"Hey, I'm the one driving. Do what you want," I said. But I really didn't mean it. A drunk Eduardo and a drunk Jon Davis could cause World War III.

"What's cachaca?" Raymond asked.

Eduardo whistled softly. "Pure sugar cane, my Haitian brother. Pure sugar cane. You gotta try some."

We crossed the Springville/Fairview town line and almost immediately everything seemed more white. I never noticed this when I lived up here but now the contrast just slapped you in the face.

"Nice town," Raymond said, almost in a whisper.

Eduardo chuckled. "Come on, not much different than Bricktown."

I started feeling a strange sense of dread as we pulled off Washington Street and drove onto Crossbridge Lane. Ashley lived on Ginger Drive, the last street off Crossbridge. I checked the rearview mirror to make sure that Sal was still driving behind us.

As we drove up to the Novack residence, I noticed about ten or fifteen cars parked on the street. This could turn out to be a big party. I was happy when I saw Paul's BMW sitting in the driveway.

"Honey, I'm home," Eduardo said as he opened the passenger door.

"Is her father Bill Gates or something?" Raymond asked while viewing Ashley's mansion.

"Nah, he's a heart surgeon. He also invented some kind of mechanical thing for pacemakers. He's rich but he's a pretty good guy. Kind of a scary guy, though," I answered.

"He's not home, is he?" Eduardo asked.

I shook my head. "Everyone's around back. Let's go."

I heard the music blasting, the typical punk pop favored by the Fairview crew. "Those tunes are awful, amigo," Eduardo said.

"Don't say nothing about it, Eddy," Sal said.

Eduardo raised his brow and made a face. "Não se preocupar, camarada...I won't cause no trouble."

There were about twenty kids hanging around out back. Ashley had set up chairs on the patio and around the pond. Everything seemed pretty mellow. There were two coolers of beer and another cooler full of soda. Ashley had ordered a bunch of pizzas from Dominoes.

Paul saw us first and immediately offered a loud greeting. "Hey, the Crandall boys are here. How you guys doing?" he said, vigorously sharing handshakes and hugs with Eduardo, Sal and Raymond. "I didn't forget you, Eddy. Look at this."

Paul retrieved a bottle from under the porch and gave it to Eduardo. "There it is, buddy. Genuine cachaca. Beleza super premium."

"Ooh, this is nice. Thanks, amigo," Eduardo said.

"You guys want some pizza, beer, soda? Everything's over there on the patio," Paul said.

"Don't mind if I do," Sal said. He and Angela walked over to the patio and Eddy and Raymond followed.

"How you doing, man?" Paul asked.

"Okay, not bad," I responded.

He moved to closer to me. "Make any decisions yet?"

"What are you talking about?" I asked.

"Come on...Fairview's a small school," Paul whispered. "Almost everyone found out yesterday in the locker room. Todd asked Coach Pearson about it and he verified it, buddy."

"So everyone knows?" I asked.

Paul shrugged. "I would think."

"What about Ashley?" I asked.

"I guess so. I haven't talked to her about it, though. She's been real busy. A bunch of little minority kids from Boston spent a couple of days at the school. It was kind of embarrassing the way they were treated."

"What do you mean?"

"I mean, everyone's being extra nice and tiptoeing around them and all that. It was like these kids were aliens or something. Annoyed the hell out of me. Anyway, you didn't tell Ashley?"

I shook my head. Nope, didn't tell Ashley. And now I'm sure she knew. That will make for a pleasant conversation later.

"You gotta figure that out, man. Either you go out with her or you don't. How long you gonna go like this?"

"I don't know but..."

"There he is...you coming home or what?" It was the extremely loud voice of Jon Davis. He had a bottle of Sam Adams in each hand and balanced a slice of pizza with his right thumb and middle finger. And he was headed in my direction.

I glanced over at the Crandall boys and Angela. They looked to be having a good time on the patio. I hoped they couldn't hear Jon.

"What's up, Jonny?"

Jon put his arm around my shoulder, the way he always did, drunk or sober. He wasn't spitting on me which meant he was still sober.

"You brought the homeys from Crandall, huh?"

"Yeah, you want to meet them?" I asked.

He laughed. "Not particularly. Don't think I'll be seeing them again." Jon dropped his voice. "More importantly, when are you starting school up here again? Monday?"

I laughed a very fake, insincere laugh. "Don't know, yet, Jonny."

"What do you mean? You're coming back, right?"

I cleared my throat and looked around for help. Paul had moved over to the patio and was joking around with the Crandall boys. "Haven't made a final decision. It's a big decision, Jonny, you know what I mean?"

Jon released his grip. "Hey, Todd and Jerry...get over here!"

Todd Gardner and Jeremy Stein were both almost as big as Jon. The left side of the Fairview offensive line surrounded me.

I greeted Todd and Jerry and then Jon said, "Kyle hasn't made up his mind about coming back. You believe that?"

"You kidding me, Kyle?" Todd asked. He had a red crew-cut

and a grungy red goatee that only accentuated his acne. But he was built like Stone Cold Steve Austin so no one ever mentioned his skin condition. "Come on, you gonna stay at Crandall? Crandall?" Todd looked over at Jon and Jerry who were both laughing. "Freaking hole, dude. You'll be lucky if you graduate without getting stabbed or getting an STD from one of those hoes down there." He then high fived his fellow linemen who all found the whole thing hilarious.

"What Todd is saying, Kyle, is that you're one of us, you know? You belong here...not in the ghetto with those punks," Jon said, pointing to the Crandall guys. "Look at them. Give me a freaking break." He put his arm around me again. "You gotta come back home, dude."

I felt trapped and their words really upset me but, for some reason, I didn't defend Crandall and I didn't defend Crandall girls and I didn't defend Eduardo, Sal and Raymond. I just stood there like a coward.

Eduardo must have sensed something was wrong because he came over and stood next to me. Jon released his arm and Todd and Jeremy stepped back.

"What's going on, amigo?" Eduardo asked. This was not the happy go lucky, smiling Eduardo. This was the scowling Bricktown Eduardo.

"Nothing. Hey, Eduardo, meet Jon, Todd and Jerry. They're all offensive lineman just like you."

Eduardo offered his hand but the scowl never left his face and he didn't say a word. The three Fairview guys shook his hand but none had anything to say, either.

As they walked over towards the pond area, Jon said, "Remember what we said, Kyle. You belong here."

"What's he talking about, Irish boy?" Eduardo asked with a puzzled look on his face.

I breathed deeply. "I'll tell you later. Go have a good time."

Just as Eduardo was about to walk away, I noticed Ashley walking towards us.

"Hey, Kyle," she said, kissing my cheek.

"Hey Ash. You remember Eduardo, right?"

"Oh sure...how are you?" Ashley asked.

Eduardo was still in full Bricktown mode and he had already made his decision about Ashley. He simply nodded, looked at me one more time and returned to the patio.

"So, were you ever going to tell me the news?" she asked.

I thought quickly and said, "I told you I tried to call you a couple of times this week."

Of course, Ashley was too smart for this game. "Come on, Kyle. I talked to you yesterday. I talked to you online at least three times this week. Don't treat me like a fool."

"I've just been thinking about it so much. The only people I talked to were my grandfather and my coach." There was no need for Ashley to know about my conversation with Katie earlier in the day.

She punched me gently on the arm. "Come on. I told you I'd be there for you...always."

"Yeah, I know. I'm sorry." Actually, I wasn't sure if I wanted Ashley there for me always and I wasn't even sure if I was really sorry. But apologizing sure made things easier most of the time.

"So when are you coming back?" she asked.

I looked over at Eduardo and Raymond who seemed to be enjoying themselves talking and laughing with a couple of

Fairview senior girls. "Don't know."

"What do you mean, don't know? You don't know when you're coming back or you don't know if you're coming back?"

"Exactly," I said.

Ashley sat on the stone wall. "Wow. You might actually stay at Crandall High? What about your future? What about us?"

I sat down next to Ashley. "There's just a lot to consider, Ash. My grandfather is sick, I like the guys...I don't know. It's just tough."

Ashley had this astonished look on her face. "All I can say is wow. I know it's not easy, Kyle but..."

Suddenly, the Fairview guys were all yelling, "Artie! Artie! Artie!"

I knew right away that Artie Robinson, 'Artie the Party', had shown up. Arthur Randall Robinson IV, the resident drug dealer at Fairview Prep. He was literally a one man pharmacy. Anything you wanted, Artie could hook you up. He was usually stoned but Artie was pretty likable and he had become sort of a folk hero around the school. The fact that he was still enrolled in the school should have been amazing. The fact that the brand new library was donated solely by Artie's grandfather explained Artie's continued presence at Fairview Prep.

"I really didn't want him to come," Ashley said. She looked very worried. "I didn't want any drugs at this party."

"You want me to get rid of him?" I asked.

We watched as Artie was hugged by Jon, Todd and the boys. "No, it might cause a riot," she said. "We'll talk later, okay?"

I watched as Ashley made her way over to the group near the pond. Artie was obviously stoned and within minutes most of those guys would be also. Maybe it was time to leave.

Sal and Angela walked over to the wall and Angela said, "Who's that guy, Kyle?"

"Artie the Party Robinson. Number one drug dealer in Fairview. Probably the only real dealer in the whole town."

Angela laughed. "Doesn't look much like the dealers at Crandall."

Pretty soon, Artie led Jon, Todd, Jerry and a couple of other guys out of the back yard.

"It's cannabis time," Sal said.

"At least they're out of the yard. Ashley's pretty nervous."

Sal laughed. "Come on, Kyle. What are the chances the cops will show up here? Maybe if they knew me, Eddy and Raymond were here, maybe."

Eduardo had switched the CD in the stereo and the rap of Ludacris blasted through the yard. Eddy and Raymond were now dancing with the two senior girls on the patio.

I sat on the stone wall, drank a Pepsi, finished off a couple more slices of pizza and enjoyed the view of Eduardo and Raymond dancing with the two preppie girls. I think the boys actually had a chance. They'd have to find their own way home to Crandall.

I felt a slap on my back and knew it was Paul.

"Having a good time yet?" he asked.

I shrugged and drank the last of my Pepsi. "Those guys are," I said, pointing to Raymond and Eduardo.

Paul chuckled. "Yeah, they are."

All of a sudden, a booming voice shattered the peacefulness of the party. "ASHLEY!!" I recognized the voice. It was Ashley's dad.

Dr. Novack stormed onto the patio and turned off the stereo.

"ASHLEY!"

Artie, Jon and Todd skulked into the back yard. "Stay right there!" Dr. Novack ordered.

He held up the bag of weed and seemed almost too upset to speak. Ashley came out the back door and said, "Dad?"

"What's going on here, Ashley? What's going on here?"

Everyone stood in stunned silence. Even Eduardo took a few steps back from the potentially lethal Dr. Novack.

"Ah, Dad, I thought you were coming home tomorrow night," Ashley stammered.

He held out the large bag of marijuana. "We go away for a couple of days and this...this happens!"

"I don't know where that came from, Dad. I swear!" Ashley said.

"These boys," Dr. Novack said, pointing to Artie, Jon and Todd. "And a few others too, probably, were smoking right on our front lawn, Ashley. Now where did this come from? I want an answer or I'll call the Fairview police right now!"

"Don't blame Ashley, Dr. Novack," Jon Davis said. "Kyle's friends from Crandall showed up with the weed. It's not Ashley's fault. She didn't even invite them. Kyle just brought them on his own." He looked at me and said, "Sorry, man."

Eduardo took a few steps towards Jon. "Yo, that's it, man. I've had it with you."

Raymond stepped in front of Eduardo. "Let it be, man. This is no win, Eddy. We'll get this cracker later," he said softly.

"That's ridiculous. Those guys didn't bring the weed. Ashley knows who brought it. Tell your dad, Ash," Paul said.

Dr. Novack turned and said, "Ashley, who's telling the truth here?"

I saw Ashley take a deep breath. She looked at me, opened her eyes wide and then said, "Jon's right, Dad. I didn't know anything about the drugs. It was just supposed to be a little party with a few Fairview kids. I guess Kyle's friends from Crandall brought the drugs. I didn't know anything about it."

I couldn't believe what I was hearing.

Dr. Novack looked at me and said, "Kyle, take your friends and leave right now or I'll call the police." He waved his hand at Eduardo, Sal and Raymond. "I never want to see these people again." He shook the bag of marijuana. "I'll be flushing this down the toilet."

"This is crap, Dr. Novack. The Crandall guys didn't bring the weed...come on, Ashley, tell your Dad the truth," I said.

Ashley shook her head. "It definitely didn't come from anyone from Fairview. That I know. No one's blaming you, Kyle. It's your friends."

And then Eduardo lost it. He charged at Jon Davis, lowered his shoulder and threw Jon to the ground. Raymond then lunged at Todd and suddenly there was a near riot at the Novack residence.

Paul and I jumped in and dragged Eduardo off Jon. Raymond had Todd's shoulders pinned on the ground but wasn't throwing any punches.

"Let me at that bitch, Kyle...Eu matá-lo-ei, você filho de uma cadela!" Eduardo said as Paul and I pushed him away.

"Kyle, get these boys out of here...NOW!" Dr. Novack commanded.

I knew that Dr. Novack was seconds away from calling the police and then the Crandall boys would have no chance at all. Paul and I pushed Eduardo out of the yard and towards the

Buick. Sal opened up the back door and we managed to squeeze Eduardo onto the seat. He was still screaming in Portuguese.

Raymond took the passenger seat in the front and I turned the ignition quickly. I sped off Ginger Drive, probably for the last time.

We drove in silence for a couple of minutes. As we left Fairview and entered Springville, Raymond looked in my direction and said in a tone of resignation, "You should have never invited us, Kyle."

Chapter Nineteen

I woke up at seven thirty on Sunday morning and felt like I had a massive hangover even though I hadn't drank a drop of alcohol at Ashley's house.

I stumbled out of bed and into the bathroom where I ran some water through my hair and brushed my teeth.

Naturally, Grandpa was already awake and reading the Sunday Tribune in the parlor. "Hey, Grandpa, can I take your car to church?"

"Yeah, sure...hey, how'd it go last night?" he asked.

"You don't want to know. I'll talk to you when I get home." I grabbed the keys from the hallway table and ran out the door. Mass started at 7:30 and I really didn't like being late. It was already going on 7:40 so I'd probably just stand in the back.

Saint Teresa's was about half full when I arrived just in time for the Gospel reading. At least that meant that I officially made Mass. Grandpa Butch had informed me that you have to get to Mass by the Gospel reading or Mass didn't count.

Father McGrath said the Mass. He was a Jesuit who taught Religion over at Archbishop Walsh and helped out at St. Teresa's on the weekends. He wasn't your typical priest. He was obsessed with sports, especially the Patriots, and he had actually run the Boston Marathon a couple of times. I kidded him a lot after we had beaten Walsh earlier in the season and he gave it right back to me.

When Mass ended, I just sat in the pew for a few minutes. A few old timers recited the Rosary loudly while I tried to sort out a few things in my mind.

"I wish the Walsh kids stayed in Church this long after Mass."

I heard Father McGrath's voice and turned to see the priest standing and smiling beside the pew. He was about forty years old but looked a little younger. Father McGrath wore his reddish hair in a short Marine style crew cut and smiled and laughed a lot. He just seemed like a guy who really loved his job.

"Hey, Father," I said.

"Everything okay, Kyle?" Father McGrath asked.

I nodded.

"That wasn't a real convincing nod," Father said as he sat in the pew behind mine.

"I have a tough choice to make...at least it seemed tough until last night," I said.

"Choices are usually tough, Kyle...what makes this one tougher than usual?" Father McGrath asked.

So I told Father McGrath the whole story and he sat there listening, letting me get everything off my chest. I told him about my parents, Grandpa Butch, the scholarship, the party, Ashley...everything I could think of. I talked more about the situation than I had with Grandpa Butch or Katie or anyone.

When I finished my story, we sat quietly for a couple of minutes. I looked at Father McGrath and could see that he was thinking. I breathed deeply out my mouth and said, "I'm sorry, Father. I don't mean to burden you with all this." I took the prayer card out of my pocket. "Another priest said Jesus wanted to take all my burdens."

Father McGrath laughed softly. "He's there for you, Kyle. Always, always there. Talk to Him like he's your friend, like you're sitting around the kitchen table."

I nodded. "I've been trying to do that...I think He's actually listening. Like I said, I shouldn't burden you with this."

Father McGrath smiled and said, "Come on, Kyle, it's my job. By the way you're talking, I'm thinking that you already made your decision."

I shrugged. "Yeah, I guess so."

"Are you happy with your decision?" Father McGrath asked.

I nodded. "In a strange way, yeah, I am kind of happy that all that stuff happened last night. Not happy, really, but relieved. You know what I'm saying?"

"I think I do," Father McGrath said. "Sometimes, certain things have to happen to clarify a situation. Last night, you were kind of caught between your two worlds and those two worlds collided, in a sense. I think it comes down to, which world do you see yourself part of? In which world, are you most comfortable?"

"I thought I was part of both worlds but last night taught me different, I guess," I said.

"It's good when we receive clarity because usually it's pretty elusive. Are you going to be okay with Ashley and the rest of the Fairview crew?"

I grimaced. "No, I don't think that will ever be the same...except for Paul. But that's alright. I have enough on my mind. It's time to focus on reality."

Father McGrath smiled. "Keep praying, Kyle. The Lord can offer you plenty of guidance."

"Yeah, you're right, Father."

Father McGrath rose from the pew and offered his hand. I stood and returned the handshake. "Anytime you want to talk, you let me know, okay?" he said.

I nodded and said, "Thanks for listening, Father. No more Walsh jokes from now on."

He laughed and said, "There's always next year's game, Kyle. Say hi to your grandfather for me."

I blessed myself, genuflected and left the church. I couldn't find a cloud in the sky and the air was cool and crisp. I zipped up my sweat jacket and walked to Grandpa Butch's Buick. I climbed into the car, took out my cell phone and dialed Ashley's number.

The phone rang twice before Ashley picked it up.

"Hi," she said.

I paused for a moment. I had so much to say to her but now the words wouldn't come forth.

"I don't know what to say," Ashley said. "I panicked when my dad came home and then...and then I just went along with Jon. It was stupid and mean and...can you forgive me?"

I took a deep breath and said, "Not right now, Ash. Maybe never. I just can't believe you did that." Ashley responded with silence. "I'll just never know why."

Ashley's voice began to break when she said, "I was just so nervous. You know me well enough to know that it was way out of character."

"Yeah, but why protect Artie Robinson? Who's he to you? He's a drug dealing loser and my friends are really good kids."

"I have to see Artie and Jon and Todd and all those guys everyday. Can't you understand that? You don't live up here anymore...you forget what it's like."

"You have to make things right with your father. You gotta tell him that the Crandall guys had nothing to do with the weed," I said.

Ashley's silence said everything.

"It's over, Ashley," I said with conviction. Again, she said nothing. I heard some sniffling but no tears would change my mind. "You understand, Ash? We're through."

Now the crying became louder. "I'm hanging up, Ash."

Finally, she said, "Kyle?"

"Yeah?" I answered.

"Can we just take a break for a while? Sort everything out and try again?"

I softened my tone. "No, this is best, Ash." And I hung up the phone, breathed in the autumn air and turned the key in Grandpa Butch's Buick. It sounded like a new Lexus.

The rain had started midway through the first quarter and just wouldn't stop. I always kind of liked playing football in the rain, but playing in a monsoon was a different story. Luckily, Clinton High School had installed field turf instead of natural grass, so the footing wasn't completely horrible.

There were about two minutes left in the game and we were losing 10-7. Clinton's field goal kicker, a kid who was born in England with a super human leg, had given Clinton the lead with a thirty yard field goal two minutes before. I didn't think anyone but Adam Vinatieri could kick in weather like this. No wonder the kid would be kicking for Oregon State next fall.

Incredibly, most of the crowd remained despite the ridiculous weather. The Clinton fans sensed a huge upset. Our record was 8-0, and Clinton had already lost four games. To quote a cliché, they were playing for pride. We were playing for the playoffs, and that dream was starting to slip away.

The main problem was holding on to the ball. Marco had fumbled three times in the game, and Clinton had recovered two of them. One of the fumbles set up their only touchdown.

I had only carried the ball eight times and I hadn't fumbled...yet.

Sammy Griffin had somehow returned the kick to the Clinton thirty five yard line. Sal gathered us in the huddle and said, "Okay, boys, what can I say? We have to score...forget the field goal. We have one minute, twenty seven seconds to score or, let's face it, the season's over. Kyle, this is you. Eye right, 32 blast, eye right, 32 blast, on one, on one, ready, BREAK!"

The linemen sprinted to the line and I reminded myself to hang onto the ball. The rain was so heavy I could barely see the line of scrimmage and I strained to hear Sal's cadence.

At the snap of the ball, I collected the handoff cleanly from Sal, and pressed the waterlogged football tight against my stomach. I surged into the line and, surprisingly, found a huge hole. I ran straight ahead for at least ten yards, and then cut to the sideline to get out bounds and stop the clock. Amazingly, I had plenty of open field in front of me. I kept going, gained another ten yards, and then slid out of bounds. It was a twenty three yard gain.

The whole offense was slapping me on the helmet and pads. I struggled to catch my breath and jogged back to the huddle.

"Alright, alright...nice run, Kyle. Way to go, line. Here we go, same thing. You okay, Kyle? Thirty two blast, on one, on one, ready BREAK!"

My turn again. I held the ball tightly but the hole wasn't there this time. I bounced outside, put my head down, and gained four yards. The ball was at the eight yard line with fifty seconds left in the game. Plenty of time for three plays.

On second down, Sal somehow completed a flare pass to Marco who caught the ball behind the line of scrimmage and was able to make it to the two yard line.

We lined up without a huddle and Sal called the play from the line. It was another 32 blast. I took the handoff and ran into an absolute wall of Clinton defenders. I managed to stumble forward for a yard. After the whistle, Sal called our final timeout.

Billy Tropea, the manager, brought bottles of water to the huddle and I could have drunk a gallon more. We were all too exhausted to speak but Eduardo simply looked at me and nodded. If I were Coach B., I'd run behind Eddy.

Sal hustled back to the huddle and said, "Okay, boys, seven seconds left. One play...that's it. We're gonna sneak it. Eddy, you move to right guard...Hector, you play tackle this play. I'm right on your ass, big guy...make the block! On one, on one, ready BREAK!"

This was it. Sal calmly called the signals and the ball was snapped. I saw Eduardo absolutely bury the defensive tackle and Sal, with his left hand on Eddy's back, dove into the line. The referee raised both hands in the air and blew his whistle. The scoreboard was barely visible through the driving rain but I could see that there was no time left on the clock. That was it.

The whole team jumped on Sal in the end zone. I hugged Coach Brennan and I could swear that he was crying but it was probably just the rain.

I grabbed Eduardo and said, "Ir bom, menino gordo!" I think that I said, 'Good going, fatboy!'

Eduardo laughed, grabbed me by the shoulder pads and dragged me to the ground. A bunch of other players then jumped on top of us and Eddy and I lay on the ground beneath the pile, facemask to facemask, grinning like madmen.

"You can't leave, Irish...you can't leave!" Eduardo shouted through the rain and mayhem.

I smiled and said, "I'm staying, Eddy...I'm staying, buddy!"

Some Crandall students had taken off their shirts and were running all over the field, screaming and sliding in the puddles. I took off my helmet and searched the park for Katie.

She was standing with the rest of the cheerleaders, covered with a red Crandall poncho. I jogged over to the track and called, "Katie!"

She turned and smiled and that lump returned to my throat. "I'm staying, Katie. This is where I belong. And I want us to be together!"

Katie said nothing and, despite the fact that I was soaked to the skin, hugged me and held me tight. "I'll wait for you at my car back at school," she said.

I saw a few of the Clinton players walking slowly to their locker room. I ran over and shook hands with each of them. They wished me luck in the playoffs. I remembered that our bus driver, Frank Sullivan ('Sully' to everyone in Crandall) was famous for leaving promptly and wouldn't think twice about leaving any stragglers behind. I sprinted to the bus before Sully pulled away. I think I made it by a couple of seconds.

I was the last player on the bus and everyone yelled and cheered when I entered the bus. Sully looked at me and said, "Nice going, Kyle. That was some Irish pride there, I'll tell you that. Your grandfather's gonna be real proud."

"Thanks, Sully," I said and searched for an open seat. There was only one seat, up in the front directly behind Coach Bonfiglio and Coach Brennan. I removed my shoulder pads and slumped into the seat.

Coach B. turned and said, "That was a helluva effort, Kyle...one helluva effort. I'm proud of you, son."

That meant a lot coming from Coach Bonfiglio. "Thanks, Coach. One more win and we're in, right?"

Coach B. raised his black eyebrows. "You gonna be here for the game?"

I nodded. "Yeah, I'm staying right here, Coach."

Coach Brennan turned around and whacked me on the shoulder. "That's great news, Kyle, great news!"

Coach Bonfiglio looked at Coach Brennan and said, "This improves the game plan for next week, huh?"

Coach Brennan glanced at me and smiled, "It sure does, Coach, it sure does."

After showering and leaving all my equipment outside my locker so it could dry, I hurried outside to meet Katie. As I walked down the ramp to the door, I heard Sal's voice, "Hey Kyle, wait up!"

I turned around and saw Sal, Eduardo, Raymond, Ricky, Marco and Peter Sousa. What the heck was going on?

Sal shook my hand and said, "Great job today, man. Couldn't have won without you. Right, Marco?"

Marco then shook my hand and said, "That's right, amigo. Hey, man, we're glad you're staying. We all know about the scholarship and...and, well, we're glad you're staying, Menino Irish. We're happy you came to our school, amigo."

Eduardo barged forward and said, "Plus, he's so pretty...he looks just like Brad Pitt!"

I was almost speechless but I managed to say, "Thanks, guys. This year, we win it all, right?"

They turned to leave and I grabbed Raymond and said, "Hey, man, I'm real sorry about the other night."

Raymond shrugged and said, "Not your fault, Kyle. If we play Fairview in the playoffs, I'll remember every one of them, though. Every one."

The rain had finally stopped and I saw Katie standing beside her Malibu. I hugged her and she said, "So, it's definite, then? You're passing up a full scholarship to one of the best prep schools in the country to stay here?"

I nodded.

"And you have no other commitments up there in Fairview?"

I nodded again and said, "The only commitments I have are right here in Crandall."

Katie smiled and said, "That's good...because you were running out of time. A girl has to have some pride, right?"

I climbed into the passenger side of the Malibu and Katie started the ignition and we drove out of the parking lot. I glanced over at Katie as she drove and the lump returned to my throat.

CHAPTER TWENTY

I sat on Grandpa Butch's front steps as Paul's BMW pulled up in front of the house. As he climbed out of the car, I noticed a pretty good shiner underneath his left eye.

"Jesus, what happened to you?" I asked, rising from the steps.

Paul smiled and shrugged. "Part of the cost of going to Fairview Prep, I guess," he said.

"No really, what happened?" I said as we shook hands.

Paul leaned against the wrought iron railing and said, "I had a little altercation with Gardner, that steroid freak. He was giving me crap in the locker room about Ashley's party so I tried to tackle him...he got me good when I was charging at him."

"I'm sorry, man," I said.

"I don't even care anymore." Paul stared at the sky. "This is it for me at Fairview, anyway. After the season, I'm leaving. I already talked to my parents. Not that they really care but they pay the tuition, you know what I mean?"

"I just can't believe what happened at Ashley's. I still can't believe it," I said.

"I tried to talk to Ashley a few times about it, but she just ignores me. Davis and Gardner and Stein told everyone I stuck up for the Crandall kids so basically everyone hates me now. Or at least they pretend to hate me. It's over with you and Ash, huh?"

I nodded. "Yeah. It was probably over a while ago, anyway but it's official now. I just can't get it out of my head that she protected that scumbag Artie Robinson over Eddy and the Crandall guys."

Paul chuckled. "Come on, man. It's not that surprising. She's having a party, she probably really didn't want the Crandall guys there at all and now her parents come home early. Davis acts like a turd but gives her a way out. I think it was a pretty easy decision for her. Hey, she's gotta see all those guys every day, you know?"

"Yeah, but so do you."

Paul sighed. "It's different. I just don't really don't care. Ashley does. That's not right or wrong, it's just fact. She's not a bad person, dude."

I wasn't sure of that anymore. "Sometimes, you gotta do the right thing, though."

"She probably wasn't thinking of right and wrong when her dad was screaming. She just wanted to get out of the mess. Like I said, Ash really cares about what people think. Not that unusual."

It was still wrong. And Paul was still right for what he did. There's a big difference.

"So, where you gonna go after the season?" I asked.

Paul smiled. "Hey, Crandall may need a tight end next year, right?"

I laughed. Although Paul was joking, we could really use him next year. Our tight end, Joe DeCaro, was graduating. This was all wishful thinking, of course.

"I don't know, maybe Fairview High. We know a lot of kids over there...the team is horrible but I think I may be done with the whole prep school thing. And my father won't have to pay the twenty five grand. I know that will make him happy." Paul sat down on the limestone step. "You know, I wasn't lying when I said I was a little jealous of you. You know that scene in 'Good Will Hunting' where Robin Williams is the shrink and he tells the MIT professor that anyone of Will's friends would take a baseball bat to help protect Will...you know?"

I nodded although I wasn't really sure where Paul was going with this but I knew from experience to just to go along.

"That's what Eddy and Sal and Ray are like. Those guys always have your back, you know what I'm saying? No matter what. Just can't find that in Fairview. And Butch, too. You know that he would take a baseball bat to anyone who bothered you. I don't know. I just think it's cool." Paul turned away and tapped the railing with his car keys. "I doubt even my parents have my back. I told my mom I got the black eye from falling into a locker and she believed me. Didn't even ask another question. I visit my dad this weekend and he flies to New York for business. So I'm sitting in this condo in Beacon Hill alone for the weekend. I ask to see him, he says yes and then he flies to New York and tells me the fridge is full and to enjoy the plasma TV. So, I say screw it...I'm going to Crandall."

We went into the house and Grandpa Butch cooked some bacon and eggs. I watched Grandpa as he stood over the stove. Dr. Patel said the treatments were working and I could see Grandpa getting stronger by the day. I went with Grandpa to his appointment the other day and Dr. Patel said the old man was the mentally toughest patient he ever had. Eighty four years old, colon cancer and he looks like he still could bang nails all day.

Later, we met Eddy, Sal and Raymond down at Palermo's and the guys treated Paul like a conquering hero. Too bad he didn't live in Crandall. I think he'd be happy.

Paul dropped me off and before I opened the passenger door, I said, "So now what? You gonna finish the season?"

Paul nodded. "Yeah, I have to. Hey, I just love playing football and I can't let those fatheads screw that up, right?" He smiled and said, "Football always makes sense, you know? You can depend on it."

The season was winding down. An unbelievable, confusing season was almost over. We had two games left, Friday night against Gibson-Packard and then the Thanksgiving event against Seward High School. In Massachusetts, some of the Thanksgiving rivalries went back one hundred years. Massachusetts high school football may not equal the popularity or skill level of Texas or Florida but the Turkey Day football tradition was pretty cool...and intense.

So, here's the story. If we defeat Gibson-Packard, we clinch the playoffs for the first time in four years. If we lose to Gibson-Packard but beat Seward, we're in the playoffs. We needed one more win.

The hatred of Fairview was reaching epic proportions. The whole school seemed to be buzzing about the incident at Ashley's house. Mr. Amaral had even called me into his office to find out what was going on. Somehow, Freddie Andrade had gotten word of what had happened and he was preparing to head up to Fairview with a few of his M-13 friends. I basically begged Freddie not to go and, for some unknown reason, he agreed to let us settle things on the gridiron. He did say, however, that he and his friends would be present at any playoff game. As much as I wanted to pummel Fairview's, I was getting a little worried that there could be actually be dead bodies lying in the stadium by the end of the game. Jon, Todd and the rest of those guys had no idea of what they had gotten themselves into.

I know I had a lot at stake if we did end up playing Fairview but I kept reminding myself that we had to win three games before we even potentially played them. Next up was Gibson-Packard. These two towns had combined their school systems a few years ago because of declining population and this move had greatly improved the athletic programs. They were a Division II school but had won the Division II football championship two years in a row. In other words, they were a real dangerous opponent particularly at this point in the season.

It was Thursday, the end of a not very inspiring week of practice. Some of the guys were not taking Gibson-Packard very seriously. There was kind of a reverse snobbery at work. Both Gibson and Packard were pretty rich towns and most of our guys just didn't believe that rich kids were any good at contact sports. Of course, there was a ton of evidence to the contrary but the Crandall kids didn't care. Rich kids just weren't tough. To most of them, I didn't become tough until my father went broke and I moved to Crandall.

Coach B. was beside himself. He knew that we had a lousy week of practice and he tried every coaching trick in the book to try to shake us out of our stupor. None of them worked.

Even Sal and Marco, whose intensity levels sometimes even scared me, weren't themselves this week. I was worried but, as a Junior and being the new white kid, I really couldn't say much.

I took the bus to Hubbard Square and stopped at CVS after practice. I grabbed a sub with Katie during her break and then rushed home. I had a huge US History-Advanced Placement test first thing in the morning.

There was a maroon Subaru wagon parked behind Grandpa Butch's Regal in the driveway. I knew that Bingo drove a Mercury Marquis and Ralphie Greco drove an old Lincoln Town Car and I couldn't imagine anyone else visiting. I became a little nervous about Grandpa Butch and hurried up the stairs.

I opened the front door and I caught the scent right away. She had to be here.

I saw the back of Mom's head in the kitchen. I heard her laughing, probably at one of Grandpa Butch's corny old jokes he stole from the old Henny Youngman video he always watched when there was no Red Sox or football on television.

I walked into the kitchen and there was Mom, sitting, drinking coffee and eating Pecan Sandies with Grandpa.

"Mom!" I said. She turned around and I saw that face for the first time in almost three months. Mom looked a little paler and thinner than she used to but her eyes lit up when she saw me and a huge smile dominated her face. She dressed stylishly in a waist length beige corduroy blazer and jeans. She didn't look depressed at all.

Mom stood up and we hugged. I put my chin on her shoulder and hugged her as tightly as I could. My face became moist from her tears and I tried to discipline myself not to cry.

Grandpa Butch sat at one end of the butcher block table with this silly grin on his tanned face. His grin made me laugh and then Mom turned around, looked at Grandpa and also started laughing.

We walked out to the back porch and Mom sat down on the chaise lounge with the torn blue cushion.

"How you doing, honey?" Mom asked.

Suddenly, I was at a loss for words. I had spoken to my Mom on the phone a couple of times a week since September but, for some reason, I wasn't prepared to see her in person.

"It's pretty strange, isn't it, Kyle?" Mom asked.

I nodded. "Yeah, I've been looking forward to this day for so long but now...but now, I don't know what to say."

So Mom took over the conversation, just the way she used to in the old days. She talked about her treatment, about Dr. Ellis, the miracle worker, and about the reasons why her breakdown occurred. I just sat there hanging on every world.

It got really quiet for a couple of minutes. And then I said, "Was it my fault, Mom?"

The smile left Mom's face and she stood and put her arm around me. "Listen to me, Kyle Francis Donovan. None, and I repeat none, of this is your fault. Whatever happened to me, to your father, to us...none of it was your fault. You have to understand that, okay?"

I nodded and I think that I finally started to believe it. Mom took my hand in hers and said, "Now, fill me in on your life in Crandall. And I want to hear everything...from the beginning."

And we sat on the back porch and talked until all the house lights on Lodge Avenue were turned off. We talked until even the next door neighbor, Mr. Napoli, shut off his television.

Finally, Mom looked at her watch and said, "Oh my, it's two o'clock in the morning, Kyle. You have school in the morning, and a game tomorrow night."

"You coming to the game, Mom?" I asked.

Mom looked away. "No, I have to go back tomorrow morning, Kyle. I'm almost there...almost. But I need a little more time. Plus, Uncle Ray will have his own breakdown if I don't get his precious car back. Pretty soon, though, we'll be together again. Although I will say that it looks like you're in good hands with your grandfather." She shook her head. "It's amazing how a person can surprise you."

We walked back into the house, hand in hand. Grandpa Butch had made up the pull out couch in the parlor with new sheets, pillows and blanket. Mom looked at the bed and laughed. "I'm glad I'm getting to know the real Butchie Donovan."

Mom kissed me good night and said, "I love you, Kyle. I can't tell you how proud I am of you. And I'm so sorry for everything that's happened." She blew her nose into a tissue. "I promised myself I wouldn't cry."

"Good night, Mom." I started up the stairs and then stopped, the silence in the house interrupted only by Grandpa's snoring. "Don't be sorry, Mom. Trust me, there's nothing to apologize for."

CHAPTER TWENTY ONE

The aroma of freshly brewed coffee woke me up. Mom must have done the brewing because Grandpa Butch usually bought his coffee at Dunkin Donuts every morning.

I walked downstairs and saw Mom placing a plate of French Toast on the kitchen table

"I wish you got more sleep," she said.

"I'm fine," I responded. I sat down at the table. "Homemade French Toast?"

Mom smiled and said, "Remember how this was your favorite when you were little? I haven't made it in quite a while."

I sat down at the table. "Where's Grandpa?"

Mom laughed. "Went to Dunkin Donuts. I offered to pour him a cup but he insisted on going to Dunkin Donuts. Can't teach an old dog new tricks, I guess."

My mother sat down and she poured some Mrs. Butterworth syrup on her French toast. "Butchie doesn't go for the low fat stuff, huh?"

"We have a very high fat, high carb diet in this house," I said between bites.

After I finished the plate of French toast, I brought the dish over to the sink and carefully washed and dried it.

"Wow, I am impressed," Mom said.

I shrugged. "Marine Corps rules."

Mom lifted her pocket book off the chair. "Well, time to go."

I stood and walked Mom to the door. She stopped at the door, grasped my hand and said, "Pretty soon, Kyle...pretty soon, we'll be together again."

I hugged Mom and watched as she headed to the Subaru station wagon. She waved, blew me a kiss and drove away.

I turned and walked upstairs to shower and get ready for school.

I did horribly on my AP US History test. I couldn't concentrate and literally almost fell asleep three times. I must have looked terrible because the teacher, Mr. Irwin, asked if there was anything wrong. There were sixty multiple choice questions on the exam and I honestly knew the answers of about thirty five. I guessed a lot.

Hopefully, I could grab a nap before the game against Gibson-Packard. We got out of school at 2:15 and the bus was leaving at 4:45 so there was a slight chance for some sleep. I had a study last period and planned on asking Mr. Amaral if I could leave.

I basically slept walked through the rest of the school day and Mr. Amaral did let me go home early. Once I hit the bed, I fell asleep. I had set the alarm for 3:30 but I snoozed right through it and didn't get up until 4:00. I forced myself to get out of the bed. I called for Grandpa Butch but remembered that he had an appointment with Dr. Patel at 3:00. Now I was in trouble.

I called Sal's cell phone but he was already at the school. The

87 bus left Hubbard Square at 4:10 and I'd have to hurry.

I threw on some clothes and sprinted to the Square. As I reached Main Street, I saw the 87 start pulling away. I waved and screamed and hoped that Al, the regular driver was behind the wheel. At least something had gone right because Al was driving and he stopped the bus to let me on.

"Don't you have a game tonight, Kyle?" Al asked as he closed the door behind me.

"Yeah, I overslept a little."

Al smiled and said, "We'll get you there on time."

It was Crandall so there was plenty of traffic. It didn't matter the time of day. Main Street had only one lane each way and Hubbard Square was always jam packed with cars. Grandpa Butch explained that the city planners never expected the volume of cars on the road and there wasn't much they could do about it now except change the traffic light cycle in the middle of the square but that only seemed to make things worse. Anyway, none of this was helping me get to school on time.

The bus rolled in front of the high school at 4:29. I thanked Al and ran around the back of the school to the locker room. I flew through the door and saw that everyone was dressed and patiently waiting on the benches for Coach Brennan's "Get on the bus" call.

"Hurry up, Kyle," Sal said. "I called your phone like ten times. Where you been?"

I shrugged and threw my girdle and game pants on at a record pace. Luckily, I had already put my knee and thigh pads in the game pants after practice yesterday. I didn't even bother getting taped and somehow was ready at 4:35 when Coach

Brennan yelled, "Let's go, boys. On the bus!"

Sal and I always sat next to each other on the bus as we traveled to away games. For most games, he was usually so geared up that he couldn't even speak. Today on the bus, Sal sounded like a co-host of "The View." He talked about school, the Patriots, his girlfriend Angela's druggie brother, the eggplant he ate last night...all I wanted to do was put my headphones on, chill out and try to get ready for the game.

We drove into Gibson and, if I had more courage, I would have mentioned how cool the foliage was. When I was younger, the whole family went apple picking in New Hampshire every year and I loved it, even though I never admitted that until now.

There was actually some goofing around on the bus, which hadn't happened the entire season. Coach Bonfiglio had to get out of his seat and tell us to shut up. Not a good sign.

We drove through Gibson Center, which reminded me a lot of Fairview Center. Same small boutique stores, a Starbucks...although Gibson had a Bertucci's restaurant. The Fairview Board of Selectmen would have never gone for that.

Sully finally pulled the bus into the stadium parking lot and I immediately noticed that a lot of fans were milling around and it was almost 75 minutes before game time.

Some of the guys seemed lethargic as they put on their shoulder pads and helmets. Marco and Sal walked around the visitor locker room, pounding guys on the pads, trying to instill some life but even their efforts seemed kind of halfhearted.

Coach B. spent less time on warm-ups and pre-game than usual. He led us into the locker room. The room was completely silent and Coach B. lit into us like I had never heard before.

"You guys are headed for a loss tonight unless you get your

heads on straight. This team is ready for you. You see the crowd? Huh? They smell an upset...they think you're ripe. Our whole week of practice sucked. You guys want to go to the playoffs? You better change your attitudes RIGHT NOW! Seniors, where are you? This team can play, boys and right now, you're not ready to play. Now get your heads out of your asses and LET'S GO! Come on, let's go! Everybody up!"

Coach B. led us in the customary pre-game Hail Mary and we all asked Mary, Queen of Victory to pray for us. I noticed that the guys seemed a little more excited.

The game started off as an absolute disaster. G-P scored on their first possession on one of those eighty yard drives that just tears the heart out of a defense. But then Sammy Griffin returned their kick for a touchdown and tied it up. Maybe things would be okay. Unfortunately, the next time G-P got the ball, they executed another long drive and kicked a field goal. Our offense didn't even take the field until the second quarter.

Our defense simply couldn't stop their running game. They ran an old Wing T which, if executed correctly, can be real hard to stop or even slow down. And, on this night Gibson Packard executed flawlessly. It got so bad in the second half that Coach B. pulled the entire starting defensive line out of the game midway through the third quarter.

We made a serious run in the fourth quarter. Everyone seemed to come to life at the same time but we were already down by two touchdowns. Marco scored on a screen pass from Sal. Eduardo absolutely buried the cornerback which shook Marco loose for the score. The sidelines came alive and Coach B. called for an onside kick. We were down by six points with a minute, ten seconds left.

I was on the onside kick team. I looked across at the G-P kids ten yards away and knew that if Ricky made a decent kick, I could get to the ball.

Ricky didn't get the football high enough in the air and the ball rolled right into the hands of Gibson Packard. The crowd went crazy and you could almost hear the Crandall Hawks deflate completely. The G-P offense ran out the clock and the final score was Gibson-Packard 23, Crandall 17.

For me personally, it was my worst game as a Crandall Hawk. I only carried the ball six times for about twenty yards and I blocked terribly. Their middle linebacker was smart and quick and I ended up chasing him a lot more than I hit him. I'm sure that Coach Brennan would notice it all when he reviewed the film.

There was no goofing around on the bus on the way home. When we reached the Crandall High parking lot, Sully stopped the bus. Coach Bonfiglio spoke so low that I could barely hear him.

"I hope we all learned a lesson tonight, boys. You have to prepare for every opponent the same way. We're not good enough to take anyone lightly. One more game...Thanksgiving against Seward. We win, we're in the playoffs...we lose, the season's over." Coach B. paused and looked around the bus. "I don't know about you guys, but I'm not ready for the season to end. But, in the end, it's up to you, not me, not the other coaches." He pointed at us. "It's up to you. What's in here." He pointed to his heart. "That's what's gonna make the difference. Take the weekend off. Think hard about everything. Film and lifting on Monday right after school." He then walked off the bus.

Everyone filed off the bus quietly. I thanked Sully but didn't speak to anyone else. I was angry at the team, but most of all, I was mad at myself. I had played like crap on a night when the team needed a spark.

Katie gave me a ride home and I barely spoke in the car. I could tell that she understood, though. I kissed her good night and promised to call her tomorrow.

As I entered the house, I wished Mom was still around so I could talk to her. I just didn't feel like talking to anyone else, not even Grandpa Butch. I was glad that he was sleeping. Maybe tomorrow I'd tell him the whole sad story of the game.

I got to my room, threw my cell phone on my desk, undressed quickly, climbed into bed and hoped that everything would be better in the morning.

CHAPTER TWENTY TWO

"My mother's gonna kill me if she finds out I'm eating this stuff," Sal said as I passed along a huge bowl of spaghetti and red sauce.

I laughed and said, "Hey, why do you call the sauce 'gravy'? Isn't gravy supposed to be brown?"

Sal looked at me like I was an alien who escaped from Area 51. "Irish people call it sauce...sauce is what you find in Spaghettios and Ragu and all that ketchup the Irish eat. We call it gravy...I don't know why, it's just gravy."

I'd only rarely seen Sal upset but I think if I continued the conversation a little more, he'd actually be angry. So I just shrugged, like I've learned to do a lot since I moved to Crandall.

It was Wednesday, the night before Thanksgiving and the Hawks Nest booster club had sponsored a spaghetti dinner for members of the football team and cheerleaders and their parents. Most of us had recovered from the loss to Gibson-Packard, although I wasn't sure about Coach Brennan. He still looked kind of dazed and confused. All of us were focused on the Seward game now.

I thought I might meet Katie's mother but she was working at the dental office. Grandpa Butch was there, shooting the breeze with some old friends in the club. I wondered why he looked a little paler than usual and I noticed that he sat down in the middle of the conversation. He had finished his treatments the week before so that wasn't the reason.

We sat in the dining room of the local Knights of Columbus. The walls were covered with light oak veneer paneling and a maroon carpet covered the floor. A massive chandelier from the 1970's hung from the ceiling.

Frankie Fitzgerald, a sixtyish plumber and vice president of the Hawk's Nest, tapped the microphone and said, "Ah, welcome everyone. Hello, is this thing working?" He tapped the microphone again. "Okay...we appreciate you all coming out tonight. I'll be brief. I just wanna say how proud we are of you boys. You've brought pride back to Crandall. You can just feel it everywhere you go. Reminds me of the old days." He cleared his throat. "Anyway, I'm as proud of how you guys handle yourselves off the field as on the field. You're winners all the way, even if we lose to Seward." He paused and observed the silent room. "But that ain't gonna happen." Everyone broke into loud cheers and Frankie soaked it all up with this big smile on his face. "Okay, okay. Now I want to introduce the man responsible for all this success. He's a great Marine, a great teacher and a great coach...Tony Bonfiglio!"

The players stood and clapped and the cheerleaders and parents followed suit. Frankie slapped Coach on the back as he handed him the microphone. Coach took a deep breath and said, "First of all, how about a big hand for all the parents." Coach motioned for the parents to stand and they did, some, like Grandpa Butch, reluctantly. I noticed how few men were present. I would say about sixty to seventy percent of the team came from single parent households.

All the players and cheerleaders stood and clapped and

whistled. I saw Eduardo's mother and Raymond's mother look at each other with wide grins and all of a sudden I just felt good about staying in Crandall.

Coach B. looked down and then said, "This has been a special season, a real special season. This group...this group of young men..." Coach held the microphone away from his body and composed himself. The hall was silent. "Okay, sorry about that...just an old Marine getting emotional for a minute. You know, they talk a lot about diversity in this country. People also talk about how screwed up our teenagers are, how the future is bleak." Coach paused. "Well, I wish they'd come to Crandall and see these kids every day. They'd see African Americans, Haitians, Brazilians, Italians...heck, we even got more than a couple of Irish kids this year. These kids represent America. And you should see how they get along. They laugh together, give each other a hard time, they win and lose together. But it's always together. I've never been prouder of any group of young men. I've never had a more enjoyable season coaching. And Frankie's right about Seward. Oh, we're gonna beat them but, in the end, it's really secondary. What these boys have already accomplished will go down in Crandall history." Coach Bonfiglio again stepped away from the microphone. "I want all the players to look around at each other...make eye contact." I turned and immediately saw Eduardo and he nodded with a small smile on his face. I nodded back and then I saw Sal who grinned.

"Never forget each other because you're making history this year. You're showing the world that money doesn't matter, that race doesn't matter, that the only thing that matters is believing in yourself and believing in your teammates. Thank you guys...for everything."

And then Coach B. sat down and we all stood again and applauded even louder than before. Coach saluted us and then raised Coach Brennan's arm and the whole crowd went crazy again. This was a great night to be a Crandall Hawk.

After dessert was served, we started filing out and I walked over to Grandpa's table. He was still sitting and was looking paler by the minute. "Are you okay, Grandpa?" I asked, grabbing a chair.

Grandpa nodded. "Yeah, Boyo. Just a little bug I've been fighting."

"Wait here...I'll go get the car."

Katie was waiting for me at the front door. "Hey, is everything alright?" she asked.

I shrugged. "Grandpa doesn't look too good. He says it's just a bug but he said that about his colon cancer, too. I'm gonna get the car. Come on with me."

Katie and I walked briskly to Grandpa Butch's Regal. It finally felt like New England was supposed to feel like in the late fall. It had been so warm that I was really beginning to believe all that global warming stuff.

I pulled the car in front of the tan brick building and said to Katie, "I'll be right back."

Grandpa was sitting on a chair near the coat rack right inside the front door. Frankie Fitzgerald was talking a mile a minute and Grandpa was nodding a lot. He saw me and a look of relief enveloped his face. He rose and said, "Okay, Frankie, I'll probably see you at the game tomorrow. Thanks for all this tonight. This was really something."

Frankie shook his hand and then turned to me. "We're

proud of you, Kyle. Proud of everything you've done this year. I know it wasn't easy. Good luck tomorrow."

I thanked Mr. Fitzgerald and helped Grandpa put on his Crandall Hawk's Nest jacket. He leaned on my arm as we made our way to the car.

Katie held the front passenger door open and Grandpa Butch gingerly climbed in. "Old timers just cause a lot of trouble, don't they Katie?" Grandpa asked as he settled in the seat.

Katie laughed and it struck me again how much I liked her laugh. We made eye contact and she smiled. The lump in my throat returned.

I dropped Katie off at her house first because I didn't want to leave Grandpa alone tonight. As usual, Katie understood. After I walked her to her front door and sat in the driver's seat, Grandpa said, "I know you're only seventeen, Boyo, but don't lose her. I guess that sounds silly but she's special. Take it from an old man."

After we got home, Grandpa took some ibuprofen and almost immediately fell asleep.

Grandpa was up early as usual the next morning and seemed a little better. He was busy at the stove, cooking up some French toast and home fries. I sat down at the kitchen table and said, "How you feeling, Grandpa?"

"Fine, sonny boy, just fine. Told you it was just a little bug...one of those twenty four hour things," he replied as he pushed three pieces of French toast onto my plate. "How about getting the syrup and butter, or do you want an old man to do everything around here?"

I devoured my plate of French toast and hash browns but Grandpa didn't eat much. He sat squinting at the sports page.

"Hey, the Tribune has Seward upsetting us today," he said.

I shrugged. "Come on, Grandpa, you know those guys are never right."

He nodded. "Yeah, just like the weathermen."

I heard a key unlocking the front door. I turned in my chair and saw Dad making his way into the kitchen.

"Happy Thanksgiving, boys," he said. Dad seemed really happy. He was clean shaven and the black droopiness under his eyes didn't seem as bad.

Dad put his hands on my shoulders and said, "Big one today, Kyle. You guys ready?"

I nodded between bites. "I think so, Dad. It'd be horrible if we blew the whole season today.

Dad hugged Grandpa and a look of concern appeared on his face. "You alright, Dad?"

Grandpa scoffed. "Yeah, I caught this bug. Feeling much better. I think I had "flu like symptoms" like Manny Ramirez gets when he wants to sit out a game."

Dad sat down and said, "What time you got to be there, Kyle?"

I glanced at the clock on the microwave. "Jeez, I gotta get going. Supposed to be dressed and ready to go at 8:45." It was already 8:00.

I threw some sweats on, said goodbye to Dad and Grandpa Butch and drove the Regal to the high school. It was a home game and, believe it or not, this was my first Thanksgiving Day game. The private schools all finished their seasons the weekend before Thanksgiving. I actually felt pretty nervous.

The locker room was quiet, much quieter than usual...even Eduardo seemed really serious. For the first time, I had the feeling that a lot of guys realized that they weren't just playing this game for themselves. Instead, we were playing for the school, for the city...particularly after listening to Mr. Fitzgerald and Coach B. last night. Anyway, I know I felt that way and it made me kind of anxious. Now, I just wanted the game to start so I could hit someone.

As we ran out to the field, I noticed that there wasn't an empty seat in the entire Hawks Nest. Spectators lined the track around the field and police stood inside the ropes separating the track from the actual field. The crowd went absolutely berserk when we won the coin toss and elected to receive.

As I stood at the twenty yard line awaiting the kickoff, I patted my thigh pad for good luck. Today, I had squeezed Grandpa Butch's Sixth Division patch in between the pad and my game pants.

The whistle blew and the short kick landed directly in my arms. The blocking wedge formed instantly and I immediately ran straight behind the wedge.

After about ten yards, the Seward kamikazes on their kickoff team broke the wedge so I darted horizontally, hoping to turn the corner along the sideline. I avoided one tackler and saw some daylight up the sideline. Peter Sousa appeared out of nowhere and absolutely leveled a would be tackler and I headed back into the middle of the field with a lot of open space in front of me. There was only one potential tackler left and that was the kicker. I had already made a pact with myself to never allow a kicker to bring me down. I easily faked him out and dashed the final twenty yards into the end zone.

When I reached the end zone, I tapped my thigh pad again. I was then buried by an avalanche of my teammates. Some Crandall kids climbed under the rope and joined in the celebration. It took the police a few minutes to get the kids off the field so we could line up for the extra point.

The run back set the tone for the game. Seward was no match for us on this Thanksgiving. Our starters pummeled them and then our second and third teams pummeled them. The final score was 40-6 but I'm pretty sure we could have scored 100 points if Coach Bonfiglio would have allowed it. Of course, there was no way Coach B. was going to embarrass any team so we had to settle for forty points.

The fans mobbed the field after game. They climbed the goalposts and generally created mayhem. A couple of small scuffles broke out and more police cars had to show up to restore the peace. As I walked to the locker room, I looked at the field and it kind of reminded of a scene from The Terminator.

I hugged Katie on the way and scanned the crowd for Dad and Grandpa. I finally saw Dad but no Grandpa. I shouted, "Where's Grandpa?" over the crowd and Dad yelled back that he was home sleeping. Grandpa would never miss a Thanksgiving Day game...in fact, he hadn't missed a game all year, even during his treatments.

Dad and Grandpa had reserved a table at the Palermo for a Thanksgiving meal. We planned to hold a chair for Mom but she had said that she didn't think she'd be able to make it. But I was holding out hope anyway. After we ate, I was going over to Katie's house to meet her mother for the first time.

After the postgame prayer and Coach Bonfiglio's talk, I

showered and changed quickly. As I rushed out of the locker room, my phone rang.

"Hey, Kyle, you on your way?" Dad asked.

"Yeah, Dad, I'll be home in five minutes. What's going on?"

Dad sighed. "It's your grandfather. I'm going to take him to the hospital. He's not good."

Grandpa Butch? "Wait for me, Dad. I'll be right there."

I flew out of the parking lot and swerved to avoid some of the tailgaters. I got home in four minutes and ran up the front stairs. When I entered the house, I saw Grandpa lying on his recliner in the parlor, looking white as the walls and shivering under three blankets.

"Jeez, Grandpa, what's going on?" I asked.

"I'll be fine," Grandpa said. He took a paper cup and spit some greenish bile.

"How long you been spitting this up?" Dad asked.

"Just since this morning...a little while after you left for the game." Grandpa was shivering almost uncontrollably now.

Dad grabbed his coat and said, "We're going to the hospital. Kyle, you can drive."

Grandpa protested weakly but Dad and I already had his shoes on and were helping him out of the recliner. We basically carried Grandpa down the front stairs and placed him gently in the back seat of the Regal. Dad sat beside Grandpa with his arm around his shoulders. I glanced in the rear view mirror and turned the ignition.

Chapter Twenty Three

"It's definitely pneumonia," Dr. Patel said to Dad and I as we sat in the emergency waiting room. Dad and I looked at each other and then Dad asked, "So how serious is it, Doctor?"

Dr. Patel took a deep breath. I knew that wasn't a good sign. "Well, with elderly patients, pneumonia can be serious...very serious. Butch is pretty weak right now and he's having a lot of difficulty breathing. With pneumonia, your lungs fill up and that's what causes the wheezing and coughing. With young children and the elderly, their immune systems aren't as strong so pneumonia can do a lot of damage quickly. You need strength to fight it off. How long have the symptoms been present?"

"Just a couple of days. I noticed on Wednesday night that Grandpa seemed kind of weak and pasty. But then this morning, I woke up and he seemed like his regular self," I said.

Dr. Patel nodded. "That's not atypical. Symptoms present themselves differently in the elderly and sometimes they come very suddenly. How's his memory and alertness been?"

"Fine, I think. Until yesterday, he seemed the same as he's always been," I answered.

"We're pretty sure it's bacterial pneumonia. Normally, because I think it's pretty early in the game, we'd treat him with antibiotics right away. He's just very weak right now so we have to be careful with everything." Dr. Patel reached out and shook both of our hands. "I'll be in touch. I'm on call until eleven tonight so I'll be checking in on Butch. In the meantime, they're moving him to the ICU where they can take good care of him."

"Could he die from this, Doctor?" I didn't want to ask the question but I had to. This was my best friend in the world.

Dr. Patel raised his eyebrows. "I hope not, Kyle. It can be serious, though and Butch has never had a vaccination. So..." and his voice trailed off. I'll take that answer as yes, Grandpa Butch could die from pneumonia.

After Dr. Patel left, Dad and I sat in the emergency room staring blankly at the "Montel Williams Show" repeat on the television. Dad reached over and put his arm around my shoulders. "Remember how strong Grandpa is, Kyle. Okinawa, cancer...there's not a tougher guy on the planet, remember when I said that about the colon cancer?" I stared at the television and just nodded slowly. "He's not ready to die, Kyle. I know that. Your grandfather is not ready to die."

About a half hour later, a nurse came out and told us that they had moved Grandpa to his room in the intensive care unit.

We took the elevator to the ICU on the seventh floor. The floor was so quiet that you could hear the muted Christmas music coming from the radio at the nurse's station. We searched for Room 712 and found it, the last room on the right hand side of the unit.

The bed next to Grandpa's was empty and a curtain was pulled around Grandpa Butch's bed. I cautiously followed Dad into the room. A nurse was adjusting an oxygen mask wrapped around Grandpa's face. She smiled at us and then left us alone.

Dad walked up to the bed and gently put his hand on Grandpa's left arm. There seemed to be all sorts of wires and hoses covering his chest. Grandpa slowly opened his eyes and blinked a couple of times. I saw my father's face tense up and then return almost immediately return to normal. Dad glanced at me and motioned for me to come to the bed.

I did what Dad did, placing my hand on Grandpa's arm. He opened his eyes again and a tear streamed down his cheek. I began to fill up myself so I looked out the picture window and stared at the half full parking lot. I kept my hand on Grandpa's arm and he drifted back to sleep.

For the next few hours, Dad and I sat in the two chairs surrounding Grandpa's bed. The critical care nurse would periodically appear and check Grandpa's vital signs and adjust some of those wires. At six o'clock, Dr. Patel showed up. Dad and I stood and greeted him.

Dr. Patel studied the chart and paperwork hanging from the side of the bed. He gave Grandpa a brief exam and then turned to us and said, "Breathing's about the same. He's pretty stable for now. We're going to start him on antibiotics and try to force this bacteria out of his system. I just want to make sure his system can handle the antibiotics because he's very weak at this point. Why don't you guys go down to the café and get something to eat? This is a tough Thanksgiving for you."

Dad nodded. "That's a good idea, Doctor. Come on, Kyle."

We each got a sandwich and soda from the vending machines and sat quietly eating our Thanksgiving dinner. As I stood to throw away my trash, my phone rang.

"How's he doing?" Katie asked.

"He's still in intensive care. The doctor thinks he'll be there for a while. They're starting him on antibiotics, if his system can handle it."

"Can I come over?"

"Wish you could but the ICU only lets family members visit."

"Are you coming home tonight?"

I hadn't really thought of what I was going to do. "Nah, I'm gonna stay here until he's better."

"When's your next practice?" Katie asked.

"Tomorrow...the game is Tuesday. Not much time to prepare."

"I know this sounds goofy, Kyle but I think your grandfather would want you to play in that game."

I took the phone away from my ear and held it at my side for a moment. I put it back to my ear and said, "I can't think of any of that right now...games, practices, school...whatever. I can't leave him...I just can't leave him."

"I understand, Kyle."

Dad and I headed back to the room and I dozed off for a while sitting in the chair. Grandpa constantly slept, opening his eyes briefly every once in great while.

At 10:30, the nurse, Kathy, came in the room and said, "I hate to say this but visiting hours are over."

"We'd like to stay the night," Dad said.

Kathy frowned. "Unfortunately, only one family member can stay with any patient in the ICU. You understand...it's hospital rules. Also, we don't think Mr. Donovan's pneumonia is contagious but we naturally we want to limit exposure. I'm sure you understand."

"I want to stay, Dad."

Dad looked at me and smiled slightly. "Okay, Kyle...I'll be back first thing in the morning. Call me if anything happens. I'll bring some clothes for you tomorrow."

"Now, you have to be eighteen to spend the night. I'm assuming Kyle is eighteen, right?" Kathy asked.

"Oh yeah, just turned eighteen," I said quickly. Dad just nodded. He's a terrible liar.

"Okay then," Kathy said with a smile that indicated that she knew I was stretching the truth. "I guess I don't have to check i.d.'s."

Dad took the keys to the Regal, patted Grandpa on the arm, hugged me and left. I settled in on the cot beside Grandpa's bed and fell asleep once my head hit the two hospital pillows.

My phone woke me up the next morning. I had no idea what time it was. I did know that I had slept for at least a few hours uninterrupted since the one of the nurses had taken Grandpa's vital signs around 3:00 AM. I sat up and said, "Hello?"

"Kyle, how are you honey?" Mom asked.

I rubbed my eyes and saw that it was 8:00 AM. "Hey, Mom...how you doing?"

"Dad called me and said that you were staying at the hospital. How's Butch?"

I looked over at Grandpa Butch, who still had the oxygen mask stuck to his face. He seemed to be sleeping pretty comfortably. "I don't know, Mom. They still have him hooked up to the oxygen but he's still sleeping away."

"Okay, honey. I'm on my way down."

"Do you have Uncle Ray's car?"

There was a short pause, and then Mom said, "I bought an old Toyota Corolla up in Vermont. I'll be driving it to Crandall."

"When do you have to go back?" I asked.

Another pause and then Mom said, "I'm not going back, Kyle. I'm coming home...it's time to be your mother again."

A strange mixture of emotions came over me. On the one hand, here was my grandfather in basically a life or death situation. And still, my mother was coming home. My mother was coming home. But where was home?

"Your doctor said it's okay?" I asked.

Mom chuckled softly. "Yes, Dr. Ellis thinks I'm ready and, more importantly, I think I'm ready."

I didn't want to ask this question but I just couldn't help myself. "Are you and Dad ever gonna get back together?"

Mom cleared her throat. "No, it's over, honey. The divorce is in the works. It's okay, though. We're going to be friends. It sounds like your Dad almost has a steady job in Hartford. Things are going well for him."

Dad didn't tell me anything about a steady job in Hartford. No way I was moving to Hartford.

"Are you gonna stay with us?"

"Yes," Mom said. "I spoke to Butch last week and we worked everything out. He's been wanting to move into the vacant apartment downstairs ever since Mrs. DiLoreto died last year. So he'll live downstairs, and we'll rent out the upstairs apartment, where you're living now."

Wow, nobody told me anything. Mom coming home, Dad getting a job, Grandpa Butch moving downstairs: this was all news to me. It was all good news...but it was still news.

"I should be at the hospital by ten," Mom said.

"Alright, Mom...I'll see you then," I answered.

"Bye, Kyle."

"Hey, Mom?" I asked.

"Yes, what is it, honey?"

"I'm glad you're coming home," I said.

"Me too, honey. Me too," Mom answered.

I hung up the phone, sat down on the cot and listened to Grandpa snore for a few minutes. I then realized how incredibly hungry I was.

As I was putting on my Crandall Hawks Football hooded sweatshirt, Dr. Patel entered the room.

"You stayed the night, Kyle?" he asked.

I nodded.

"You're a good grandson," Dr. Patel said. He read Grandpa's chart and then conducted a quick examination of Grandpa Butch. Dr. Patel said nothing.

"How's he seem?" I asked.

Dr. Patel took a deep breath and said, "It's hard to say. His body seems to be accepting the antibiotics so let's hope that does the trick. We should know by the next day or two. It's just that...this pneumonia hit him hard, Kyle. It hit him hard and quickly...we'll keep checking his vital signs and, hopefully, he'll stabilize. He's a tough guy, Kyle. You know that."

After Dr. Patel left, I took the elevator down to the cafeteria, which was located on the first floor. Crandall Hospital had installed a new café within the past year so there were plenty of choices for breakfast. I ordered a ham and cheese omelet and bought a Tribune from the machine next to the cash register.

I scanned the sports page while devouring the omelet. I

almost resisted the urge to buy another omelet but the smell of the grill was too much.

After I finished eating, I found the chapel on the other end of the first floor.

The chapel was empty. I chose a pew in the back and sat down. I tried to pray but my mind kept wandering. I thought of Grandpa Butch lying in the hospital bed but I also thought of him dressed in that starched white tee shirt, standing in the kitchen, flipping pancakes. For some reason, I thought of his two tattoos, the shamrock and the Marine Corps emblem. I reached into the pocket of my sweatpants and took out the Sixth Division patch.

I thought of Mom coming home and Dad with his new job in Hartford. I thought of Katie and Eduardo and Sal and Coach Bonfiglio. Images rushed in and out of my mind. There was Paul and Ashley and Mr. Amaral. I couldn't control these thoughts but I really had no desire to do so. None of it made much sense but maybe it wasn't supposed to make any sense. I don't know.

I knelt down and said an Act of Contrition. I asked Jesus to give strength to Grandpa Butch. And then I asked Jesus to give me the same strength. I blessed myself, stood up, genuflected and walked out of the chapel. In my heart, I knew Grandpa Butch was going to be okay.

CHAPTER TWENTY FOUR

I was trying hard not to doze off but it was really difficult. It was 8:30 on Monday morning and Grandpa had been in the hospital since Thanksgiving, last Thursday. I had just talked to Dad on the phone and he was on his way to the hospital with some coffee and donuts.

Throughout most of Saturday and Sunday, Grandpa Butch slept. Every once in a while, his eyes would open and I'd say something but then he'd be fast asleep again before saying anything in response.

Dr. Patel told us that they were still monitoring his vital signs, which were stable. However, the doctor also warned us constantly that Grandpa Burch was very weak. Today was the last day Grandpa would spend in the ICU.

Mom came down on Friday and she looked like her old self. Her eyes still seemed a little sad but, overall, she seemed okay. Mom spent most of Friday and Saturday sitting with me in Grandpa's hospital room.

She and Dad seemed to be getting along alright although only an idiot would fail the notice the tension whenever they spoke to each other. But I think they wanted to make the best of it for my sake. They were divorcing...there was no doubt about that but they loved me too much to let their resentment affect their only son.

Sal and Eduardo helped Mom move her stuff into Grandpa's house. They also started bringing Grandpa's belongings downstairs to Mrs. DiLoreto's old apartment. Katie, Raymond, Peter Sousa, Ricky and Marco (believe it or not!) came over after practice on Sunday morning and scrubbed the whole apartment. And then they finished moving Grandpa's stuff. What can I say about my Crandall friends?

My main concern was that Grandpa would be actually going home. Saturday and Sunday weren't particularly great days so I tried to read Dr. Patel's face when he checked in on Grandpa Butch. Dr. Patel was an expert, though, and he hid his emotions better than Bill Belichick.

I got up out of the chair, stretched and yawned. I walked over to the window and looked at the big digital clock on Crandall Savings Bank across the street. 47 degrees with a very light rain. Perfect football weather. I hoped that I could play tomorrow but it all depended on Grandpa Butch. I wasn't leaving him even if there was an earthquake in Crandall.

I leaned on the sill below the big picture window and stared out the window across the parking lot to the bank's clock. I heard some rustling and then I heard Grandpa Butch spit. I could be in the middle of Times Square at noon time and I would be able to hear and recognize that spitting sound.

I turned around quickly and there he was, sitting up and spitting into a paper coffee cup. Grandpa stared into the cup and said, "No more of that yellow crap." He then looked at me and smiled. He was pale and thin and still pretty weak looking but he was alive and smiling.

I walked over to the bed and hugged him, being careful not to interfere with the various wires and tubes that would undoubtedly be annoying Grandpa Butch within seconds. He felt thin but I felt his vise like hands on my shoulders and I knew that he still had his strength.

Sure enough, he immediately began fumbling with the tubes and wires. "What the hell is this stuff?" Grandpa asked.

I went out to the hallway and told Brenda, the nurse on duty, that Grandpa Butch was sitting up and coherent.

Brenda rushed into the room and said, "Now, what do you think you're doing?"

Grandpa looked up and said, "I gotta get this stuff off of me...brings back some bad Okinawa memories."

Brenda checked Grandpa's vital signs and then looked at me, shook her head and smiled. "Your grandfather is something, really something."

"Now, Butch, you lay back down and the doctor will be right in, okay? And leave the i. v. alone, okay?"

Grandpa grudgingly agreed and lay back down. "Hey, Boyo, could you raise this bed a little?"

After I had lifted the bed, Grandpa said, "What day is it?"

"Monday," I said.

Grandpa tried to whistle but his mouth was too dry. I poured him a glass of water and then he said, "How come you're not in school?"

I shrugged.

"Have you been here the whole time?" Grandpa asked.

I shrugged again.

Grandpa was about to speak again when Dr. Patel entered the room.

"Well, it's himself," Grandpa Butch said.

Dr. Patel smiled and said, "Butch, how are you feeling?"

"Pretty hungry and thirsty. A little weak but not too bad."

Dr. Patel studied the chart and examined Butch carefully. "Well, the antibiotics really worked. There's not much I can say, Butch. You're one in a million, my friend." Dr. Patel then turned to me and said, "Hopefully, if all goes well, your grandfather can go home tomorrow. And you, why don't you go home, take a shower and get some rest."

Grandpa Butch grasped my hand and said, "The game's tomorrow, Boyo. You have to go to school."

That's right, I did have to go to school if I wanted to practice this afternoon. If I didn't practice today, there was no way Coach B. would let me play in the game on Tuesday.

"Yeah, I'll take a shower and get to school. I have to be able to practice today." I put on my jacket and said, "Okay, Grandpa, it looks good, I guess. I'm gonna take off. I'll be over after practice."

As I turned to leave, I felt Grandpa Butch grab my hand. He looked into my eyes and said, "Thank you, Boyo."

I nodded, hugged him and walked out of the room.

As I entered Crandall High School, I chuckled to myself. I remembered my first day of school, how nervous I was, my obsession with dressing correctly, the near fight with Eddie. Now I could greet almost everyone by name and it felt like I had been a Hawk my entire life. Life is funny.

Mr. Amaral greeted me as I walked into the main office.

"Kyle, how's Butch?" he asked.

I smiled and said, "He's gonna make it, Mr. Amaral. He's still pretty weak but I think he's gonna be okay."

Mr. Amaral extended his hand and said, " No way he would miss the championship game, Kyle. You look pretty tired...why don't you go home and get some sleep."

"I have to practice this afternoon. You know Coach Bonfiglio...if I don't practice today, I won't play tomorrow. And I have to play tomorrow."

Mr. Amaral nodded. "You're right, Kyle." He laughed and said, "I'm glad Coach Bonfiglio is on our side."

I got my pass and glanced at the wall clock in the office. It was 10:30.

I hurried to my locker and retrieved my Algebra II text book. I entered the classroom and heard Mr. Bruno explaining inverse functions with the intensity of Eduardo attacking a quarter pounder with cheese.

I handed my pass to Mr. Bruno who smiled and said, "Good to see you, Kyle. Now hurry up, you're missing all this great material."

Katie looked at me with surprise and I gave her a thumbs up. Raymond patted me on the shoulder as I sat down.

I later found myself almost nodding off during English class but I wouldn't have missed much even if I had fallen asleep.

I was really exhausted by the time the final bell rang. I had to drag myself to practice and find out what Coach Bonfiglio and Coach Brennan had planned for Monsignor Casey, our opponent on Tuesday.

I hadn't been in the locker room for a few days but it felt like a year.

"Here he is, The Great White Hope!" Eduardo announced as I walked toward my locker.

I shook Eddy's hand and said, "Thanks, man, for helping out

with the apartment. You're a good amigo."

I felt a slap on my back and Sal said, "Well, we like your grandfather, Irish boy. Not sure about you, though."

Pretty soon, it seemed like the whole team was gathered around my locker, shaking my hand and giving me a hard time.

"Let's go, boys...you forget about a little game tomorrow?" Coach Brennan yelled.

I caught his eye and he said, "Well, look who's here...Kyle Donovan, the pride of Fairview."

"How you doing, Coach?" I asked.

"Much better now that I know you're playing tomorrow. How's your grandfather?"

"He's gonna be alright, Coach."

Coach Brennan smiled and nodded. "Okay, then...hurry up and get ready. We put in some new plays and I know you're easily confused."

It took me a while to shake off my fatigue but practice went well. I started the practice as the second team fullback but I was starting again by the end of practice. The new plays weren't very complicated. Come to think of it, Coach Bonfiglio's entire offense isn't that complicated.

I could barely walk by the end of practice but thankfully Sal offered me a ride home. I saw Mom's Corolla in the driveway and Dad's Taurus parked out front. I sighed and prepared for the worst.

When I walked in, Dad and Mom were speaking quietly in the kitchen which by now I realized was the absolute center of activity in Grandpa Butch's house. It wasn't that way in Fairview.

I caught Dad's eye as I entered the kitchen. He stood and

smiled. "Kyle, how you doing buddy?"

I shook Dad's hand and glanced at Mom who sat at the table, smiling. Maybe this wasn't going to be that painful after all.

I opened the fridge and grabbed a Mountain Dew and took a seat at the table. "What's going on?" I asked.

Mom and Dad looked at each very briefly and then Dad said, "Your mother and I have been talking, Kyle. We both agreed that it would be best for you to live here, with your mother and grandfather, in Crandall...if that's your choice, too."

Thank God. "That's awesome, Dad. Not that I wouldn't want to live with you or anything. It's just..."

"You don't have to say a word, buddy. I saw you in the hospital...with your grandfather. You belong here. I'll be around a lot, though. You're not getting rid of me, right?" Dad said. "I'm taking Grandpa home tomorrow. You friends did a great job getting the place ready. Those are good friends, Kyle. Really good friends."

I nodded. "Yeah, they are, Dad. You gonna stay in Hartford?"

"Yeah, it's really working out. There's a startup company that needs a guy like me, believe it or not. If everything goes well, they're expanding to Worcester next summer. So hopefully, I won't be far away at all."

"That's great, Dad. I'll be down to visit all the time."

Dad got up and yawned and stretched. "Okay, then. I'll sleep downstairs tonight. Good night, Donna...good night, Kyle." He turned and began to leave the kitchen.

I stood up and patted Dad on the shoulder. "Hey, Dad."

Dad turned and said, "Yes, Kyle?"

"Everything's gonna be okay, isn't it? I mean, everything's really gonna be alright."

Dad looked at Mom and smiled. He nodded and said, "Yeah, son...everything really is going to be okay."

CHAPTER TWENTY FIVE

In Massachusetts, high school playoff games are always played on neutral fields so the venue for our game against Monsignor Casey was going to be Rockford Stadium. Rockford was a pretty small town located along the coast, about twenty miles northeast of Crandall. I guess the Rockford school system had spent a ton of money rebuilding the stadium, track and field. It had the new field turf and seated around 10,000 people.

It was really cold and the wind was whipping off the ocean as we climbed off the bus at Rockford Stadium. I'm not sure that God had planned for football to be played in New England in December and I was glad that I had worn the all-weather Under Armor Mom had bought the week before. Eduardo and some of the linemen were still wearing short sleeves shirts under their pads. It was a macho thing. I may not have been as macho as those guys but I know I was a lot warmer.

The locker room was brand new and it didn't even have that funky locker room smell yet. We threw on our pads and headed out for warmups.

The crowd steadily filed in and the seats were almost full by the time we finished our calisthenics pregame. Coach Brennan called for us to jog back inside.

I had gotten used to the cold and was hoping that Coach B. wouldn't have us in the locker room for too long. As I slowly ran towards the locker room door, I heard a familiar voice.

"Hey, Donovan, you suck, you traitor!"

I looked in the direction of the voice and saw Jon Davis standing behind the chain link fence separating the track from the stadium area. His face was beet red and I wondered if the color was caused by the cold weather or alcohol. Probably a combination of both.

Fairview had won the first playoff game easily and would play the winner of our game in the state championship. The whole team was probably scouting this game.

I looked over at Jon and waved. He yelled again; this time, his words were clearly slurred. "You're a traitor, Donovan. Get ready for the beating of your life on Saturday."

Todd Gardner stood beside Jon. He looked at me and shrugged. Todd even looked a little embarrassed. Maybe that was progress.

Unfortunately for Jon, Eduardo heard his voice. He ran closer to the fence and said quietly, "You just wait, Tolo. You just wait. You're gonna be mine, Homeboy."

Jon made a motion like he was going to climb the fence and go after Eduardo but I honestly don't think he wanted any part of Eddy. Jon looked like he was just waiting for Todd to hold him back.

There was more bad news for Jon. Raymond had been running behind us and he just stopped and glared and pointed at Jon and Todd. I hadn't seen fear on the face of Jon Davis much but now doubt definitely dominated his face. He knew he was messing in the big leagues.

I wasn't even upset by the whole scene. In fact, it just provided more motivation. I was ready in every way possible for this game. Dad had brought Grandpa Butch home from the hospital this morning and the game was being broadcast on the local cable access station. He and Bingo Lonergan would be eating frozen pizza and enjoying the game together.

The team was ready, too. There was just this sense around the guys that we weren't ready to be done yet. We were confident but it wasn't cockiness. It was a quiet confidence, a feeling that we had come a long way and the story wasn't over. Hey, I could be wrong too.

Coach Bonfiglio called us together. He paused and then said, "Alright, here we are. This is what we worked for, gentlemen. I don't have much to say except remember double sessions, remember all the lifting in the off season, remember the sweat and the work and the blood that got us to this point. You know I think every one of you is a winner...but let's show everyone else that." Coach B. turned to me and said, "Kyle, will you lead us in prayer?"

I still had constitutional questions about the prayer but I said an Our Father and yelled, "Mary, Queen of Victory, pray for us!" Everyone charged out of the locker room, screaming like maniacs and almost frothing at the mouth. We were ready.

Monsignor Casey was ready, too. They had beaten Archbishop Walsh for the Catholic League championship in a thriller on Thanksgiving. Their quarterback, Kevin Coleman, was one of the best in the state and headed to Boston College. The Casey defense had a huge defensive line and had only allowed 82 points the entire seasons. They were big, disciplined and all business. There would be a minimum of trash talking in this game. Their coach, Jimmy Hughes, had been at Casey for twenty five years and wouldn't allow it.

As I ran onto the field, I scanned the crowd and couldn't find an empty seat. I saw Katie jumping around with the rest of the cheerleaders. I breathed out and rubbed my hands together. Sal and I performed our game day ritual. He slammed me on my shoulder pads five times and I did the same to him. He whacked me in the face mask and we both were screaming at the top of our lungs.

We lost the toss and I hopped around, trying to stay warm on the sidelines.

The Coleman kid was good, close to the best I've seen. Monsignor Casey ran a type of West Coast offense and they threw the ball on almost every down. Coach Bonfiglio had our defense well prepared, though, and it seemed like he and Coach Hughes were playing a chess match.

Raymond sacked Coleman on third and three and forced Casey to attempt a thirty five yard field goal. The kicker had the wind at his back but the kick skidded off to the right. It was our ball.

We came out in a shotgun on first down, which seemed to confuse the Casey defense. I lined up beside Sal, and Marco split out wide. The Casey linebackers were yelling out adjustments when the ball was snapped.

Sal slammed the ball into my stomach and I barreled into the huge hole created by Eduardo and Peter Sousa. Casey wasn't expecting a draw play.

I ran north to south and I ran hard. I eluded the reach of the mike linebacker and headed into the defensive backfield. Their safety hauled me down from behind but not before a gain of twenty six yards. We were in Monsignor Casey territory.

Coach Brennan was mixing up the offense, alternating

between short passes and running plays. We were running the offense without a huddle and all of the sudden movement seemed more confusing than I thought. We had rolled down to the Casey fifteen yard line when I went into motion at the wrong time. The referee threw the flag and pushed us back to the twenty yard line. I saw Jimmy Killoran sprinting to the huddle with a petrified look on his face. I knew that he substituting for me.

I ran off the field and Coach Brennan called me over. "You alright, Kyle?" he asked.

"Yeah, yeah, I'm fine, Coach. Just got confused for a play."

Coach Brennan nodded and adjusted his headphones. "Okay, we need you. No more mistakes, okay?"

Jimmy had missed his block and one of the Casey defensive ends threw Sal for a loss. It was now third and seventeen.

I returned to the huddle. Eduardo slapped me on the pads and said, "Come on, Irish boy. Stay in the game...focus, menino!"

"Okay, boys, big play," Sal said. "Twins right, draw left, twins right, draw left, on one, on one, READY, BREAK!!"

This was my turn for redemption. Another draw play out of the same formation as our first play from scrimmage. I hoped for the same result.

The ball was snapped back to Sal. He faked a pass and then placed the ball in my arms. We needed yardage and I couldn't let the team down. I bulled straight ahead and lowered my shoulder into the Casey outside linebacker. He fell back but I kept my balance. I picked my head up and saw daylight in the middle of the field. I drove towards the end zone and saw a defensive back moving towards me for the tackle. At about the two yard line, I leapt forward and my momentum carried me over the Casey defender and into the end zone. Touchdown, Crandall Hawks!

I tapped my thigh where Grandpa Butch's Sixth Marine Corps Division patch lay under my pad. I blessed myself and thought that this touchdown was for my grandfather. And then I was mobbed by five crazed offensive linemen.

"Three carries, fifty seven yards," Coach Bonfiglio said as he slapped me on the helmet. "That's a pretty good pace."

I grabbed some water and tried to catch my breath on the bench. I felt great. There was no way we could lose now.

Unfortunately, Monsignor Casey marched down the field and tied up the game within four minutes. Coleman completed six passes, including a thirteen yard touchdown throw. Just like that, the score was 7-7.

I glanced at Coach B. quickly because it was pretty obvious that we were in a shootout. Coach Bonfiglio was a defensive mastermind and he hated this type of game. However, he had this look of resignation on his face, as if he knew what was in store. The team that held the ball last would probably win the game.

At the half, we led by a score of 21-20. The holder had fumbled the snap after Casey's second touchdown...that's the only reason we were winning.

There wasn't much for Coach B. to say at halftime. We all knew what was happening. Our defense was being torn apart by Coleman, who looked like a young Joe Montana. Our offense just had to keep pace and hope that the defense could rise to the occasion at least once.

Raymond was furious, as mad as I've ever seen him. He was

usually real quiet, kind of that scary kind of quiet. It actually made him more intimidating...until you got to know him. And then you found out he was terrified of his five foot mother.

Today, though, was different. Raymond called the defense together and basically tore their heads off for two minutes. The whole locker room was silent except for the sound of Raymond's voice.

Coach B. gathered the team together and said, "You heard Raymond. I don't have anything to add. Defense, suck it up...you know what you have to do. Offense...just keep scoring points." He then paused. "And you know who's waiting for us in the championship. You know them well."

Even the thought of Fairview Prep drove a lot of the team into a frenzy. Coach Bonfiglio unleashed that gem just at the right time. Raymond literally looked like he was going to kill someone. I felt like rushing out of the locker room so it wouldn't be me.

The second half resembled the first half. The two teams traded scores until their defense stopped us on fourth and two at the Casey twenty seven yard line with about three minutes left in the fourth quarter. The score was 35-35.

I jogged to the sideline and prayed that the defense could give us one more chance to win this thing. I saw Coleman break the huddle and coolly stroll to the line. Ten thousand fans screaming and he looks like it's a preseason scrimmage.

Coleman wet his fingers with his lips and the center snapped the ball. He took a quick three step drop and fired the ball fifteen yards across the middle to the big, Harvard bound tight end, Billy Duffy. Duffy carried Ricky for another six yards. First down, Casey, near mid field.

Casey didn't huddle and our defense was getting tired. Coleman called for a quick snap and threw a little swing pass to the halfback. The halfback sprinted to the sideline and darted up field for another sixteen yards. The ball was at our thirty six yard line. We couldn't stop them.

Casey kept going without the huddle. Our defensive line looked exhausted. Coach Hughes must have noticed the same thing because he called for a running play for only around the tenth time all game.

Joe Collins, the halfback, collected the perfect pitch from Coleman and followed the pulling guard and tackle. Marco was playing cornerback and managed to knock Collins out of bounds. But Collins had gained another eighteen yards.

There was 2:08 left in the game. Casey would have to run another play before the two minute warning.

Coleman barked out the signals and then dropped back to pass. There was virtually no pass rush and it seemed like the quarterback had all day to pick out an open receiver. This time, however, our defensive backs just wouldn't give their receivers an inch. Coleman threw the ball far out of bounds.

The whole offense stood on the sidelines, yelling encouragement. I saw Eduardo bless himself after the incompletion.

Second and ten on our eighteen yard line. 1:56 left to play.

Coleman completed a screen pass to Collins and Raymond dragged him down after a gain of seven. Coach B. called a timeout and summoned the entire defense over to the sidelines.

The ball was on the eleven yard line, well within their kicker's field goal range. On third and three, Coach Hughes wouldn't settle for the field goal. Coleman attempted to hit

Duffy on a slant pattern in the end zone but Marco was able to knock the pass away at the last moment. The Casey crowd cried for interference but there was no flag. The Casey field goal team jogged onto the field. It would be a twenty eight yard attempt.

With 1:43 left, the long snapper expertly hiked the ball. Coleman calmly placed the ball on the turf and the kicker made contact. Out of nowhere, Marco burst through the left side of the Casey line and dived forward. The ball grazed his left hand and fluttered through the air. It bounced off someone's helmet and Raymond quickly jumped on the ball. Crandall ball on the thirteen yard line with 1:31 to play.

The sideline mobbed the defense as they ran off the field. Sal tried to calm the huddle.

"Okay, boys, calm down, calm down. We got one timeout left...they got one, too. We have to get to their twenty yard line and give Ricky a chance to win this game. You okay, Marco?"

Marco was breathing heavily. He had played just about every snap of this game. He nodded and said, "Okay, Sal...Eu estou pronto, homem."

Sal dropped back to pass and hit Marco with a short pass. Marco sprinted up field, running with absolute abandon. He crossed the thirty yard line, tripped and went down at the thirty five. 1:12 left.

"Okay, Kyle, your turn. Clock's running...gonna run that draw play again. They won't be expecting it. Remember, we call timeout right after this play."

For the fourth time in the game, the draw play surprised the Casey defense. I couldn't believe the size of the hole...I could have walked through it and gained ten yards. But I decided to run. We'd been throwing most of the game so my legs were pretty fresh. I wasn't even touched for fifteen yards. I had to work for the other ten yards and the draw play gained twenty five yards. We were at the Casey forty yard line but the running play took plenty of time off the clock. Sal screamed for time and the clock stopped with forty five seconds remaining.

Our offense was pumped up. I glanced over at the Casey defense. They were all on one knee and guzzling water. One more big play and we had this game.

Sal hit Sammy Griffin down the sideline for another first down but Sammy wasn't able to get out of bounds. The clock continued to run as we lined up. Sal spiked the ball with twenty nine seconds left.

"No timeouts, boys. One more first down and we'll get Ricky out here to end this thing," Sal said.

Sammy made a spectacular catch on the Casey sideline which took the ball down to the nineteen yard line. It would be a thirty six yard field goal for Ricky, which probably was slightly out of his range. Although I'm certain he believed it was well within his ability to make the kick.

"Last play. If there's nothing, I'm throwing it out of bounds. No one gets tackled in bounds, okay?" Sal said.

I flared out to the sideline and was open for a split second. Sal spotted me but he was late with the pass. As he threw it, I instinctively turned into a defensive back myself. I was able to knock the ball away from the Casey cornerback. An interception would have meant a touchdown for Casey.

There were seventeen seconds left when Ricky came out to attempt a thirty six yard field goal. I was part of the field goal team and I concentrated on trying to protect the kick from the Casey kick block team which was now playing for the season and, for many of them, to continue their high school careers for one more game.

Peter Sousa's snap was a little shaky but Sal handled it perfectly and positioned the ball. I handled my block and turned and saw Ricky keep his head down and slam his foot into the football. I watched the ball sail towards the goal post.

I wasn't sure if it was good or not but I recognized the Crandall red of the crowd behind the end zone. And they were all going crazy. The kick was good!

I got to Ricky first and tackled him to the ground. The rest of the kick team jumped on top of us. The referee was blowing his whistle and threatening a penalty. I heard Coach Brennan screaming at us from the sidelines to get off the field.

There was still twelve seconds left in the game. Ricky had to collect himself and kick it off to Casey. He squibbed the kick and a Casey player smartly just fell on the ball and stopped the clock with seven seconds left. Time for Kevin Coleman to try one Hail Mary pass.

Monsignor Casey had the ball on their own forty yard line. Normally, I would figure that no high school kid could reach the end zone but I had watched Coleman the whole game. Coach Bonfiglio wasn't taking any chances.

"Donovan!" he called.

I ran to the coach. "Yeah, Coach."

"Go in for Deron, stand in the end zone and play center field," he said. As I started to run onto the field, Coach B. grabbed me. "And Kyle, don't let anyone catch that ball, you understand? I know that kid can throw the ball sixty yards."

I called Deron off the field and sprinted towards the end zone. I hadn't played a snap of defense in two years. And I hadn't played baseball in three years. And I wasn't a centerfielder, I was a third baseman.

Five Casey receivers ran towards the end zone. We only had one player rushing the passer so Coleman had plenty of time to set up and heave the ball as far as he could.

Coleman reared back and threw and I saw the ball spiraling in my direction. Two Casey receivers were readying themselves to leap for the ball. Marco, Ricky and Sammy Griffin were all converging on the ball.

Amazingly, the ball was going to reach the end zone. Six players leapt at the same time for the ball. I reached out my right hand and tried to bat the ball to the ground. Ricky was trying to do the same thing but the ball bounced off someone's shoulder pad and floated in the air. I dived and slapped the ball again and, this time, it fell harmlessly to the ground. We were playing Fairview Prep in the championship game.

Ricky, Marco and I hugged each other and fell to the ground. "É nosso destiny, homem, ele é nosso destiny, it's our destiny, Irish boy. Fairview's next!"

I ran to catch up with Kevin Coleman, who was slowly walking off the field.

I tapped his shoulder pad and said, "Great game, man. You're a great quarterback. Good luck next year."

Coleman shook my hand and smiled. "Thanks. Don't let the preppies win this thing. Good luck, Donovan."

After more celebrating in the locker room, I showered and hurried so I wouldn't miss the bus. But I doubted that even Sully would leave anyone behind today.

As I walked to the bus, I heard a familiar voice. "Kyle, Kyle."

I turned and Ashley was standing in the parking lot.

"Hey," I said.

"Hey," she said. There was a really awkward silence and then Ashley said, "Great game. You guys are really good."

"Thanks."

She took a step closer. "I'm so sorry, Kyle. I just wasn't...I just wasn't ready for all this. I am now, I promise. I want to be part of your life."

I looked around and saw Katie standing beside her car.

"Good luck, Ashley," I said, and I reached my hand out.

Ashley shook my hand and said, "I am sorry, Kyle."

"Bye, Ashley."

I jogged over to the Malibu and hugged and kissed Katie. I looked at her and said, "We're playing Fairview, Katie. Fairview."

CHAPTER TWENTY SIX

The sound of my cell phone woke me up. I rolled over and checked the alarm clock. 2:30 AM. I stumbled to my desk and picked up my phone. It was Paul.

"Uh, Paul?" I said.

I heard a big sigh on the other end. Paul then said, "Hey, man. Any chance of crashing at your house tonight?"

"Here, in Crandall? Don't you live in Fairview?"

"Yeah...but...it's a long story," Paul said. He sounded sadder than I could remember.

"Yeah, yeah, of course you can stay here. Where are you?"

"Look out your front window," Paul said. Sure enough, there was Paul sitting on the hood of his car, waving.

"I'll be right down," I said.

I went downstairs, opened the front door and let Paul in the hallway.

After we climbed the stairs to the second floor apartment, we both sat in the kitchen.

"You want something to drink or eat?" I said. I felt like Grandpa Butch.

Paul shook his head. "Nah, I'm all set, thanks."

I took a seat and said, "What's going on?"

Paul remained silent for a few moments. He then said, "My mom threw me out of the house last night. She invited this guy over for dinner and..."

"What'd you do?"

"The guy's a loser, Kyle. He and my mom have been going away almost every weekend. I don't think he even knows my name. Anyway, I come home for supper after practice and here's this guy sitting in the living room watching some stock market show. He didn't even acknowledge me. Imagine that? So, I ask my mother if there's anything for supper and she said we'd all be sitting down in a few minutes. Sitting down? All of a sudden we're the Cosby show...one, big happy family."

"Doesn't sound too bad so far," I said.

Paul shrugged. "Maybe not to you but it just ticked me off, you know? I mean, I don't even know this guy's name. So, I say that I'll go out and eat and then this guy says, 'Hey, your mother cooked for you.' She cooked for me? She's barely cooked in at least three years since Dad left! So, I said to the guy, 'When did this become your business?'

"Uh oh," I said.

"Yeah. So he stands up and says, 'Like I said, treat your mother with some respect.' The guy weighs about 150 pounds," Paul said with disdain. "Butchie would kick the crap out of him. So I look at my mother and say, 'Mom, who is this guy?' And she says 'This is Robert, son.' Well, I made it clear that I didn't want Robert telling me anything. So then my mother said it would be best if I left."

I sat silently. What could I say? His mother kicked him out of the house to eat dinner with some guy named Robert. That sucked.

Paul continued. "So I call my father and he doesn't pick up his cell phone. I say, screw it, I'm just gonna drive into Boston and find him. I drive into Beacon Hill and I see him walking up the front stairs of his place with some girl. I say, 'Dad!' No response. So I say, 'Dad' again. This time he turns around and says, 'Paul?'

"What happened next?" I ask.

"I say to my father, 'Hey, could I stay here for the night, Mom kicked me out.' He walks real fast over to me and pulls out his wallet and says, 'Busy time for me, son. I don't really have any food in the fridge either.' He takes a hundred bucks out of his wallet and just hands it to me. Then he turns and says, 'Call me tomorrow, buddy.' And he left me standing in front of my car with a hundred bucks. So then I came here. I didn't know what else to do."

I looked at Grandpa Butch's two family house and then noticed the lack of trees, the postage stamp front yard, the chairs on the street protecting precious parking spaces shoveled out from a recent dusting of snow. And I felt lucky to be here. And I felt really badly for my friend.

"Alright, man. Come on upstairs. You can sleep in the living room."

Paul took his bag and followed me up the stairs. Mom was waiting at the top and said, "What's going on, Kyle?"

"Hi, Mrs. Donovan," Paul said.

"Hi Paul," Mom answered.

I looked at Mom and raised my eyebrows. She nodded and grimaced slightly. Mom knew all about the dynamics of the Elliot household.

I grabbed a blanket and a couple of pillows for Paul. "Can you tuck me in, too, Uncle Kyle?" he said.

I laughed. "I'm not gonna read you a story either."

As I started to my room on the third floor, Paul said, "Hey, Kyle."

I turned around. "Yeah?"

"Thanks, man."

I nodded and went to bed.

At 6:15, my cell phone rang again. I could barely sputter out a "Hello?"

"Hey, I got breakfast all cooked down here," Grandpa said.

Home from the hospital a couple of days after almost dying from pneumonia and he's cooking breakfast.

"Yeah, okay, Grandpa, I'll be right down."

"And wake Paul up. I got something for him, too," Grandpa said.

I had no idea how Grandpa Butch knew that Paul was staying with us but, for some reason, it really didn't surprise me. He always seemed to be a step ahead of everyone else.

I whacked Paul on the arm and took the pillows away from underneath his head.

"Hey, what are you doing?" he asked.

I motioned downstairs. "Come on, wipe the drool off your face. Grandpa Butch cooked some breakfast."

We both went downstairs and I could smell that familiar aroma of Jimmy Dean sausages and scrambled eggs.

"Hey, Grandpa," I called as we entered through the front door.

Grandpa Butch emerged from the kitchen, looking a bit pale but pretty healthy, his white tee shirt freshly ironed, the tattoos visible under the short sleeves.

"Well, well, well, there's himself and some refugee from Fairview. Sit down, boys," Grandpa said.

We both dived into our plates full of eggs, French toast and sausages. After he briefly came up for air, Paul said, "This is good, Butch...real good."

Grandpa smiled and said, "Good, good, Paul. Now, what's going on with you?"

Paul glanced at me and then said, "Ah, same old stuff at home, Butch. Just a little worse, that's all. My parents...it's just..." His voice trailed off.

Grandpa nodded. "Yeah, parents can really screw up sometimes. Believe me, I know that." We sat in silence for a minute or two, the quiet broken only by the sound of my chewing.

"But sometimes, parents need a second chance," Grandpa said. "Maybe, sometimes, you have to give them a chance to fix stuff."

Paul looked at the table and said, "I don't know, Butch. I don't know if I can forgive them this time."

Grandpa Butch looked him the eyes. "You gotta be able to forgive, Paul. I'm an old man...take it from me, you have to forgive, even when you don't want to sometimes. That's your family." Grandpa looked at me. "That's all you got, when it comes to it."

Paul's phone rang. "Hey, Mom," he said.

I brought my dishes over to the sink and Grandpa put the eggs and milk into the refrigerator. Paul stood and walked into hallway. After a couple of minutes, he returned to the kitchen.

"I guess I'll go home this morning," he said with a shrug. He stuck his hand out to Grandpa Butch. "Thanks for the advice,

Butch. My mom deserves another chance. But my dad...I don't know."

Paul went upstairs and grabbed his bag. I walked him out to his car.

"Alright, I guess I'll see you Saturday," Paul said. "That's gonna be kind of weird, isn't it?"

I nodded. "Yeah, at least you're not playing defense."

"Yeah." Paul started walking to his car and then turned around. "I didn't want to tell you this, man but..."

"What?" I asked.

"Some of the meatheads are out to get you, you know what I mean? Jon Davis and a couple of other skumbags. Mainly Jon, though. They're talking about it all the time in school. Jon said he'd give anyone a hundred bucks if they sent you out of the game."

I scoffed. "Not scared of them, Paul. Not scared at all. It's just a football game, you know? Just a football game. One team will win and then life will go on. I'm glad you told me, though."

Paul shook my hand and said, "My last game for Fairview Prep. Next year, who knows?"

I started talking in a PA announcer's voice. "Starting at tight end, for Crandall High School, PAUL ELLIOT!"

Paul laughed. "You never know, you never know."

He turned the key and I watched the BMW navigate around the various cones and chairs up Lodge Avenue.

I checked the clock on my cell phone. It was 7:30. Time to get to school.

The school was literally in a frenzy over the game against

Fairview. Even the school police working the metal detectors were in the spirit. One of them flipped me a Ring Ding when I showed up at school on Wednesday morning. When a kid in line asked for a Ring Ding, the guard scoffed, "That's Kyle Donovan... Now empty your pockets."

I felt a little bad about the special treatment but the Ring Ding tasted good.

The whole school had been decorated by the cheerleaders and the newly formed Spirit Committee. Red streamers, posters and photos lined the walls of the school halls. I think that even the rival gangs had called a truce for this week.

Kids were yelling, "Donovan!" and waving or flashing gang signals at me all day. I always just waved back, never returning the gang sign. The thought of me in a street gang was just too ridiculous to imagine, anyway.

I was hanging out in the computer lab after lunch when a junior in my Algebra II class came over to my chair.

"Hey, Donovan."

I nodded and said, "How you doing, Andre?"

There was an awkward pause as I returned to surfing the internet.

"You gotta beat them, Donovan."

I looked up at Andre. "Yeah, we'll beat them."

"No...I mean, you gotta beat them, man."

Andre was staring at me like I had some sort of magical power to guarantee Crandall the victory.

"Yeah, okay, Andre. We'll try our best, you know what I mean?"

Andre sat on the table beside the computer and said, "My mother worked in Fairview...she cleaned a house for a rich family. She took the bus out there every morning and worked for them for four years. Then one day, they fired her for stealing...just like that, it was all over. They accused her of stealing...my mother...stealing!" Andre grimaced and looked away. "And then they threatened to call Immigration on her. She barely speaks any English...she never took anything her whole life and now she's a thief and she's gonna be deported back to Haiti."

I sighed. "That's too bad, Andre."

He nodded. "Yeah, it is...it's too bad. But you're from there, you know what it's like. This game means a lot, Kyle...not just to me, either. A lot of people think we got something to prove."

I shook Andre's hand and said, "Alright, like I said, I'll do my best."

"We gotta win, Kyle," Andre said and then walked away.

Now I was starting to feel some pressure. A football game had turned into some type of war.

I logged off the computer and went down the café to buy a burrito. Mrs. DeCaro, the lunch lady, greeted me with her heavily Italian accent.

"How you doing, Kyle?" she said.

"Good, good, Mrs. DeCaro." I almost called her Mrs. LoGrasso because we always kidded Sal that they resembled each other. "Could I have a burrito, please?"

"Sure, sure, we get you a burrito. Big game on Saturday, huh?" Mrs. DeCaro asked with a smile.

"Yeah, big one."

"You guys gotta win, Kyle. You win for everyone around here, capice?"

I nodded. "We'll win, Mrs. DeCaro."

I think she was satisfied with that answer because she flashed a big smile as she put the burrito on my tray.

I took out my wallet and prepared to pay at the cash register. Mrs. DeCaro looked horrified. "No, no, Kyle...you no pay. You win Saturday."

I shrugged and walked over to an empty table. I had already eaten one lunch but I was still hungry. I was hoping to quickly eat alone but my History teacher, Mr. Irwin, was supervising the cafeteria and he took a seat across from me.

"Hey, Kyle," he said.

Mr. Irwin was one of my favorite teachers but I prayed that he wasn't going to talk about the game against Fairview.

He folded his hands and said, "So, big one on Saturday."

Wrong again. Mr. Irwin hadn't discussed football at all throughout the season. He seemed too mesmerized by Westward Expansion and War of 1812. But here we were.

"Yeah, big game, Mr. Irwin."

He leaned back and said, "Must be a little weird, playing against your old school in such a big game."

I tried to follow my mother's advice and not talk with my mouth full. After I swallowed, I said, "Yeah, it's a little strange."

Mr. Irwin was about to continue the conversation when the sound of a student shouting a loud profanity shattered the relative calm. He looked at the student, smiled and said, "Well, back to work. See you in class."

I devoured the rest of my burrito, grabbed my backpack and hurried out of the café. I tried to think of a safe place where no one wanted to discuss the Fairview game. But I just couldn't think of any.

CHAPTER TWENTY SEVEN

Wednesday was a light day of practice. We hit the field with helmets and no shoulder pads for about an hour and then we headed inside to watch the film of the Fairview playoff game.

During the film, the Fairview advantage became very obvious: Size. When I played at Fairview, I never really focused on how big we really were. Now, from an opponent's perspective, it was ridiculous.

Jon Davis must have weighed 280 pounds. Gardner and Stein were easily 260-270 pounds each. I glanced over at Eduardo, who was eating a big bag of Doritos. Eddy weighed around 255 pounds but I think that he had lost some weight during the season. Peter Sousa was the next biggest at around 240 pounds. The rest of the guys were smaller...but incredibly tough. That was our hope: our toughness. I was pretty certain that there wasn't physically or mentally tougher team in the Commonwealth of Massachusetts than the Crandall Hawks.

The coaching matchup was even. There wasn't a whole lot of difference between Coach Bonfiglio and Coach Pearson. I think that Coach B. could win in Fairview and Coach Pearson would do well at Crandall. It was like choosing between Belichick and Parcells.

There was no question that we had major work to do before

Saturday and not much time.

After the film, Coach B. said, "Alright, boys, there they are. Big, strong and well coached. Definitely the best team we've played all year. Their size is impressive, no doubt about that. But we can beat them...I know that we can beat them. We only have two days of practice so we have to make them count." Coach Brennan stood up and started handing out packets. "This is everything we got on Fairview."

The packet was twelve pages of detailed player profiles, tendencies and Fairview formations and plays. Now there was conclusive evidence of what I had always suspected: that Coach Bonfiglio and Coach Brennan never slept.

We broke into meetings for a while and then Coach B. sent us home at around 7:00. Thankfully, I had hardly any homework. Most teachers weren't even bothering to assign homework this week. Although Mr. Bruno couldn't resist scheduling an Algebra test for Friday. He just can't help himself.

Katie picked me up and we stopped at Dunkin Donuts on the way home. I didn't realize how hungry I was until I saw the picture of the bacon, egg and cheese croissant in the window.

"You okay?" Katie asked after we sat down with our food.

I nodded as I took a massive bite of my croissant.

Katie smiled. "Why don't you finish chewing before you answer."

I swallowed and then said, "Yeah, we're ready to go. This is it, you know?"

Katie shook her head. "I didn't ask about the team, I asked if you were okay."

More proof that girls were much smarter than guys. "Yeah, I'm fine."

Katie wouldn't let go of this. "You seemed kind of, I don't know, jumpy in school."

I shrugged. "I'm pretty nervous, you know? There just seems to be a lot of pressure to win this game and I guess I'm feeling that pressure...maybe even more than the other guys because of everything.

"I've never seen the school like this before. It's like this game means so much to everyone. It's actually kind of scary," Katie said.

"You're a native Crandallite or Crandallingian or whatever. Why is this so important? I know Fairview's a rich town but there a lot of rich towns. Why does this mean so much to everyone? I know why it means so much to me but that's a whole different story."

Katie took a sip of water. "You're right. It's like something has happened to the whole city. A lot of people know what happened at that party you guys went to." She paused and then said, "What exactly happened at that party, anyway? You never told me the whole story."

I really didn't feel like rehashing that again. "I told you, remember? The Fairview kids had weed and blamed it on Eddy, Ray and Sal. There was a fight and we took off. That's what happened." Of course, I had left out Ashley's role in the story.

Katie nodded with a look on her face that she knew that I wasn't telling the entire truth but she was going to let it go.

For some reason, when I was with Katie, I just talked way too much. "There's other stuff, too. Paul says that one of the Fairview meatheads has put a bounty of a hundred bucks on my head for the game. If someone knocks me out of the game, he gets the hundred."

"Oh my God, that's terrible!" Katie said.

I shrugged. "It's really not that big a deal. I keep telling myself it's only a football game, you know? Most of the Fairview kids are pretty clean players and the coach is a really good guy. So, I'm not worried." Actually, I was a little concerned.

"Shouldn't you tell Coach Bonfiglio?" Katie asked.

I laughed softly. "No, Katie, I'm not going to do that."

"Now, I'm worried," Katie said.

I reached for her hand. "Don't worry about anything. It's all talk, that's all. Everything will be fine. I just wish the game was tomorrow. I don't know if I'll make it to Saturday."

Katie dropped me off at home. I climbed the stairs and heard Mom singing as I opened the front door. It still seemed a little strange that Grandpa Butch was no longer living upstairs.

"You hungry, honey?" Mom called from the kitchen.

"Nah, I'm all set, Mom. I ate at Dunkin Donuts. I think I'll just go to bed...I'm pretty tired."

Mom walked into the hallway and said, "Is everything okay?" What was it with women? Were they all mind readers?

I nodded. "Yeah, I'm just tired."

"Any homework?" Mom asked.

"No teacher is assigning anything this week. It's like the whole world has stopped for this game."

"I was kind of getting that impression. You alright with all of that?" Mom asked.

I wasn't ready for another long discussion about my feelings about the Fairview game. "Yeah, I'm fine. Like I said, just really tired."

Mom looked at me skeptically...kind of like the way Katie

looked at me. "Okay, then, get some sleep."

I lay in my bed and stared at the ceiling for a while. Eventually, I drifted off to sleep.

I woke up feeling guilty. I felt guilty about the stupid party at Ashley's house. I hoped that wasn't the reason why everyone was so hyped up about the game. I asked myself over and over why I wanted to bring the Crandall guys to the party. Was I trying to prove something to Fairview? Was I looking for some trouble? Was I trying to drive Ashley away? I shook my head. I was feeling a big headache coming on.

As I was getting some books out of my locker after second period, I heard someone say my name. I turned and Freddie from MS-13 was standing in front of me.

I wasn't as intimidated by the tombstone tattoo or the scars anymore. But I never wanted to upset Freddie in any way. We had been on very good terms since our near fight on the first day of school and I wanted to keep it that way.

"Hey, how you doing, Freddie?" I asked.

Freddie shook his head, his black eyes reflecting what I thought was sadness. "Not too good, muchacho. I don't like what I'm hearing, don't like it at all."

Uh oh. "What's the matter, man?"

Freddie looked up and the sad eyes had turned very menacing all of a sudden. "I heard about the bounty, Irish. The bounty, man. I'm not down with any bounty, you know what I'm saying, amigo?'

I nodded.

Freddie took a step closer to me until I could smell the last cigarette he smoked. "I'm gonna take care of it, amigo."

As much as I now disliked Jon Davis and friends, I wasn't looking for a driveby. I had to think fast.

"Thanks, Freddie, I mean, I really appreciate it but there's not gonna be any bounty. It's just all talk, you know? Believe me, nothing's gonna happen. It's all talk."

Freddie took a step back and seemed to be pondering what I had just said. He suddenly nodded and said, "Okay, Irish." He started to walk away and then turned around. "But listen to me. If I see anything, and I mean anything, homeboy, that looks, you know, not right, they're gonna pay. I'm talking a twisted ankle, anything man, there's gonna be some Fairview blood spilled." Freddie then smiled and winked at me. I think he was rooting for the sprained ankle to happen.

So now I could feel guilty about a potential gang war, too.

All I wanted to do was to go home and hibernate until the game on Saturday but school and practice kept getting in the way.

We didn't wear pads at Thursday afternoon's practice. The temperature had dropped about thirty degrees over the course of the day. It was freezing but the weatherman had said that it would warm up a bit by Saturday. I hoped so.

We ran through our entire offensive and defensive game plan. No conditioning at the end of practice. If we weren't in shape by now, a few sprints weren't going to get us there.

After practice, I took a long hot shower, trying to push the cold out of my system. As I dried off in front of my locker, Eduardo came by.

"This is it, Irish boy, this is it," Eddy said.

"Almost there, Eddy, almost time."

Eduardo grimaced. "Payback, man, payback. That's what's on my Brazilian mind, menino."

I nodded. "It's still a football game, Eddy. Remember that."

Eduardo chuckled and raised his eyebrows in surprise. "Just a football game? Hey, Monsignor Walsh was just a football game. This is different, man. This is payback." Eduardo slapped me on the shoulder, put in his earplugs and walked away.

As I threw on a pair of sweatpants and sweatshirt, I thought about what Eddy had said. It was payback for Eddy and Sal and Raymond. It was pride and a whole lot of other stuff for Andre and Mrs. DeCaro and a bunch of other people in Crandall. What was it for me?

I shook my head and sighed. It was more than a football game. Much more. I couldn't really explain what it was, but it was more than a football game. How could I wait until Saturday?

Wasn't there a movie about World War II called "The Longest Day"? Well, Friday was my longest day. A forty five minute class period seemed like an eternity. At least Mr. Irwin showed a movie on Andrew Carnegie, which was pretty interesting. And thankfully, Mr. Bruno decided to postpone the Algebra test until Monday. Even the great Mr. Bruno had to cave to the reality of this situation. Although he wasn't happy about it at all.

I kept staring at the clock but it never seemed to move. By some miracle, the bell rang at 2:20 and school ended. Another short practice and then a spaghetti dinner in the café sponsored by the Spirit Club.

Even though we hadn't worn pads for three days, I think that this could have been our best week of practice for the year. There was this quiet confidence. The guys were going about their business but no one was acting like this was just another game. We all understood the importance of the game (you couldn't escape that with everyone in the city reminding you all the time) but not one player was scared, not even the sophmores. We had proven a lot to ourselves over the past three months. This was the biggest test but we had passed every test before.

At the end of practice, Coach B. gathered us around and said, "No senior rituals this year. This game tomorrow is enough for all of us. You know I've said too much this year. Let the captains say something. Marco, Sal, Peter...come on up front."

The three stood before us and we cheered loudly. Peter Sousa spoke first and was brief. Not surprising since Peter never said much. His blocking usually spoke volumes.

Sal spoke next. He was probably the most popular kid on the team, always willing to help someone out, making sure the younger kids weren't picked on, encouraging everyone. He cleared his throat and said, "I really don't know what to say. I mean, what a season, right? This has been a dream come true, fellas." He pointed to the entire team. "Everyone one of you has made this dream come true." Sal paused and then screamed at the top of his lungs, "FAIRVIEW, BABY! This is it...Crandall High, SUPER BOWL CHAMPS!" We all went crazy, yelling and clapping.

It had started to rain softly but I bet most of us wanted to stay on this field for as long as we possibly could. Marco smiled and said, "Can you believe it? Huh? Here we are, man, last game for Crandall for a lot of us. Yo, this is the biggest game in history coming up here. The Super Bowl, man...Bacia Super! Crandall gonna make history tomorrow, meninos. I ain't much of public speaker but..." Marco paused and looked at the ground and then looked up at us through the rain. "I love you guys."

There was silence on the practice field for a moment. Forty three high school boys, by this time dirty and completely drenched by rain and sweat, stood alone in their own thoughts. And then Eddy yelled, "SUPER BOWL, BABY!" and everyone raised their helmets to the sky. "Okay, boys, bring it in...one last time!" Sal said.

I felt this weird mixture of emotions as I walked off the field. The rain was coming down hard now but I didn't feel wet or cold. I just felt really emotional. I mean, I wasn't going to cry or anything but it was a different feeling. Different than when I found out my parents were splitting up, different than when I moved in with Grandpa Butch, different than when Grandpa Butch got sick, different than when Mom came home...a lot has happened these past three months.

Someone slapped me on the back. I turned and saw Marco. "This is it, Irish boy. You ready, boy?"

I nodded.

Marco smiled. "Remember that first day in the weight room?"

I chuckled. "I'll never forget that, buddy."

"I was a tolo, man, you know that, right?"

"Oh yeah, Marco, that's all in the past. You painted my grandfather's apartment, remember?"

Marco smiled again. "That's right, I did do that, didn't I?"

We walked together for a few more yards and then Marco said, "I heard from Bentley, man."

I stopped and said, "You're kidding me. What's going on?"

Now Marco sported a huge grin. "Full boat, menino. Full ride, playing football right up there in Waltham. My mother and sister can come see me play every week, man"

I shook Marco's hand and slapped him on the shoulder.

"You let me do it, Irish boy," Marco said.

I shrugged. "Hey, it was best for the team."

"Yeah, but most guys wouldn't have done that. Thanks, man."

I nodded.

"Next year, that's your year, Irish. Two thousand yards. I'll be disappointed if you don't get that much."

After I showered, I sat in front of my locker for a long time. It was noisy as usual, guys talking about girls, music, movies, lunch...just about any subject you could think of.

Finally, I stood up and changed. It was six thirty...the spaghetti dinner started in fifteen minutes.

I just couldn't get over this emotional feeling I had inside. I wasn't even really nervous about the game. It was anxiety, not nervousness...at least that's what I kept telling myself. I checked my cell phone. Paul had called me at 5:30. I wondered how he was feeling.

The clock read 6:35. In eighteen hours and twenty five minutes, the ball would be kicked. I wonder if this feeling would be gone by then.

Chapter Twenty Eight

I woke up like a shot on Saturday morning. It was 7:10...pretty early, but I had a real good sleep. I immediately rose from the bed and wandered downstairs. I ventured outside briefly to get the Tribune and felt the rush of cold air. It was cold but what could you expect in December? At least the sky was only partly cloudy. A great day to play football.

I knocked on Grandpa's door knowing that he would be awake. Sure enough, he quickly answered the door. "Well, it's himself," he said. I still hadn't figured that "himself" thing but Grandpa's buddies said the same thing to each other all the time.

I followed Grandpa into the kitchen and took my customary seat.

"So, we ready?" he asked with a smile.

Tough question. Was I ready? I think so but I was nervous...like can't stop shaking type of nervous.

I nodded. "Yeah, I'm ready, Grandpa but..."

Grandpa scrunched up his eyes. "But what, Boyo?"

I sighed and said, "I'm nervous, Grandpa. I never felt this way before a game. It's not like I'm nervous about getting hit or anything like that. It's just a different feeling, something really different."

"It's been quite a run for you, Kyle," Grandpa Butch said. "Quite a run." He laughed that familiar deep laugh. "Who would have thought it, huh? The Super Bowl...against Fairview. Sounds like one of those sports novels or movies."

We sat in silence for a couple of moments and then Grandpa said, "I'm not sure if I've really told you this, Boyo, but...these last few months, well...I can't tell you how much they mean to me." Grandpa stared straight at me, the lines in his permanently tanned face appearing deeper, the eyes bluer than ever. "To have you with me at this stage in my life, through cancer, through pneumonia...you're a special kid, Kyle, a special kid. And I'm not talking about football because, in the end, it's just not that important. But who you are as a person, you're special, Boyo." He paused and smiled. "Can't believe that you have some of my genes. No matter what happens today, think about who you are as a person, what you've accomplished. You've been tested in so many different ways, too many tests for a seventeen year old. And look at you, a man among men at age seventeen. I'm proud of you, Boyo, prouder than you could ever imagine."

There was quiet again, not an awkward silence but a peaceful, satisfying quiet that I think could only happen between best friends.

"Of course, you're nervous," Grandpa said, breaking the silence. "You can't let all this hype around town get to you. Go out and play the game like you've played every game this year. And then walk off the field with your head high. That's all there is...you play with pride, you play like Kyle Donovan always plays."

I nodded. Grandpa made sense, like he always makes sense.

Grandpa stood and walked over to the refrigerator. "You hungry?" he asked.

I shook my head. "Nah, my stomach's doing cartwheels right now."

Grandpa chuckled. "You gotta eat something. What time does the bus leave?"

The game was to be played at the new field over at Paulsen University in Boston. "Bus leaves at 9:45," I answered.

"Don't be late, Sully will leave without you. He'd leave without Tom Brady if he was late. Have an English muffin or something."

My stomach was feeling better so I accepted Grandpa's offer of English muffins. They tasted good and my stomach stopped doing flips. I'm sure they'd come back at game time.

Sal picked me up and we made our final drive of the season to the Crandall High School locker room.

We stopped at a red light in Hubbard Square and Sal said, "You ready, *Paisan*?"

I nodded. I was going to say something but any words at this point would be useless. We both knew what was at stake.

It was tough for Sal to sit in silence. "Hey, I heard from the Westfield State coach. I'm making a visit up there on Tuesday. You ever been to Westfield?"

I shook my head. "Nah...I think it's off Route 2 somewhere. It's outside of Route 128 so you'll probably get lost."

Sal laughed. "Yeah...I gotta get that GPS. You think they would put it in a car this old?"

I chuckled. "No way. But seriously, man, congratulations. You'll do great up there."

As we approached the high school, the Spirit Club and the

Hawks Nest were waiting for us in the parking lot. When someone spotted Sal's car, they all started screaming and cheering. It was two and a half hours from kickoff and the lot was almost full. Some of the kids were tailgating and the Hawks Nest guys must have bought twenty dozen donuts. They also had enough coffee to supply the whole city. Everyone was fired up for the game.

Sal pulled into one of the few remaining open spots and parked the car. As he took the key out of the ignition, he said, "What a year, huh? What a freaking year. Who would have thought it." And then he added, "Not over yet, though, Irish boy. Not over yet. We gotta get it done today."

As I climbed out of the car, I started to feel more confident. We were ready for this game. Our coaches were ready, the captains were ready, the whole city was ready. We may lose but it wouldn't happen because of lack of effort.

The locker room was quiet. Guys were carefully inserting pads into their freshly washed and dried uniforms. Marco sat with his back against his locker, his eyes closed, head nodding, listening to the constant beat of hip hop music.

I took my game pants out of the backpack, reached into my locker and began putting the pads into the slots. I always did this slowly. I slid Grandpa Butch's Marine Corps patch and the prayer card under the right thigh pad.

As I was pulling on the pants, I heard Coach Brennan yell, "Kyle Donovan!"

He didn't have to say anything else. Once Coach yelled your name, your only option was to get to the coach's room in thirty seconds or less.

I rushed to put on my pants and then jogged barefoot to the

coach's office.

Coach Bonfiglio sat in his office chair, looking calm, almost serene. He smiled and said, "So here we are, Kyle. Would you believe it?"

I nodded. "Unbelievable, Coach...unbelievable."

Coach glanced at Coach Brennan and then said, "I heard about the bounty on your head. Through the grapevine. You okay?"

"Yeah, I'm fine, Coach. To tell you the truth, I don't really take it seriously. Most of those guys aren't "bounty" types, you know what I mean?"

Coach B. leaned back and put his hands behind his head. "Well, I'm planning to speak to Coach Pearson before the game about it."

Oh no...please don't do that, I thought to myself. Everything would just escalate.

"It's pretty serious stuff, Kyle," Coach Brennan said.

I sighed and said, "Coach, could you please not say anything to Coach Pearson? I'm telling you...nothing's gonna happen. It's just one loudmouth up there. I'd appreciate it, Coach."

Coach B. looked again at Coach Brennan, the way he always did. They were able to communicate without words. I was convinced of it.

Coach B. leaned forward. "Okay, Kyle. But if anything weird happens, anything at all, I'm stopping the game and informing the referee. You got that?"

I nodded.

"You ready?" Coach Brennan asked.

I smiled. "Ready's not the word, Coach."

I hurried back to my locker and gathered up my shoulder

pads, cleats and helmet. Sully was already beeping the horn and it was only 9:40.

There wasn't much traffic and we arrived at the field at about 10:15. Paulsen University had installed new turf two years earlier and the campus was beautiful...trees and flowers everywhere. It was hard to believe we were in the middle of a major city.

We took our gear to our locker room. The backs and receivers would go up to the field, stretch out and play catch for a while. The linemen would meet with their coaches and then go up to the field and beat the crap out of each other. I kind of felt badly for linemen before the games. There really wasn't much for them to do.

There were a few people milling around the concession stand as we walked to the sideline. As I stretched, I noticed the Fairview bus rolling into the parking lot. I tried not to look as the players exited. Coaches usually encouraged their players not to look at the other team. Coach Bonfiglio was just the opposite. He noticed the bus and then said, "Take a good look, boys. Take a good look. The preppies have arrived. Thought they'd be taking limos to the game." I glanced up at Coach B. and he winked. Even great coaches had to play the socioeconomic card every once in a while.

We finished stretching, played catch and ran through some plays for about a half hour. Coach Brennan whistled us together and then we headed back to the locker room to put on the pads and get ready to play for real.

It was after 11:00 and the stadium was filling up quickly. I noticed Coach Pearson leading the Fairview boys out of the visitors' locker room and toward the field. They all wore their helmets but I recognized every one of them.

I found Paul and he smiled and nodded. As I passed the team, I heard Jon Davis' voice. "It's all over today, Donovan. All over, boy." He started clapping. "Oh yeah, all over for Kyle Donovan today."

For some reason, I stopped and said, "Shut up, Davis. Just shut up."

This was a huge mistake. I had told myself over and over that I wouldn't take any bait, that I would just play the game and then move on with my life. But I just couldn't help myself.

Jon started laughing loudly. "Listen to this...big tough guy with his Crandall friends. You're really scary, Kyle...real scary. Hey, do me a favor, will you? I need my lawn raked next weekend. Maybe you and a couple of your amigos can take care of that for me."

I was about to respond when I saw Sal rush past me like a lightning bolt. He lowered his shoulder into Jon's ample waist and actually brought the big guy down. Within seconds, there was a full-fledged brawl which got worse when our linemen came storming out of the locker room.

Coaches from both teams jumped in the middle of the scuffle and the whole thing lasted less than a minute. I felt someone grab me from behind with a death grip and I figured it was Paul.

He released me and I turned around. It was Todd Gardner.

"Hey, Kyle, don't pay attention to that fathead." He stuck out his hand. We shook and then Todd said, "Hey, man, no hard feelings about that party, I hope. We were losers, man, real losers. Good luck today." I shook Todd's hand again and then he said, "Don't worry about that bounty stuff. No one took

Davis up on his offer. Everyone knows he's a jackass." Coach Pearson was screaming at his team to gather up. Todd smiled and jogged away.

I felt a light tap on my helmet and Jeremy Stein ran by, yelling, "Don't listen to Davis, Kyle. Good luck, man." I felt better.

By this time, Coach Bonfiglio was screaming at us to get into the locker room. It was hard to hear him above Eduardo yelling in Portuguese but we all got the message.

When we got into the locker room, I had never seen Coach Bonfiglio so worked up. "Get your pads on," he yelled. He slammed his forearm against an empty locker. "So this is what it comes to, huh? Wanna fulfill every stereotype, every fear people have?" Coach lowered his voice. "No way...no way. We've come too far, men, we've come way too far."

Coach pointed at Eduardo and said quietly, "Is this what you want, Eddy? You want all those nice people out there from Fairview to be talking about the big Brazilian fool from Crandall? Some out of control thug from the ghetto with no discipline? Huh?"

Coach walked up to Eduardo and grabbed his facemask. "You beat him on that field, Eddy, you beat him on the field! That's where you show them you're better than him. Because you are better than him...better in every way possible, on and off the field. And then, after the game, you smile at them and point to the scoreboard. You don't say anything...just point. You understand?"

Eduardo nodded silently but there was this fierce look in his eyes. If I were Jon Davis, I would be afraid, very afraid.

Coach B. sighed deeply and said, "Everyone up here boys.

We have time for a story." He looked around the locker room for a moment, at 43 kids who probably represented every possible human emotion. "When I was nineteen, I dropped out of college. I was playing ball up at Dartmouth." Coach stopped and smiled. "Ivy League? Imagine that? Anyway, I had a great freshman year, I was doing pretty well in school, the rich girls liked me but the season ended and I started drinking and goofing around. Drinking to forget, drinking to remember, I guess...I won't bore you with the details. I was this kid from Crandall with all these rich kids and then I just started acting like I thought everyone expected me to act. Hey, everyone loved me...life of the party and all that. Then one morning at about 3:00, I took a baseball bat to the Dean of Students' car. Smashed the thing to pieces...I was out of my mind. Don't ask me why...I barely remember doing it. Anyway, I have a hearing and they end up throwing me out of school. There were two kids with me...both kids' fathers were distinguished alumni of Dartmouth. I get expelled, they do community service and pay a fine. My mother..." Coach B. stopped and shook his head. "She was a single mother...we lived down in the Brickworks and she was so proud of me...just like your parents. And I disappointed her, and everyone, so much. So I said, screw it and I enlisted in the Marine Corps. It was 1970 and I was headed to Vietnam when most of the other guys were coming home." Coach B. paused and stared at the floor for a minute. "Vietnam, boys...just like Iraq but worse. So I play the fool and land in a hospital bed with half my foot blown off. And I start drinking again and I kept drinking...until I quit seventeen years ago. Haven't had a drop since. So what's this story all about?"

I think everyone in the room knew what the story was all

about. Coach Bonfiglio was speaking almost in a whisper. "Don't play the fool, guys. Don't make the same mistakes I did. Show this team, these fans, show everyone how we play football in Crandall. We play clean, we play hard and we kick butt." Coach straightened his shoulders and his voice began to rise. "You take it to this team and you keep on taking it to this team! No one deserves this more than you, NO ONE!" Coach B. was pointing his finger and my heart was pounding like I don't remember it pounding before. "You are the Crandall Hawks! You play with pride, you leave everything on that field and every last person here will remember THIS for the rest of their lives: they saw the toughest high school team they've ever seen stomp all over Fairview Prep!!"

By this point, Coach B. was screaming at the top of his lungs and we were in such a frenzy that we might not be able to wait until kickoff to hit someone.

We sprinted onto the field sounding like crazed escapees from some other planet. It was game time.

Chapter Twenty Nine

City kids versus the preppies. The local news media had been playing this theme the whole week. All the news stations were there and the game was being broadcast live on local cable. Paulsen Stadium seated over twenty thousand and there wasn't an empty seat in the house.

The sun that shone so brilliantly in the early morning had given way to clouds and I could already feel a mist in the air. Both teams were run oriented so a little drizzle or rain wouldn't favor either side.

My heart just wouldn't stop bounding. I tried not to bounce around when last season's tenth place finisher on American Idol sung the national anthem . I knew that Grandpa Butch would be watching and any sign of disrespect for the flag would not be received lightly.

Finally, the pregame festivities were over and the captains met at midfield. Sal took Coach Bonfiglio's advice and grudgingly shook hands with the Fairview captains. He wasn't happy about the situation but he had no choice. Coach B. would definitely sit him, championship game or no championship game.

We won the toss and I strapped up my helmet and now I started bouncing. Coach B. called us together for the final Hail Mary and "Mary, Queen of Victory, pray for us!" of the season.

I raced onto the field and tried to soak in the atmosphere. I slapped Marco and Sammy on the pads. I glanced over at the Fairview sidelines and saw Coach Pearson pacing, a student manager furiously trying to keep up behind him so the coach's headphones would remain intact.

The whistle blew and the ball landed in Marco's arms on the fourteen yard line. We set up the wedge and I looked for someone to block. Sammy and I led Marco straight up the middle where we double teamed number 33. Marco then cut to the sidelines and picked up another ten or twelve yards. Crandall first down on their own thirty eight yard line.

Marco rose slowly and limped into the huddle. "You alright, amigo?" Eduardo asked him.

Marco nodded. "Yeah, yeah, I'm fine...just landed on my ankle a little funny, that's all."

Sal sprinted into the huddle and took charge. "Here we go, boys. First play...make it count. Tight I, toss right, on one, on one, ready BREAK!"

This was our bread and butter play. I would go slowly in motion, the offside guard would pull, Sal would toss the ball to Marco and he'd follow us through the hole.

Sal yelled out the signals and I went into motion. When the ball was pitched, I sealed the outside linebacker and tried to move him inside so Marco could use the sideline.

I knew Chris Supino, the outside backer. He was pretty tough but lacked quickness so if I positioned myself correctly, I could move him.

I got a good hit on Supino and I could almost feel Marco breeze past my block. The safety, Matt Stevens, dragged Marco down but only after a gain of seven.

There was bad news, however. Marco really struggled getting to his feet and limped badly to the huddle. He was grimacing and leaning on Eduardo's shoulder.

The referee noticed and immediately blew the whistle and motioned to our sideline. Coach B. and the trainer, Johnny Cabral, ran onto the field.

By this time, Marco could no longer stand and sat on the turf.

"No good, Irish, no good," Eduardo said.

We stood together and watched Johnny help Marco to his feet. Marco swung an arm around Johnny's shoulder and hobbled off the field. Before he turned and headed for the sidelines, Coach Bonfiglio said, "You're at halfback, Kyle. Get ready to carry the ball."

So this was it...back to halfback. With Jimmy Killoran blocking for me. When Jimmy ran into the huddle, I patted him on the shoulder pad and said, "We need you now, Jimmy." Jimmy looked at me and nodded enthusiastically and I was a little more encouraged than I was thirty seconds ago.

In true Coach Bonfiglio/Coach Brennan fashion, we ran another Toss Right on the second play. Jimmy got a decent block and I followed Peter Sousa for five yards. First down.

As much as I had come to appreciate the contributions of playing fullback, it was like another world playing halfback. The coaches were aiming for a long punishing drive to start the game and we were sticking to the gameplan.

The seconds and then minutes rolled off the clock as we methodically drove the ball down the field. Toss Right, Toss Left, Pick Right, Pick Left...not much mystery to the strategy but it was working to perfection.

With two minutes left in the first quarter, I caught a screen pass from Sal and maneuvered my way into the end zone from the eleven yard line. Ricky knocked home the extra point and we led 7-0. The Crandall fans were beyond hysterical.

I took a seat on the bench and tried to catch my breath. I had carried the ball six times on our first possession and I wasn't used to it. But it felt good, real good.

I heard someone scream my name and for some reason I turned to the crowd and Freddie flashed me his gang signal. Despite the seriousness of the situation, I had to laugh. I waved at Freddie and he laughed and flashed the sign again.

Unfortunately, our lead didn't last long. Ryan Barrett, a senior return specialist, took the kick back to our twenty yard line. Two plays later, the quarterback hit Paul in the end zone from the twelve yard line.

I guess I felt a little happy for Paul in a weird way but that didn't last long. I rose from the bench, buckled up my helmet and got ready for the kickoff.

I walked over to Marco, who was sitting with the trainer. There was obvious pain on his face. I nodded at him and Marco said, "Okay, Irish, your game now, man." I nodded again and jogged onto the field.

Sammy returned the kick to our thirty three yard line. As we waited in the huddle for Sal, I glanced over at the Fairview sideline. Jon Davis had his helmet off and was screaming inaudibly in my direction. I shook my head and concentrated on Sal's play call.

After six plays, the drive stalled. Coach Pearson had made some adjustments with his defense and it was getting tougher and tougher to run successfully. Sal was going to have to play a major role with his arm and that hadn't been necessary for most of the season.

As the second quarter began, the Fairview offense really began to click. The quarterback, a Sophomore named Brian Fisher, was picking our secondary apart. Losing Marco on offense hurt but losing him defensively was devastating. The backup safety, Justin Monroe, just couldn't keep up with the Fairview receivers. Paul already had four catches.

When Fairview reached our twelve yard line, Coach Bonfiglio called timeout. I heard him yell, "Donovan!" I rushed onto the field where Coach was speaking to the entire defensive unit. "Kyle, you're in at safety!"

I played some scout defense during practice but had only taken a couple of defensive snaps during the season. Coach B. was taking a chance. And Paul would be my responsibility on some pass plays.

I didn't get much of a chance to prove myself because Fisher scored on a bootleg on first down. They made the extra point and the score was Fairview 14, Crandall 7.

The referee blew the whistle signifying the end of the first half.

A bunch of Fairview kids stood by the fence as we jogged to the locker room. There were a couple of comments but, all in all, not too bad. Maybe the sight of Freddie and his buddies standing on the other side of the field helped calm them down.

You can tell a lot about a football team at halftime. You can immediately sense nervousness, cockiness, fear once you walk in the room. When I entered the locker room today, I sensed confidence.

Coach McGee spoke quietly to his linemen at one end of the

room. The backs were waiting for Coach Bonfiglio and Coach Brennan.

Sal sat next to me on the bench in front of the lockers.

"Hey, can I ask you a question?" he asked.

"Ah, yeah," I responded.

He looked at me earnestly. "How come rich people can't dress casually?"

You have to be kidding me. Halftime of the most important game in Crandall history and he's asking me this?

"No, no, I mean it. I'm walking off and I notice they're all wearing these weird hats and boat shoes and jackets tied around their waists. What's the deal?" Sal asked.

Thankfully, I didn't have to answer because Coach Brennan called us together.

It was a very businesslike halftime. Not a lot of yelling or emotion. We knew what had to be done and now we had to prove that we could do it.

As we gathered to prepare to head back out to the field, Coach Bonfiglio pulled me aside. "Alright, Kyle...you're playing safety now. You okay with that?"

I nodded. What could I say?

As we walked out of the locker room, Eduardo said, "Hey man, I heard Urban Meyer is here today? He's scouting, amigo...looking at Davis. Can you believe that, man?"

I shook my head. I used to root for Ohio State. Not anymore.

We kicked off and Barrett returned the ball to the thirty. Our coverage was better.

I ran into the huddle. Raymond stood in front and relayed Coach B.'s signal to the team. I caught Paul's eye as he broke the Fairview huddle. I noticed him raise his eyebrows in surprise.

On the first down, Raymond caught Barrett from behind and threw him for a three yard loss. I jumped on the pile as he was going down and it felt good. I saw Jon Davis as I rose from the ground and I said, "I'm right here, Jonny. Hundred bucks, right? Here I am!"

Davis didn't respond and I ran back to our huddle. Ricky slapped me on the helmet and said, "There you go, Irish. You're getting to be one of us!"

On the next play, Fisher hit Paul across the middle. Raymond missed the tackle but I charged over and gave Paul a pretty good lick and dragged him down. As we lay on the ground, we looked at each other. Paul chuckled and then I did the same.

We held them on third and four. Ricky returned the punt to the Fairview forty. I had barely caught my breath when I returned to the field.

Coach B. threw caution to the wind and called a long pass play on first down. Sal threw a perfect spiral to Sammy Griffin who handled the throw expertly and took the ball down to the Fairview six yard line. I think we actually caught Coach Pearson by surprise.

Two carries later, I scored my second touchdown of the afternoon. Ricky kicked the extra point and the score was 14-14.

As I jogged off the field, I scanned the crowd for Grandpa Butch. Sure enough, I saw him standing and cheering with Bingo Lonergan, Mom and Dad. I tapped my thigh pad and pointed in his direction.

The drizzle was steady by this point but it wasn't affecting either offense. By the time the fourth quarter started, we led by a score of 24-21.

With about three minutes left in the game, we had driven down to the Fairview ten yard line. My body ached and my head was spinning but I tried to focus on pushing in one more score. It would be tough for Fairview to score twice against our defense, even with me playing safety.

Sal called the play and pitched the ball to me. I attempted to cut around the left side. As I turned upfield, I tried to maneuver past Supino, the outside linebacker. For a split second, I lost concentration and my grip on the ball loosened slightly. At that moment, Supino reached out with his right hand and pounded down on the ball. The ball squirted from my arm and I fell to the ground.

Supino dived on the ball as I lay helplessly on the ground no more than five feet away. He jumped up with the ball and was mobbed by the Fairview defense.

I felt a hand grab my shoulder pad and helped me to my feet. Eduardo tapped my pads and said, "Come on, *Menino*. You got to shake it off, man. Time to play some defense, Homeboy. Get that ball back!"

I shook my head and tried to get my mind straight. The noise in the stadium was deafening. Two minutes and twenty nine seconds left in the game. Raymond grabbed my face mask and yelled, "Come on, Kyle. Forget about that! We need you on defense now! Stay in the game!" He slapped me on the helmet and we broke the huddle.

Momentum is a funny thing. You think that Fairview was done...all we needed to do was gain ten yards in four plays. Even if we only kicked a field goal, we could have run down a lot of the clock. Instead, I fumble and it's a new game. Yeah, that's right...I blew the Super Bowl for our team and the whole city of Crandall.

I couldn't push that thought out of my mind as the Fairview offense lined up. The quarterback, Fisher, barked out the signals. As their flanker went into motion, Raymond looked back at Ricky and me and screamed something inaudible. It was probably important but I just couldn't stop thinking about that fumble.

Fisher ran a play action fake and then hit the flanker, Beazley, at the sideline. Ricky tried to keep him in bounds but Beazley was able to stop the clock. Gain of twelve.

In the huddle, Raymond took charge. "Yo, you gotta listen to the calls, Ricky. Come on, man, we seen that play fifty times in film this week! Come on, boys, this is our game!"

Fisher completed his next pass to Paul, who must have made ten catches by this point in the game. Paul tried to angle for the sideline but Manny Garcia, the outside backer was able to keep him in bounds. The clock was ticking and Fairview had one more timeout.

Fairview hurried to the line of scrimmage. Fisher dropped back to pass. I noticed Beazley running a pattern to the center of the field. I sprinted upfield and then Beazley stopped quickly. I did the same but then Beazley accelerated and ran straight down the middle of the field. I was caught flat footed. Fisher threw the ball as far as he could. Beazley caught the ball at the fifty and kept running with Ricky and me in pursuit. I dove after Beazley at the five yard line but to no avail. He stumbled into the end zone. Touchdown, Fairview.

I knelt on the five yard line and watched as the Fairview squad swarmed all over Beazley. Now it was official: I was the goat...to be remembered by generations of Crandall football fans.

The extra point was a formality. Fairview led, 28-24, and there were just over one minute thirty seconds left on the clock.

The Crandall crowd was silent. I jogged to the sideline with my head down. I heard Katie scream, "It's okay, Kyle...there's time!" I didn't even glance in her direction. There was no time and it was all my fault.

I sat on the bench and hoped that no one would come over and sit next to me. I didn't want to be comforted or encouraged. I stared straight ahead and tried to suppress every emotion that I felt.

I heard a familiar voice yelling, "Kyle, Kyle, Kyle!"

I turned around and saw Grandpa Butch leaning against fence behind our sideline.

I nodded in his direction and focused again on the field.

Grandpa yelled again and when I turned, he was holding up a Sixth Marine Corps Division patch with both hands. "Come on, Boyo...no giving up now!"

I put my hand on my thigh pad, hoping that Jesus and that Marine patch, that symbol of bravery, but most importantly, that symbol of my grandfather, would somehow rise up and give me some Okinawa courage and strength.

I stood up and buckled up my helmet. How could I go down with a whimper after all that had happened these last few months? I turned and gave a last look at my grandfather, who remained standing behind the fence, holding the patch. I pumped my fist in his direction and he smiled. Win or lose, goat or hero...I couldn't finish the season crying and sulking on the bench.

I walked to the sideline and stood in the cold drizzle beside Sal. He turned and said, "You ready, *Paisan*? This is it, baby."

We shook hands. Coach Brennan saw us and said, "How do you want to end it, boys? We're better than that team! It's up to you two!"

Sammy returned the kickoff to our thirty two yard line. The offense jogged onto the field with one minute, thirteen seconds left in the season.

Sal stood before us and said, "What can I say, fellas? Ain't nothing left to say. This is it...we score, we win. I don't wanna lose, boys...I don't wanna lose. Alright, we got one timeout...let's not waste it. We're gonna run a toss right...Kyle, get out of bounds, man. On one, on one, READY...BREAK!"

The linemen sprinted to the line of scrimmage. They were tired and wet and cold but they were still running to the line of scrimmage.

I kept reminding myself to hang onto the ball. I took the pitch from Sal and found a burst of speed I didn't know was still in me at this point. I pushed Jimmy Killoran into Supino and headed upfield. Their safety dove at me but I was able to leap over his outstretched body. I thought about cutting back to the middle of the field and go for it all but I decided to get out of bounds and stop the clock.

I flipped the ball to the referee and was immediately hugged by Eduardo and Peter. I saw the ref place the ball on the Fairview forty one yard line. I had gained twenty seven yards.

The Crandall crowd was loud again. Rows of fans stood behind the fence surrounding the field. It began to rain more intensely. Second down, fifty two seconds left in the game.

Sal tried to calm the excited huddle. "Okay, okay, nice job Kyle...nice job Jimmy and the line. This time we're gonna throw a swing pass. To you again, Kyle. Got out of bounds or we'll have to call time out right away. I right, swing pass right, on one, on one, READY, BREAK!"

Sal faked a handoff to the fullback. I flared out towards the sideline. Sal looked left and then threw a soft spiral, leading me perfectly. I caught the ball on the run and was one on one with Supino, the linebacker. I faked left and then ran right. Supino took the fake and I sprinted down the sideline. I gained seventeen yards before I was knocked out of bounds.

The ball was placed on the Fairview twenty four yard line. There were thirty four seconds on the clock and we still had one timeout.

Coach Bonfiglio called a pick pass to the tight end, Walter Garcia. Walter collected Sal's pass and took the ball down to the eighteen yard line. He couldn't get out of bounds and the play took a long time. The clock was ticking and the Fairview defense was getting up very slowly.

We rushed to the line of scrimmage without a huddle and Sal quickly called the signals. I was the only back in the backfield and Sal called a draw play. I took the ball and charged directly into the center of the Fairview defense. Peter and Eddy made great blocks and momentum carried me to the Fairview four yard line. It seemed like everyone in the stadium called timeout at once. There were eight seconds left on the clock. Time for one more play.

Johnny Cabral and Ricky ran out with bottles of water. As I gulped down the water, I tried to find Grandpa in the crowd. At this point, the rain and the noise wouldn't allow me to focus.

I heard the taunts of the Fairview kids standing behind the end zone fence and chuckled to myself.

Eduardo stood beside me and said, "It's gonna be a toss

right, Irish. You're gonna run behind me and you're gonna score a touchdown. And we're gonna win the Super Bowl. You got all that?"

I looked at Eduardo. His uniform was filthy, there were smears of dirt all over his face and there was a patch of dried blood below his mouth. He looked like a model for NFL films.

We clasped each other's hands and I just smiled at Eddy. He nodded and we heard Sal call for the huddle. "Four yards, boys. Going to the bread and butter. This is it...Tight I, toss right on one, on one, ready BREAK!"

Eduardo looked back at me and grinned. This was it...four yards for redemption.

I had banged my shoulder pretty hard on the swing pass and it hurt like hell. I tried to block the pain out of my mind for one play.

I lined up behind Jimmy and prepared myself. The Fairview linebackers were screaming at the top of their lungs. I had trouble hearing Sal's signals but there wasn't much mystery about the snap count by this time.

The ball was snapped and Sal pivoted and launched a perfect pitch in my direction. I collected the football and motored towards the end zone.

A brief and small hole opened up between Eddy and the tight end. I burst through the hole, untouched for the first two yards. And then it closed as quickly as it had opened.

Three Fairview defenders met me on the two yard line. I got as low as possible and surged forward. I stretched out my entire body. My shoulder felt like it had been completely dislodged from my torso.

I fell to the ground with the Fairview defenders. The goal

line had been made invisible by the rain. I held on to the ball with every ounce of strength remaining and hoped for the best.

The referee began pulling players off the pile and there was a minor scuffle between Eddy and the Fairview nose guard. The Fairview safety made one last attempt to wrestle the ball away from my grip but there wasn't a chance that was going to happen.

Finally, the referee found me and immediately raised both hands in the air. TOUCHDOWN, CRANDALL!!

Within seconds, the entire end zone was full of Crandall players and fans. I just lay at the bottom of the pile and hoped that I wouldn't be crushed to death.

I was finally able to stand up and was tackled again by Eddy, Peter and Raymond. Crandall fans were everywhere, sprinting up and down the field, climbing the goalpost. The Boston Police detail looked on with cautious amusement.

Sal and Ricky doused Coach Bonfiglio with a bucket of water and I watched as the coaches tackled each other and rolled around in the mud.

Katie ran into my arms and I gave her a long kiss. I was hoisted up from behind and carried off the field. I felt like Rudy at Notre Dame.

By this time, Coach B. was screaming at us to get in line and shake hands with Fairview. I hugged Paul and promised that I would call him later. The shaking hands ritual was incident free. Jon Davis didn't bother shaking hands with anyone.

Coach Pearson shook my hand and tapped me on the side of my head with his left hand. "Beautiful, Kyle...just beautiful. Congratulations, son, no one deserves it more than you."

I thanked Coach Pearson and then jogged to our sideline. I

was looking for Grandpa and Mom and Dad when Coach B. grabbed me and said, "Kyle, there's someone who wants to meet you."

I had too much respect for Coach Bonfiglio (and too much fear!) not to accept his invitation. I turned around and there was Coach Urban Meyer, looking just like he did on television, wearing an Ohio State windbreaker and carrying a soaked notebook.

We shook hands and Coach Meyer said, "That was quite a performance, Kyle. The way you came back after the fumble... pretty impressive. Work out like hell over the winter and spring and I'll be in touch next year. Okay? Congratulations, son."

I was too awestruck to say a word. I just shook my head affirmatively, turned and saw my family walking through the fence gate onto the track.

Grandpa, Mom and Dad were all smiling and laughing like little kids.

I caught Grandpa Butch's eye and he smiled and reached into his pocket. He held up the Sixth Marine Division patch and nodded. I tapped my thigh pad and pointed in his direction.

My eyes were wet but I told myself that it was from the rain.

I said a quick prayer and thanked Jesus for taking on all those burdens. And I promised Him that I would always trust Him completely.

I picked up my shoulder pads and helmet and walked towards the track.

My family was waiting for me.

EPILOG

Kyle thought he heard Sully honking the bus horn as he made his way across the field towards the parking lot at the south end zone. Has to be my imagination, Kyle said to himself, smiling. Even Sully would give the team a little leeway...after all, they just won the state championship.

Shaking hands with Urban Meyer, hugging his mom and dad, seeing that look of pride in Grandpa Butch's face, the kiss with Katie...he'd walk home to Crandall if the bus had left. It'd be worth it.

"Kyle, Kyle, **Kyle**." A shrill, unfamiliar voice shouted at him from the rear.

Kyle turned and saw a twenty something reporter, a green press pass dangling over his hipster hoodie, tiptoeing carefully in an attempt to keep his skinny jeans dry.

Kyle stopped, and nodded at the reporter.

"Hey, great game, Kyle. Trevor Stewart, North Shore Daily...good to meet you. So Kyle, what's in your plans now? I saw you talking with Coach Meyer earlier?"

Kyle chuckled. "I guess he was here to watch some Fairview guys. He stopped and said hello. Nice guy."

Trevor scribbled down some notes, his look of disgust indicating his displeasure at covering a high school football game. "Anything else? Any truth to the rumor that you're going back to Fairview?"

"No, no truth at all."

Trevor smirked. "So you're staying at Crandall?"

Kyle peered at the reporter. "Where are you from, Trevor?"

"Swanton...class of 2006."

Swanton was about twenty miles west of Fairview, and wealthier, if that were possible.

Kyle put his hand on Trevor's shoulder. "You see, Trevor. I'm from Crandall." He smiled and flipped the football to the unsuspecting reporter. "Come visit sometime," Kyle shouted as he jogged to the bus.